The Pathfinder

Book 2 in the Denny Durant Montréal Crime Series

C.J. Fournier

THE PATHFINDER

Copyright © 2025 C.J. Fournier

ISBN: 978-1-7782997-4-2

ISBN: 978-1-7782997-3-5

The characters, events and some of the places in this book are fictitious. Any similarity to real persons, living or dead, is coincidental, and not intended by the author.

Published by CALAMITY ENTERPRISES

For Jen,

And in loving memory of Joel Walter Fournier (1938 – 2024)

Chapter One

The best part of Christmas, I reckoned, was being adrift on a sea of booze, watching the festivities sail by.

I was in Montréal, sitting at the bar in my local pub, the Gargoyle, on December 24, in the insalubrious company of other misfits and outcasts, some without family, some without homes, some simply seeking refuge from the season's relentless commercialism.

Through the far window, I could see enough snow swirling around outside to imagine the deepening cold—ten below zero last I checked—and to be glad I was warm and safe inside.

Out of habit, I glanced at the screen above the bar to check the score of the hockey game. But there was no game. The players and owners were still locked in a dispute about salaries. Instead, there was a news clip showing the partly frozen St. Lawrence River at a spot where a man had gone through the ice.

"That's some way to spend Christmas," said Clyde Finster from the stool to my left, watching the same news report.

The conversation burbling around me was making me comfortably numb, a protective, anesthetic layer against the fact that I would be without my children this Christmas for the first time since they'd been born. I had no idea what I would do tomorrow, except to feel even more sorry for myself. And drink. I drained my beer glass.

The decorations Virginia had put up—the small crèche at the corner of the bar, the row of red bulbs strung across the mirror, the miniature spruce laden with ornaments by the door to the kitchen—made the place homey enough to afford a little consolation.

Virginia—bartender, friend, confidante, critic.

She caught my eye and made the universal symbol for another round. I nodded and she started a fresh pint of St-Ambroise. I caught her sneaking a glance at the new diamond engagement ring on her finger.

She set the pint in front of me, deliberately using her left hand. The ring's sparkle, like a brilliant newcomer at a gathering of old friends, couldn't be ignored.

"Have you and Richard set a date yet?"

"We'll probably wait until May, when the weather improves."

I wasn't sure if she was more pleased about the ring itself, or the prospect of marrying her long-time fiancée, Richard, or the fact that Richard's proposal meant she would stay on track with her five-year plan.

"Not a bad turnout," she said, scanning the crowd. Her face radiated a post-proposal glow I found annoying, given the new, failed state of my own marriage.

"Like a convention of Christmas rejects," I said.

"Denny, you need to lighten up and get yourself in the Christmas spirit."

I took a sip. "Yeah, just missing the girls."

She leaned over the bar so that only I could hear her and placed her brown hand on my lily white one. "It's better this than living with Angie and fighting all the time."

She had a point. Then she drove the point home. "Didn't she throw an ashtray at you last Christmas?"

"Crystal paperweight." I chuckled to soften the grim recollection.

I was about to change the subject when a muffled crash and a loud curse saved me the effort. Sammy—the pub's gifted, permanently stoned chef—had come out of the kitchen carrying three plates of food and run straight into the decorated spruce. The tree was spared, but the floor was a mess.

"Sorry Vee!" he hollered. "I'll clean it up."

Virginia shook her head, muttered a few words—maybe praying for patience—and walked to the other end of the bar to tend to a customer.

The TV was now showing a curling match between—well, it didn't really matter.

Idly looking around the room, I caught the eye of an attractive, dark-haired woman sitting with a female friend at a table near the back. Our shared glance short-circuited the negative current running through my thoughts and dispelled my gloom about Angie, the kids, gifts, Christmas. It even sparked some hope.

I was about to saunter over to say hello when someone to my right roared, "Denny Durant? You gotta be fucking kidding me!"

The voice sounded both familiar and strange, like hearing a once-meaningful song for the first time in years.

It was Michael McPhee.

"Holy shit," I said.

He advanced toward me, arms outstretched, ice clinging to his beard, and surrounded with an aura of snow and Arctic air.

"Mike McPhee. What the—?" My words were stifled by his embrace.

Somewhere behind me Virginia said, "Of all the gin joints in all the towns in all the world…"

He hugged me for an awkwardly long time. I realized much later it was the embrace of a drowning man who had happened upon a piece of wreckage.

When he finally stepped back, I told him to sit down on the stool Clyde had just vacated. "Let me buy you a beer."

I signaled to Virginia to bring another glass of what I was having, though I remembered from our time together in Afghanistan that Mike wasn't much of a drinker.

The last time I'd seen him he was wearing the uniform of an officer of the 3rd Battalion of the Royal Canadian Regiment—3 RCR. We'd been standing in the dusty heat of the air base in Kandahar, and I was shipping out after a three-month stint as a wire-service reporter.

Now he was dressed in the winter uniform of a Montréaler—a toque, fleece-lined leather gloves, massive goose-down parka, and a wool scarf. He began divesting himself of the articles, one by one.

I was struck by the change in his appearance. When had I last seen him? Was it 2006? The years since hadn't been kind. He'd put on maybe twenty pounds. Except for several red blotches, his face was now grey, as was his scraggly beard. I remembered the fit soldier who could bench press more than most soldiers on the base. This was a different man.

Virginia arrived with the fresh pint as he finished taking off his parka.

"Virginia, this is Mike McPhee. We spent some time together in Afghanistan," I said.

Virginia stuck out her hand. "Nice to meet you."

McPhee glanced at the rock on her finger. "Likewise."

"Are you a reporter too?" Virginia said.

"Hell no," he said with mock disgust. "Regular army."

McPhee had been the most loved and respected officer on base: company commander, former reconnaissance platoon leader, Patrol Pathfinder. He was the hardest of the hardcore, a soldier's soldier, the kind others looked to for leadership in every situation, including the worst. And from what I heard and observed, he'd risen to every occasion. Now, I doubted whether he could lead Sammy back to the kitchen.

McPhee raised his glass. "Cheers!" We clinked and drank.

He grinned at me with bright eyes. Too bright.

"Mike, what brings you to Montréal?"

"Long story," he said, wiping his mouth with the back of a huge hand.

I took a sip of my own beer. "I've got time."

"I've got some unfinished business I need to take care of."

"On Christmas Eve?"

"I'm meeting an old friend. She's not free until a little later so I had a bit of time."

He took another deep swallow of the beer. "Truth is," he began, "the wife and I had a little falling out. I'm taking some time away."

"Sorry to hear that."

"Thanks, buddy. But, you know, shit happens."

Even while he was speaking, he seemed closed off. He avoided looking me in the eye and was gripping his glass so tightly his knuckles were white. It made me feel like I was a pier he had tied himself to while waiting for the tide to turn, or for the storm to pass, or for the coast guard to call off its search.

It was hard for me to reconcile this new version of McPhee with the old one.

Had he tried to find me? For someone with Mike's skills, I wouldn't be hard to track down. He could easily have learned which bar I frequented from any one of my colleagues among the city's press corps.

I was more than a little spooked by the off-kilter vibe he was giving off. He must have sensed this.

I was about to ask how he knew where to find me when he said, "Things haven't been going too well, old buddy."

"What's been happening, Mike?"

"I'm not really sure, to tell you the truth. I try to keep my shit tight, you know, but lately I've been a walking explosion."

"How so?"

"It's the mission. Not sure I can buy into it anymore."

He drained his glass and signaled for another. I nodded to Virginia.

"I just haven't been myself since I got back," he said.

"How long ago was that?"

"Not long."

Virginia placed a beer in front of him and gave me a concerned look. She had a good instinct for people and could tell there was something off about him.

"Came back in '08." He took a long gulp of beer then mentioned a battle near Kandahar. I'd heard about it.

"Fucking shit show," he said. "Nearly got my head blown off. Wounded enough to get sent home. But things were already bad before that."

He seemed to need to talk, and I was content to let him. He hadn't asked me any questions about my own life, how I was, where I was working, and I suspected he never would. He needed me to be the audience.

"Things went bad while I was over there, and they were worse when I came back. I have no idea how to make them right. I applied for medical release, got my temporary category in 2009, then my permanent category almost three years ago, in March 2010."

"Temporary category?"

He chuckled at my ignorance. "Medical leave. I was released six months after that. I've been dealing with Veterans Affairs ever since."

He paused and we both pretended to watch the curling on TV.

"The marriage is bad, Denny. The marriage is gone to hell."

"It's tough when that happens," I offered.

I could have told him that I knew the feeling, because my own marriage had also gone to hell, but it wasn't that kind of conversation.

In Afghanistan, whenever McPhee had spoken about his wife and kids, his love for them was palpable. It was easy to see that he felt himself to be a lucky man. Not that McPhee and I were particularly close friends. Everyone becomes friends in a war-torn environment. But it wasn't like we exchanged Christmas cards.

Still, I admired him and still felt a strong sense of camaraderie. I also felt indebted to him for helping me out after the accident. He'd gone beyond the call of duty to make sure I was okay.

"She told me not to come back until I sorted myself out," he said.

"Your wife?"

He nodded.

"She called the cops a few times, last time was a few months ago. They came to the house, arrested me in front of the kids, took me out."

This explained why he looked like a man staggering through some kind of emotional whiteout, like a ship adrift, navigating by feel because the instruments weren't working.

"I didn't put up a fight. If she wanted me out, I didn't want to stick around."

Another pause.

"But my kids—" he said. For a moment he seemed to be staring at nothing. Was the sodden ship finally about to sink?

"I can't see my kids any more."

"For how long?"

He shrugged. McPhee was unmoored. The thing that had always anchored him, his family, had been taken away.

"Until I get myself sorted out, whatever the fuck that means," he said.

We sat in silence for a while, both of us drinking steadily—the price of admission to this one-man show. Around us the revelry was building as midnight approached. But McPhee was a solo actor on the stage of his discontent. And the show wasn't over.

"Do you think we made a difference over there?" he asked

"Tough question. I don't know."

"Why were we there?"

"Because the Americans wanted Bin Laden?"

"The Taliban offered to give him up to a third party but the Americans wouldn't even negotiate."

I nodded. "When the US wants war, it gets a war."

"You know that forty percent of casualties from air strikes are children? We went over there to get Bin Laden. We didn't get him. We stayed to create, what, a democracy? More than half the country still lives below the poverty line. Sixty percent of the population is still illiterate. How much did we spend? How much blood?"

This was a McPhee I didn't recognize.

"I got a lot of buddies who are pretty messed up, you know? And I don't care what they say, the Infantry bore the brunt. You get in a vehicle to drive from this camp to that camp, knowing there's like a 75 per cent chance you're going to hit a roadside bomb, and you're like, 'Okay, is today the day I get blown up?'"

He ran a hand over an unshaven chin. "I was company commander. So it was my guys getting blown up. I was in charge, but I was helpless." He sighed. "This country wasn't ready when we switched from peacekeeping to combat. Most of the folks back here are still stuck in peace-keeper mode. We're over there in contact."

He looked at me squarely for the first time. "I have this rage now. It wasn't there before. Now it's all I have."

"If things are that bad, Mike, there must be some Veteran's Affairs services, right? You could get some help."

He laughed. "When I first got back, they offered me a shrink. Emma convinced me to go." A smile played at the corner of his mouth. "She actually cried to make me go. She told me, 'If you won't go for yourself, go for me.' So I went along with it."

"How did that go," I asked.

"It was okay. It helped. I went six or seven times, and things were starting to improve, but then it stopped helping."

He looked away, then back.

"I think about ...." He stopped mid-sentence, looked up at me and smiled. "But, hey, I don't mean to bore you with all of this."

"It's okay Mike. I'm sorry things are bad right now."

He nodded. "Thanks, man. You were always one of the good ones."

Then he looked me in the eye again. "I remember you had a bad time over there too."

"Yes."

He checked his watch. "I gotta go meet my friend. Don't want to keep her waiting."

He finished his beer and reached for his wallet.

"It's on me," I said.

"You see what I mean," he said with a laugh that made him sound almost like his old self. "One of the good ones."

He stood up to put on his parka. You're still writing stories aren't you?"

"Doing my best," I said.

"I read the one you wrote about fentanyl."

"Oh yeah?" I said, surprised that he'd been following my career.

"Heck of a story," he said. "I've got one for you." He fished into one of the big side pockets of the parka and withdrew a fat manila envelope and handed it to me.

"What's this?"

"Ever heard of Mefloquine?"

"Rings a bell. What is it?"

"Have a look at these. You'll see. I'll give you a call and we can talk about it. What's your cell number?" He pulled a phone out of his pocket, then frowned. "Son of a bitch, it's dead." He reached into another pocket and pulled out a ballpoint pen. "Here, write your number on something."

I grabbed a St-Ambroise beer mat and scribbled my number on it.

"Good man. Incredible to see you. I'll be in touch."

Incredible was the right word, but what I said was "Give me a call tomorrow. Come for Christmas dinner if you're at a loose end."

"You'll be with your family, Den, I don't want to impose."

"It's no imposition. I'm on my own. My wife has the kids in the townships. "

"I didn't even ask how things were with you."

"Don't worry, we can catch up tomorrow."

He got one arm into the parka, then swayed and almost lost his balance, and gave up on getting the second arm in. Instead, he let it hang from his shoulders, picked up his scarf, hat and gloves and shoved them into his pockets.

"I'll give you a buzz," he said, putting the beer mat in an inside pocket, a small one with a zipper on the side. "I could use a good dinner."

At the door he turned unsteadily to give me a wave, extended the wave to include Virginia and walked out into the Montréal snow.

His departure felt like the sun emerging from behind a huge, dark cloud.

It was just past midnight, and the party in the bar was in full swing, buoyed by alcohol and the solidarity of being clever enough to not be stuck at home with family and children.

Virginia came over with two shots of eighteen-year-old Macallan, one for her and one for me. "Merry Christmas," she said.

"Maybe your last one as a single woman."

We drank.

She asked about McPhee. I said he was an old friend who was going through a hard time and left it at that.

But the conversation with McPhee was playing on a loop in my mind. Virginia must have assumed I was thinking about my ex-wife, because she said, "I think that once you get some space from Angie, you'll find someone, and you'll want to take another kick at the can."

I regarded her as the whiskey warmed me. "I'm happy for you. If anyone can make marriage work, you can."

The dark-haired woman I'd spotted earlier appeared beside me.

"Hello," she said in a bold, friendly manner.

I smiled at her. "You look like you need one of Virginia's famous Christmas cocktails."

"That's exactly what I need."

Virginia rolled her eyes at the clumsiness of the pick up. "Two Christmas cocktails then," she said. "I'll go crush limes."

The woman stuck out her hand. "I'm Johanna."

"Denny." We shook. Her hands were small. She was dark and intense. She gave me a challenging look, daring me to call her bluff.

Virginia arrived with the cocktails and set them in front of us. "Banzai," she said sardonically.

Johanna lifted an eyebrow and smiled. "I think she likes you."

"We're old friends. She just got engaged."

"How nice for her," said Johanna, taking a sip of the cocktail, which was a festive concoction of rye, soda, limes, maple syrup and cherries.

"And you," she said. "Are you engaged?"

"No, freshly single."

"How nice for me."

We stood there, swaying a little, as the music played a Christmas number. Johanna's brown eyes were glittering with something like promise or maybe redemption.

The table where she had been sitting earlier was now empty. "Where did your friend go?"

"Home," she said. "We live at the university, in residence."

"You're a student?"

"I'm a graduate student, yes."

"You're Scandinavian?"

"Close. I'm from Finland."

She was just a few inches away from me, and I could easily reach out and stroke her hand with my finger. So that is exactly what I did.

"You study medicine," I said, letting my hand rest on hers.

"Norse literature."

"Close," I said.

"Very close."

She was like an arrow winging its way for the kill.

"Where did your friend go?" she asked.

"He had to meet someone."

"It looked like you were having an intense conversation."

"He's going through a rough patch."

"That's how it is sometimes," she said. "Life throws you curve balls."

"How do you know about curve balls?"

"You share a border with Russia, you learn about curve balls."

"Do they have baseball in Finland?"

"Of course," she said. "And hockey."

"I knew about the hockey."

She hooked a finger into the pocket of my jeans.

"We have lots of things in Finland."

"Ice and snow?"

"Yes."

"Vodka?"

She laughed. "The best in the world."

I was beginning to forget about McPhee. And Angie.

"Would you like to dance?"

"I'm just drunk enough to dance," she said.

We threaded our way through to the tiny dance floor, where three other couples in various stages of inebriation were swaying to "I'm Dreaming of a White Christmas."

I slipped my hand around her slim waist. She settled into the crook of my arm. We fit well together.

After a couple more slow songs we returned to the bar. We had a cocktail for the road and made small talk without mentioning what we had both already decided to do, and before long, I went to get her jacket and helped her on with it.

She leaned into me, pressing her breasts against my ribs and whispered in my ear. What she said would have made a bishop blush.

I caught Virginia looking at us and shaking her head. She pointed to her phone. I checked mine. She'd sent me a text that read, "She's barely older than the Macallan."

Johanna asked why I was laughing. I showed her the text.

She smiled. "You can tell her I just turned thirty, and thank her for the compliment."

We left the bar, closing the door on a strange evening— a precursor to the strangeness to come.

Chapter Two

I woke to a pale light filtering through my bedroom curtains. Christmas morning.

Johanna lay in a rumpled mess of pillows and bedding, her dark hair spilling over the duvet, a slim forearm draped over my chest and her lips pressed against my shoulder. She had proved as direct in bed as she had been at the bar.

I eased myself out from beneath the covers, put on my blue robe and leather slippers, and stepped quietly into the living room, closing the door behind me. Clothes were strewn everywhere as we'd hurriedly undressed as soon as we arrived.

Elliott, the family I now had custody of, came at a run and began rubbing himself against my shins. I tottered into the kitchen and fed him wet cat food, spooning it into a dish as he did increasingly energetic circles around my legs. Then I remembered the cat toy I'd bought the previous evening. I found it in my jacket pocket, gave it a squeak, tossed it into the corner, and hung the jacket on a chair. "Merry Christmas, El."

I made coffee and stood for a while at the window, looking out at the new snow, enjoying feeling at peace.

Snow was falling rapidly in large flakes, smothering the vehicles parked on the empty street, the dark, bare limbs of trees, and clinging to the dull exteriors of the buildings. A massive icicle fell from the place opposite and smashed on the sidewalk.

My kids would be awake now, and I pictured their delight, tearing open the gifts that Angie and her mother would have spent hours wrapping. The thought produced a dull longing. I boxed it up and stuffed it into the room with all the other useless feelings.

I was getting chilly from the cold seeping in from the window so I went to the kitchen for more coffee, then retrieved my phone from my jacket. It was dead. I didn't want to miss a call from my kids so I hunted around for the charger and plugged the phone in.

I wondered how McPhee had made out with his old friend. Was he already seeing someone? He didn't seem to be in the right head space for a relationship, but I was far from an expert.

Then I remembered the envelope he'd given me. Had I left it at the bar? I hurriedly checked my coat. It wasn't there. To my relief, I spotted it on the desk next to me laptop. I must have put it there last night when we'd come in, though I didn't remember doing that. I took the envelope into the kitchen, grabbed a sharp knife and slit open the envelope. It contained a sheaf of documents an inch thick, held together with a red butterfly clip.

I heard the bedroom door open and Johanna soon appeared, her hair askew, her dark eyes barely open, wrapped in the duvet like a Finnish sausage roll.

I placed the envelope with its contents on top of the fridge, next to the small dish where I kept my spare keys. "Sleep well?"

She smiled, shuffled over to me, looked keenly into my eyes and said, "I'm starving."

There's nothing like a hungry woman to bring me back to the here and now. "Eggs?"

"Perfect. Do I smell coffee?"

I poured a cup and handed it to her, then made her two fried eggs with toast.

"Merry Christmas," I said, handing her the plate. She took a few bites, then pulled me into a hug that nearly spilled the coffee.

I wasn't in the mood, so I disengaged from her and picked up my phone, expecting to have missed a call from the girls.

"How are the eggs?" I asked, while I checked the phone.

"Just what the doctor ordered," she said through a mouthful.

There had been no calls. Instead, there were notifications from an unknown number. I had received seven calls from that number between 1:30 a.m. and 4:30 a.m. I checked voicemail. There was one voice message.

McPhee, his breathing ragged, said "Hey, Denny, hate to bother you, especially at oh one thirty. I've got a situation here. Room 110...The Lorelei Hotel on rue Saint-Jacques. Something bad happened...can you get down here when you get this? Hit me back asap brother. McPhee out."

I tried calling him back. It rang several times before cutting to a canned message that said the person at that number hadn't set up voicemail and please try again later.

Joanna was looking at me. I still had the phone to my ear, even though McPhee's messages had ended. I saved the message and put the phone down, telling myself I'd try him again in an hour. Or maybe I should just go to the hotel.

"What's wrong?" Joanna said.

"That was my buddy. The guy I was talking to last night at the Gargoyle. It sounds like he's in some kind of trouble. He left a couple of messages this morning."

"Did he say what kind of trouble?"

I shook my head. "Just said he was in a hotel on Saint Jacques and wanted me to come down there. Said something bad happened. It's probably booze related."

We stood there for a moment. If McPhee needed help, I couldn't ignore him.

"I should go down there," I said.

"Okay, I'll get my things."

Chapter Three

After dropping Johanna at the Atwater Metro station, I drove on past the market and beneath the underpass and took the exit to rue Saint-Jacques. The hotel wasn't very far along.

I told myself that McPhee was probably just pulling my leg. Maybe he was suffering from some kind of booze-related meltdown.

My mild concern about him turned to cold fear when I came in sight of the hotel. Outside it was an array of emergency vehicles, lights flashing. As I slowed to turn into the hotel parking lot, I counted three police cruisers, one ambulance and the large, blue police forensics van that was rolled out only for the most serious of crimes.

"Shit," I said to nobody as I steered around the orange crime-scene tape which had gone up in a wide perimeter. I found an unoccupied spot at the side of the Lorelei and pulled in.

I walked back to the front of the hotel and stood watching for a few moments. It was about ten degrees below zero, and the sun was trying without success to break through the clouds. A blue and white fleur-de-lis flag hanging from the marquee snapped in the northerly breeze.

I looked around for someone who might know what was going on. A young man smoking a cigarette stood beside a concrete planter just outside the main doors of the hotel. He was looking off into the distance, brow furrowed, puffing for dear life.

I walked over to him and addressed him in French. "Hi, my name is Denny Durant. I'm a reporter. What's going on here?"

He replied in French. "They found a body in one of the rooms."

"Oh shit."

He nodded and kept puffing.

We stood silently contemplating this until I asked, "Do you work here?"

"Yeah, I work behind the desk. I finished my shift an hour ago but they want everybody to stay. The police want to talk to everybody who was here last night."

"That sucks."

"Tell me about it. I got two kids waiting at home to open their presents."

I shook my head in commiseration. "The person who died was a guest?"

The young man seemed to retreat farther into the hood of his parka. A scruffy red beard covered the lower part of his prominent chin. He shivered. "Yes. I think so. I'm not sure."

I nodded a goodbye. "Thanks for your help."

I took stock. Someone was dead and, judging by the number of police and the forensics van on site, it didn't look like whoever it was had died of natural causes.

I stepped away from the police tape, took out my phone and texted Bruno Castillo, an old friend who had joined the police force out of high school. After a stint in the communications department he was now back on the Major Crimes unit and was pretty plugged in to whatever was happening in the department. He was always my first contact when I needed the police viewpoint. I didn't expect him to get back to me right away, so next I phoned Charlie Hackett, an editor on the city desk at the *Montréal Gazette*.

A guttural male voice answered.

"Charlie, it's Denny Durant, Merry Christmas."

"Hey Denny. Whaddya see, whaddya hear, whaddya know?

"Listen, I got a tip about something that's gone pear shaped down at the Lorelei hotel on St-Jacques. I'm on the scene right now and there's tons of police. Apparently there's a body in one of the rooms and it doesn't look like a heart attack."

Charlie coughed and said, "You telling me we got a murder on Christmas Day?"

"I would say that's a strong possibility. Do you want the story?"

Sounds of Charlie eating something. "Yeah, sure. We got the usual Christmas skeleton staff but Feldman is covering a fire in the east end, and frankly I got nobody else so if you're there, you might as well file something as soon as you can. Give me 200 words for a web hit. You can fill in the rest as you get it."

"You want a photo as well?"

"I'd love a photo, but if I took a photo from a freelancer, I'd get in all kinds of shit with the union. So just stick to the story for now."

I said I would and hung up.

I pushed aside the nagging question of how McPhee was involved and got down to business. The man I'd spoken to earlier was still outside, smoking a cigarette. I took out my notebook and pen and approached him again.

"Would you mind if I asked you a few more questions?"

He finished a deep inhale and said, "I don't want to get in trouble with my boss. Do you have to use my name?"

"No, I don't."

"Okay, but quick because they're gonna call me inside any minute."

"Do you know what happened?"

"Not really. One of the maids came out to the reception desk around 9:30 a.m. and said there was a person who looked dead. She was really upset. The manager went with her to the room and then called 911. The police arrived in about five minutes, then the ambulance came, then there were police everywhere. They said we couldn't go home."

"What can you tell me about the person who died. Is it a male or a female?"

"It's a guy. The maid kept saying, 'He's covered in blood.'"

"Was the person a guest of the hotel?"

"I think so, yeah, but I can't really get into details." He flicked his cigarette end into a pile of snow by the door. "I gotta get back inside."

"Of course, thanks again."

He brightened momentarily. "Which paper you with?"

"The *Gazette*."

"The story will be in tomorrow's paper?"

"Yes."

I handed him a business card. "In case you think of anything else."

He nodded, stuffed it into his pocket and walked inside. Through the glass doors I could see a dozen or so people milling about in the lobby, drinking coffee, huddled in quiet conversation or sitting alone. An older woman in a cardigan sat on a worn looking sofa, clutching herself and rocking gently. A uniformed policeman stood next to the front desk, thumbs hooked into his bulletproof vest. I assumed the room they were using for interviews was out of sight.

"Can I help you with something sir?"

The policeman who had been standing sentry at the edge of the perimeter was walking toward me. Small particles of ice had formed on his mustache. His name tag said James, W.

I introduced myself, told him I was working on a story for the *Gazette*, and asked if there was any chance of an interview.

He stiffened like a terrier when I told him I was a reporter. "We'll be making a statement to the press a little later today."

I had expected something similar. I had dealt with this kind of reaction many times. Years of rejections, obstacles, prevarications, of doors slamming, of phones calls abruptly ended, of emails ignored, of people turning the other way when I approached or leaving the room when I entered, had helped me develop the skin of a walrus. This guy — Officer James — wasn't the first and wouldn't be the last to give me the cold shoulder. I'd had colder shoulders from better men than him.

"How about I just go inside and ask around."

He looked at me with amusement. "We both know that's not going to happen."

"Officer James, correct?"

"That's correct."

"Are you the officer in charge?" My fingers were numb and the ink in my pen had frozen but that didn't stop me from scribbling some notes.

He said, "I was the responding officer, I caught the call, and so therefore, I am the officer in charge."

"And it's your job to hold the scene. Is that correct?"

His amused look vanished and he said, "We're kind of busy here. If you don't mind, please step back a little ways just to let us do our work."

I said, "No problem, officer. When do you think you'll be making that statement?"

Officer James exercised his prerogative and turned his back to me. But then he did something surprising. He got on his radio. "We have some press here. When are we expecting Annie on the scene?"

I couldn't quite make out the response, but after he ended the call, he said, "Probably within the next hour or two."

I thanked him and stepped away.

A few minutes later, a female paramedic emerged from the hotel leading another woman, middle-aged and visibly shaken, to the back of an ambulance. It looked like the woman who'd been sitting on the couch inside. Was she the maid who had found the body? The paramedic opened the door and helped the woman up the steps. The door closed behind them.

Mike McPhee, I said to myself, what have you done?

Chapter Four

There was a twenty-four-hour gas station next to the hotel, so I went there to find out whether somebody saw something.

I poured myself a coffee from the urn, and as I was paying, asked the kid at the cash register if he'd seen anything the previous night.

He looked perplexed.

"Next door at the Hotel Lorelei. There's a bunch of cops there. I heard there's a body in one of the rooms."

He shrugged. "I didn't see anything but I just started my shift. Maybe the other guy saw something."

"What's the other guy's name?"

"Joachim," he said, pointing to an employee of the month placard behind him. It said Joachim B. "He does nine to nine."

"Do you have a phone number for him?"

He shook his head.

I thanked him and left, making a couple of notes once outside.

Christmas morning was turning into Christmas afternoon. Just as I was wondering why the girls hadn't called yet, my phone rang. It was them. They ran off a list of what they had received under the tree from Santa, and then thanked me for my gifts. They asked what I was doing and I was temporarily at a loss, but I told them I was just on my way to spend the day with some friends. I couldn't tell them I was at a crime scene, and I didn't want them to think I was the kind of man who spent Christmas day by himself.

After I ended the call, I went back to where I was standing. I sipped coffee and watched what was happening at the hotel.

A pair of bewildered tourists rolled suitcases hesitantly out of the lobby then crouched beneath the police tape that Officer James held up for them.

The snow was still falling steadily. The two policemen manning the perimeter stamped and blew into their hands.

The young man with the scraggly beard I'd spoken to earlier left the hotel and started walking toward the car park. I moved to intercept him. He must have seen me coming, because he picked up his pace, climbed into a dirty white minivan and drove away without letting the engine warm up.

A few minutes later, a TVA van pulled into the lot and parked on the far side. The competition had arrived. Camille Sutton, a reporter I'd known for years, stepped out. She was talking on her phone. She was dressed for the camera in black leather boots and a fuchsia wool coat fastened off center with a single, large silver button and belted to accentuate her telegenic figure.

I made my way over. She looked sour, probably speaking with the holiday editor, and acknowledged me with an eye roll. When she finished the call, she fished a pair of red, cotton gloves out of her pocket then turned to me.

"Merry fucking Christmas, Denny."

"You must have pissed somebody off, Camille."

We air kissed on both cheeks in the French fashion.

"Our holiday guy called in sick. This better be a good murder." She nodded towards the entrance of the Lorelei. "Any idea what's going on?"

"The police got a call around ten o'clock. The cleaners found a body in one of the rooms."

"Maybe a hookup gone wrong," she said.

"Maybe.

"You haven't seen them wheel it out?"

"You mean the money shot?"

She looked at me with interest. "Yeah, the money shot."

"Not yet."

"Is the victim male or female?"

"I heard it was a male," I said.

It occurred to me to tell Camille that I might know somebody connected with whatever this was, but I quickly dismissed the idea. Camille was a good reporter. She would never let something like that go. I would become a person of interest for her story. And that wasn't something I wanted to be.

Camille's cameraman appeared carrying two cups of coffee from the gas station and handed one to Camille.

We introduced ourselves.

"Victor."

"Denny. Merry Christmas."

With his free hand, Victor reached inside his parka and withdrew a silver flask. "Wouldn't be Christmas without a little Baileys."

"Amen to that," said Camille.

He doctored the coffees and offered me the flask.

"No, thanks. Still trying to sober up."

He chuckled and nodded toward the police tape. "Shitty business."

Camille took a sip of coffee and looked at me. "What the hell are you doing here, anyway?"

"I got a tip."

"In your stocking?"

"Yes, inside the lump of coal."

My answer seemed to satisfy her and we both turned back to the scene. A woman I knew from previous crime scenes—and from television—glanced over at us before detaching herself from her colleagues and approaching. It was Annie Laframboise, one of the Montréal police force's flacks. She must have arrived while I was getting coffee. She ducked under the yellow tape. Everyone shook hands.

Camille got right down to business. "Can you tell us what happened, Annie? Can we get you on camera?"

"Yes, of course."

Victor set up the camera and boom mic. I held up my small Olympus recorder to capture Annie's voice, and filmed her with my phone at the same time. Annie knew what to say.

"The police were called to this address at around 10 a.m.," she said. "On the scene, we discovered a male, late twenties, who was deceased. The death is being treated as suspicious at this time."

"Why is the death being treated as suspicious?" Camille asked.

"There are signs of violence on the upper body, and we believe the victim died as a result of this violence. We believe the violence occurred between the hours of 2 a.m. and 7 a.m. The identity of the deceased is being withheld pending notification of the next of kin."

I was about to ask a question when a voice behind me interrupted. It said in French, "This is the latest in a series of murders in this area. What are police doing about the high level of violent crime here?"

I glanced behind me. It was Robert Provost, a reporter with *Le Journal de Montréal*, a Francophone tabloid and one of the Gazette's direct competitors.

Annie looked taken aback by the forcefulness of Provost's question. She blinked a couple of times before regaining her composure. "The police have stepped up street patrols and we're using more community policing techniques in this area and in many other areas on the island."

"Do the police have any suspects in this incident?" I asked.

"Police are searching for a woman in her early twenties and a man in his late thirties, who may have information about the incident."

"Can you tell us anything about how the man died?" said Camille.

"We can't release details at this time," said Annie.

"What details can you give us of the two people the police are looking for?" I asked

"The only thing I can tell you is that the woman is in her early twenties and the man is in his late thirties."

Provost asked, "How do you know about them?"

Annie paused before saying, "We have access to security video that shows these people."

I said, "And you're sure these people were involved in the incident?"

"They are people of interest that the police want to speak to."

As we spoke, our breaths formed puffs of ice dust.

"Can you tell us again how the man died?" asked Camille. She must have wanted a better take for the final edit.

"The man died of the violence inflicted," Annie said. "There were signs of violence on the body. That's how we know it wasn't natural causes. The case has been turned over to the major crimes unit."

"Was the victim known to police?"

"Too early to say."

"Who found the body?"

"A member of the cleaning staff."

There was a pause as we ran out of questions—or rather as the questions crashed and died against Annie's stone wall of officialese—and she took that as her cue to end the presser. With a curt and almost victorious nod, she left us to rejoin her colleagues.

"Useless as ever," said Camille, once Annie was out of earshot.

Victor snorted and reached for the Baileys in his jacket pocket. "Ready for a top up?"

Camille held out her coffee.

Provost, not the warmest of humans, walked away to make a call.

"See you later," I said to Camille and Victor. "I'm going to go poke around."

Camille looked at me, her competitive side kicking in. "You filing on this?"

"Yes, the Gazette wants it."

Victor said, "Here they come with the stiff." He put his camera back on his shoulder and started shooting.

I moved aside to let Camille and Victor do their take. On a signal from Victor, Camille started speaking into the camera. "Montréal's thirty-seventh homicide of the year occurred in the early hours of Christmas morning at this hotel on the western end of rue Saint-Jacques. Police say the victim ....”

Behind her, two men in white coveralls wheeled a gurney towards a waiting hearse. I assumed they were officials from the Coroner's Office. On the gurney was a full body bag.

Several more uniformed officers were now behind the police tape, and a woman in uniform with “Identité Judiciaire, Forensics,” on the back of her jacket emerged from a police van holding a German shepherd on leash and entered the hotel.

My phone buzzed. It was Bruno getting back to me at last.

“Dude, it's Christmas,” he said.

I apologized. “News never sleeps.”

“Yeah, but I was sleeping after a hellish night shift.”

He promised to call again when he'd talked to someone working on the Lorelei case, and I left it at that.

Behind the police tape, two men in civilian clothes were conferring with another man, who I guessed was one of the investigators. He wore a leather jacket that did nothing to cover his enormous beer gut. The three of them shuffled and stamped their feet beneath a portable propane heater. I knew from covering previous crime stories that they were likely undercover cops who would have already asked their informants about the murder. That told me that whoever had died was likely connected to the underworld, someone who would be described in news reports as “known to police.”

A cop in uniform and a baseball cap carried a small, black case out of the hotel and stepped into the forensics van. I'd seen that kind of black case before, it contained the tools used to dust for finger prints. I wondered what, if anything, this cop had found in Room 110. If McPhee had been involved, if he'd been the perpetrator, he would have been meticulous about removing signs of his presence. Or the McPhee I knew in Afghanistan would have.

He would also have been aware of any security cameras, so it was unlikely they got a clear image of him.

A huge white van that looked like an RV drew into the parking lot and came to a stop just inside the police tape. It was one of the Montréal police's new mobile command posts. The two men in plain clothes made their way toward it.

I had to decide whether to tell the police about the phone calls from McPhee. It seemed possible, perhaps even likely, that he was the man in his late thirties they were searching for. But I didn't know how he was involved, or for sure even if he was involved. I didn't know anything about what had happened in that hotel room. I didn't even know why McPhee had called me. How could I go to the police when I didn't know what the circumstances of the crime were? He was in a bad way, but that didn't mean he was involved in a murder.

I took out my phone and pushed redial on the number that McPhee had called me from. It was a long shot that he would answer but I had to try. So much of journalism is making calls you don't want to make. The call went to the same canned message as before. I pocketed my phone and started walking toward my vehicle.

My chance meeting had morphed my Christmas Day into the strangest I'd ever had. A man was dead, McPhee was AWOL and I was now on deadline for the story. I was wondering whether to stay longer or leave and start writing when Bruno called to say they discovered the guy in the hotel room "cock stiff and purple" and it looked like he had been through a mincing machine.

I climbed back into my Toyota icebox and drove off.

Chapter Five

My intention was to head home and write the story, but the thought of working alone in my small, cheerless apartment on Christmas Day held no appeal. For one thing, there was barely any food there, and I was hungry. I knew a cheap Chinese restaurant on Saint-Laurent that would be open and that had Wi-Fi, so I made my way there.

It was lunchtime and the place was crowded. I took the only unoccupied seat I could see, at the far end of one of the wooden benches that ran the length of the ground floor, and opened my laptop. People were coming up and down the stairs to the lower level in a steady stream, and for a while I watched them and my neighbours, slurping down their noodles, as my mind processed all that had happened at the crime scene.

Eventually a server in his mid-fifties arrived to take my order. To keep it under twenty bucks, I went heavy on the noodles and bok choy. He set down the chopsticks in their paper wrapper, carefully avoiding my laptop, and said, "You working on Christmas?"

"The news never sleeps," I said.

"Only bad news," he said, laughing, and walked off to place my order.

The smell of roasting chicken and fried noodles was reassuring, as was the sound of conversation, and the jovial atmosphere buoyed my spirits. It was a stark contrast to the cold silence at the hotel.

I wanted to file my story as soon as possible so that Hackett could get it up on the website. I got to work. It didn't take me long to put it all together.

The headline was easy to write: "Police investigate suspicious death after body found in Montréal hotel." I led with the body being discovered by cleaning staff, gave the time, mentioned the location, added a couple of lines of police-speak from Annie Laframboise, a few lines about the victim and the two people captured on camera leaving the room around the time of the incident, and wrapped it up with the public service line that police are asking anyone with information to contact them.

The food arrived and I pushed the laptop aside to focus on my Christmas dinner for a few minutes. After getting through half the food, which was delicious, I resumed typing, adding details like police hadn't yet confirmed the case is a homicide and there had been 36 murders so far this year on the Island of Montréal.

It was as bare bones a story as you could get.

I texted it to Hackett and told him I'd phone in twenty minutes. I finished my meal, paid, and stepped outside to make the call. We went over the story briefly together, I confirmed my sources to him, and he said he would call if he had any questions.

After I got off the phone, anticipating his next question, I called the police media line to ask if there was an update on the case. The person I spoke to said the death was being treated as a homicide and the major crimes unit had opened an investigation. I relayed this information to Hackett, who said he would include it in the story. An hour later it was up on the website under my byline and with the video I'd taken of Annie Laframboise.

I walked back to my car, wondering what the police were doing now. Who was the woman McPhee had gone to meet? What had happened in that hotel room?

In Afghanistan, McPhee seemed to embody all the qualities of a warrior: He weighed the cost of acting against the failing to act. He was courageous enough, both morally and physically, to thrive in the stress of combat. He never overlooked legal considerations to further the success of a mission or his career.

One time on base, I'd overheard a couple of junior officers talking about an operational meeting, where McPhee's commanding officer had been plotting a night raid on a Taliban position near Nalgham. They were laughing at how the face of this "chalk commander" became "red as a fecking poppy" when McPhee began enumerating the reasons why the raid was doomed to fail.

Whenever a mission was overwhelmingly successful, it was a safe bet that McPhee had been in charge. But he would never brag or show any delight in being proved right. He seemed to be genuinely humble.

Another time, a sergeant from McPhee's unit and I had ended up grabbing some Thai food at the Kabul airport. He told me about the time they had been on patrol in one of the villages in the Maywand District. They were going house to house looking for Taliban fighters. This kid, a boy maybe twelve years old, steps out of a mud hut with a rifle levelled at the platoon.

"McPhee, cool as a cucumber, shoulders his weapon, walks up to the kid like he was holding a stick instead of an AK, and offers him a bar of chocolate. The kid, who was shaking like a goddam leaf, looks at McPhee, looks at the chocolate, looks back at McPhee, and hands over the weapon. McPhee was smiling the whole time. We just carried on with the patrol. It's shit like that you never forget."

I thought back to the voicemail he'd left me that morning, and once again I debated whether I should contact the police. I decided not to, for now, not until I knew more. It felt too much like a betrayal.

Chapter Six

It was half two by the time I got home, exhausted and care worn. Even though the Lorelei wasn't far from my downtown apartment, once I'd parked the car, taken the ancient elevator to the fourth floor and shut the door, the crime scene with its attendant police and forensics—the grotesquely large mobile command post, Camille and Victor and their camera that represented the dispassionate eye of a voyeuristic public—seemed far off.

Even more evanescent was the memory of Johanna. If it wasn't for the coffee cup, the plate of half-eaten eggs on the coffee table and the blanket pooled on the floor I might have forgotten she'd been in my apartment that morning. They were material evidence. Had the police found any of McPhee in the hotel room?

I brought the dishes to the kitchen, made myself a vodka and tonic, wished myself Merry Christmas and sat on the couch to unwind.

Where was McPhee now?

I retrieved the envelope of documents McPhee had given me from my desk and sat back down.

There were about two hundred pages. They looked like official letters, documents, reports from various government offices, stretching back to early 2008, as well as letters to and from various researchers. Everything was meticulously ordered and labeled.

They included copies of letters from a nurse care manager, something called a temporary medical category, or a TCAT, a list of medical employment limitations, which boiled down to restrictions to his work schedule, tasks, roles, environments, locations. There were several letters to a doctor in the U.S. who appeared to be doing research into the effects of something called mefloquine toxicity. Several dozen documents related to McPhee's correspondence with the Veteran's Review and Appeal Board and his claim to receive a disability pension for mefloquine toxicity,

I'd heard of mefloquine but I couldn't remember from where. A quick Google search told me mefloquine was an antimalarial drug.

My head was starting to spin. In the past 24 hours, I'd been reunited with an old acquaintance from Afghanistan, covered a murder that somehow involved that old acquaintance, and now I was in possession of a fistful of documents about something called mefloquine.

I tossed the documents onto the coffee table, and, after finishing my drink, stood for a while at the window looking out. Down at street level, amid the snowbanks, visible in the glow of the lamp standards a man, woman and three small children ambled along, picking their way around the chunks of hard, dirty snow and ice that had fallen from the wheel wells of cars and trucks. The children carried bags of presents, the mother and father held containers of food in their bent arms. Through the cold glass, I could faintly hear the song the children sang as they walked.

I wondered if my own kids were missing me, which only made me feel lonely, even desolate, until Virginia's words came back to me, about how it was better to be alone than to be in a relationship with a person who despised the sight of you.

At the edge of my memory, something moved. In Afghanistan, McPhee had a friend whom he'd described as "like family." I'd forgotten the man's name, but I could see his face. He and McPhee were from the same small town, somewhere in Ontario. If my memory was correct, they'd gone through basic training together. Surely this guy would know what had happened to McPhee, or at least would know where to start looking.

There was something else. I'd forgotten the particulars but I vaguely remembered that I had a problem with McPhee's friend.

His name could be in one of the notebooks from Afghanistan, all of which were now in a box in the basement storage locker. I decided it was worth a look.

I made my way to the storage locker and fumbled around with my worldly possessions: boxes of books, bags of forgotten items, mementos of past eras, long-untouched skis, baseball equipment and hockey equipment, boxes of clothes that no longer fit and of letters from long forgotten correspondents.

A few weeks ago, Angie and I had sold the house as part of the divorce settlement. The sale had thrown us a lifeline in terms of the funds it provided, but the new owners wanted to close quickly, so I'd moved all of my old possessions to this storage locker and had unpacked only what I needed.

Eventually I found, on a bottom shelf against the back wall, the green canvas shoulder bag with many straps and buckles and a lock that didn't work. On the whole it was an insecure arrangement. Fortunately it contained only materials of value to myself.

I hoisted the bag and returned to my apartment.

Chapter Seven

I spent the next half hour on the phone with my mother. I'd called to wish her Merry Christmas. She was staying with her sister's family in Toronto. Next I warmed up the leftover Chinese food I'd brought home and ate it and then realized I was just delaying the inevitable. I set the shoulder bag on the table, then I made myself another vodka tonic, because I knew I was about to open the door to a room I'd been avoiding for years.

I first removed the notebooks, many of them wrapped with the remains of old elastic bands, and laid them out in order on the table. In all, there were twenty-seven.

In general I find it relatively challenging to be organized. But I have always organized my notes well. I use the same type of notebook whenever I can, and I took a bunch of identical ink-proof ones with me to Afghanistan. They had black covers and were thread bound, meaning they opened flat. Each had an inside pocket where I stored business cards and scraps of paper containing phone numbers, maps or observations. On the front cover label, I always wrote the location—or locations if I moved around—and the dates.

I first arrived in Afghanistan in June 2006. I and a number of other reporters were tracking the approximately 2,600 Canadian soldiers based at Kandahar Air Field, or KAF for short. My time there coincided with Operation Archer under US military command, and Operation Medusa, which took place over two weeks in September and was led by the Canadians, with support from British and American troops and the Afghan National Army.

I started flipping through the earliest notebook, looking for the first time I'd written about McPhee. It didn't take me long to find this entry on 14 June, 2006:

> Major Michael McPhee, nickname Mad Mike, from Cornwall, ON, 38, Royal Canadian Regiment 3rd Battalion (3 RCR), light infantry, 2 mechanized brigade group, two half-inch stripes and a quarter-inch stripe between. Thin, ruddy, fair hair, bleached by sun, flattish nose, deep-set blue eyes, square jawed, gives impression of power and intelligence.

There followed some notes based on what he'd told me:

> −3 RCR + recce battalion in support of SOF
> −says operation was to take down compound housing reputed MVT (talib cmmdr) w/IED and poppy making capab.
> −first light, Hyderabad in central Helmand Prov., sig source of poppy prod + cash generation for Taliban, known as 'moneybelt' of Taliban
> −successful operation with 5 enemy dead, sig. intel assets, no losses
> −mud bridge across canal that flows into Helmand r.
> −north of FOB Martello
> −some ANP involved

It was my own style of shorthand, nothing like what they teach at J-school, but it worked for me. It relied upon my making full notes as soon as I finished whatever I was doing and going back to source to check on things like quotes if there was any doubt in my mind and I needed something verbatim. Usually for those I used a voice recorder and transcribed it later.

I was interviewing McPhee for a story about a successful operation the Canadians had just finished conducting. McPhee had been the commanding officer. We'd got on immediately.

As I flipped through the notebook, references to "friendly air strike," and random comments like: "KAF is a bubble" jumped out at me.

I remembered that the Canadians were trying to train the Afghan soldiers, who'd had no training at all. They were insurgents, living in the moment, doing stuff like drinking all their water in the first hour.

The notes reminded me of how much time we spent just driving around in a convoy of LAVs, with nothing usually coming of it.

I came across notes about emerging from my tent in the morning and the sun and sand being so blinding I staggered around like a drunk until my eyes adjusted. The heat was so intense that summer—sometimes sixty degrees Celsius—that the mercury in the thermometers topped out. During my first week there, I'd noted that the public affairs officer—the so-called Paffo—pointed to a spot on the map roughly corresponding to the Arghandab River and said, "That's the shit show."

I remembered how the soldiers referred to the war they were entering into as "the Suck." We reporters were routinely kept in the dark on operations, but then offered a seat at the last minute and having to let the editors back home know we were going on "opsec," which meant we couldn't give details or report on future troop movements because it could jeopardize operational security. We were forbidden to take pictures of the equipment on base, and I'd written a note once after being told off by a sergeant major for snapping a shot of a LAV.

Being on a base in wartime is a totally different way of life. You could get stuck in it and never go back. For some reporters, it was hard to return to Canada.

There were scribbled notes about eating and drinking with the other reporters and bonding by going out on high adrenaline operations; seeing the soldiers working out every day on base, benching three plates or more; the special forces guys, sporting beards and civilian clothes, sprinting around the base in forty-five-degree heat. I remembered the first time I booted around in a LAV and it being incredibly loud. There were no windows, so you had no idea where you were, you could see the legs of the rear gunner, but that was about it; keeping your helmet on, because if you didn't, you could bang your head on the steel interior and get knocked out; but some guys sat on their helmets anyway they didn't want to get their balls blown off if they hit an IED; the Johnny-on-the-Spots in rural Afghanistan, where you'd go to take a piss and the shit would be an inch away from your package.

We were always looking for IEDs. The Taliban would look for any way they could get one under the road. Sometimes the bomb would be pressure plated, so it'd go off when you drove over it, sometimes it was detonated remotely by some dude up in the hills. Our guys would go on sweeps looking for them. And if they saw something they'd have a team of engineers come in and deal with whatever it was.

I had to go back and forth a couple of times across the timelines but I finally found the entry I'd been looking for—

Background/ 27.June.06
M. McPhee / Conrad Buzsaki, sergeant, 32, from Cornwall, BT at Petawawa.
CB: One time him, McPhee, interpreter, Afghan soldier were crossing open area to get to COP, they got "lit up" by an RPK, they had to decide to cross or go back for cover.
MM: The terp got hit. But we're pinned down. Rounds snapping off all around us. I go to return fire. Sergeant says he's going to get the terp.
CB: I tell him no goddam way we got to wait for more support. He completely ignores me, sprints about 30 metres out into the open, grabs the terp, hauls him back, applies a tourniquet to his leg.
MM: It was very impressive. I wrote him up for valour in the face of the enemy.
CB was Conrad Buzsaki, or Buzzy, as he was known. He was

McPhee's buddy. I vaguely remembered the conversation. There had been some event, it might have been Canada Day. I recalled a pool table in one corner of a large room and we may have played a game. There was nobody else around, and it had been a particularly bad spell of fighting. The Taliban had been putting up more resistance than anyone had anticipated. The battalion was getting soldiers killed and badly wounded every day, and some of the troops were starting to question the mission.

I must have recorded the conversation and transcribed it. Background meant I could use the material to inform my reporting but I couldn't directly attribute it.

Buzzy was smaller than McPhee—stocky, tough—but also well-liked, competent, quiet and very close with McPhee. Buzzy was a platoon leader and McPhee's 2IC, or second in command.

Then I remembered. Buzzy and I had almost come to blows about Sarah. The memory gave me a sick feeling. Until now, I'd managed to create some distance between myself and everything that had happened in Afghanistan. But here it was again, banging down the door.

I put down the notebook and searched on my laptop for Conrad Buzsaki on various social media platforms. I found him on Twitter. His profile photo showed him in full camouflage with a helmet and a backpack, holding a rifle against the background of a poppy field. His profile said he was a former member of the Canadian Armed Forces, and there were some hashtags like #Justice4AfghanVets. The location said Cornwall, ON.

He wasn't very active on the platform. His last post was almost a year old and showed him and a boy about twelve years old, presumably his son, standing outside a business that looked like a garage of some kind. The sign read "Buzzy's Bikes and Buggies."

I wrote to him: "Hi Conrad. I don't know if you remember me. My name is Denny Durant. I met you and Mike McPhee in Afghanistan in 2006. I'm living in Montréal now and I happened to run into McPhee last night. I'm a bit concerned about him. Would you have a moment to chat by phone?"

I added my number and signed off.

I checked that my phone was on, just in case he called immediately, which seemed unlikely, then picked up the last notebook on the table, from September 2006. It had a different feel, as if it had been through something. The pages were stiff, as if they had absorbed liquid and many of them were stained black.

I flipped it open to the most heavily damaged page.

9.21.06
-In LAV, en route to Mas'um Gar, total opsec, last minute, 2 seats
-Sarah sitting next to me
-Tense feeling, supposed to be no Taliban but already some contact
-Around

My note ended there, and there were no more. It was the last one I wrote while in Afghanistan. I spent the rest of my stay in hospital on the base. Sarah was a radio reporter from France, and during my time on the base we became lovers. While I was writing this note, the light armoured vehicle that we were in ran over a roadside bomb that destroyed the vehicle. She and two soldiers were killed.

The stains on the page were blood. It could have been anybody's blood, there was so much of it. I hadn't looked at the notebook since then. All of my things at base camp had been packed up and returned home with me.

In the aftermath of the explosion, McPhee had helped me get out, visiting me in hospital, making sure I had everything I needed, offering sympathy and moral support. Buzzy, on the other hand, had only made things worse.

I put the notebooks back in the bag and noticed they left a fine layer of sand on the table. So I had brought something of that country back after all.

I sat back in my chair. The apartment was quiet, the ornaments on the tiny Christmas tree glowed dimly, hinting at celebration, at joy and warmth, like a lantern in the desert. Not far away the cold St. Lawrence rolled on through the night.

I had to get out of the apartment. There were too many thoughts and emotions circulating through my system. I needed some air.

Chapter Eight

Outside it was cold and almost deserted. It could have been the foot of new snow that had fallen in the past twenty four hours that was keeping people inside, or maybe they were saving themselves for New Years Eve. Either way, I was content to have the streets almost to myself.

As I walked, the memories of Afghanistan, shaken loose by reading the notebooks, rattled around in my mind. I was approaching rue Crescent now and I thought about dropping in to the Gargoyle, but I couldn't face it tonight. I wanted to keep walking.

I felt a twinge of resentment toward Mike McPhee. I didn't want to be derailed by this person from my past. I didn't understand what he was playing at, telling me he had a story for me and then getting mixed up in a murder.

But it was hard to maintain the anger. The noise of traffic on rue Sainte-Catherine calmed my nerves, and the bracing cold brought me back to the present and allowed me to put the events with McPhee into some perspective. Slowly the memories started to fade, and I was filled with an unexpected gratitude that I still had time. There might still be happiness in my future. My life was so different now than it had been six years go. The accident was a distant memory. I had prospects. I was finally free of a bad marriage.

Still, the questions niggled me. Where was McPhee? What had happened in Room 110 at the Lorelei?

A story I'd written two months earlier was supposed to have been the crowning story of my career. It had changed my life. It felt like a long time ago, but the reality was I hadn't yet recovered from everything that had happened. It's hard to predict the effect of witnessing violent death, as I'd learned in Afghanistan.

I had pushed everything to the back of my mind and just got on with things. But even now, two months later, I still didn't feel quite myself.

And there was still the police investigation. I would be called as a witness. In this city, it wasn't unusual for witnesses to go missing. I'd just read about one who was shot a few days before he was due to testify in court.

The truth was there were some people—some organizations—you couldn't hide from, not here in Montréal, not in any city. There was no protection. If they wanted to find you, they would find you. And justice was whatever they decided it was.

I was under the illusion that at some point, things would go back to the way they had been. But maybe that's not how it worked.

My thoughts were disturbed by a sudden feeling of being followed. I turned and caught a glimpse of someone disappearing into a doorway about twenty meters behind me. McPhee?

Had he been watching my apartment? Had he been standing out in the cold waiting for me? The idea was ludicrous. But it wouldn't be difficult for a Pathfinder to track me down. He would only need my address, and that wouldn't be hard to find. I had utility bills, a phone bill. My driver's licence had my address on it. He would only need one friend in law enforcement to do a quick search. He could pay an investigator to find it. He could have pieced together bits of information from my social media profiles. He could have chatted to any of a dozen or so reporters in the city who knew me well to get information about me.

I looked back again. There was nobody there. The streets were empty.

Still, my heart was thumping and my throat felt dry.

Following an instinct to seek higher ground, I turned up rue de la Montagne and climbed until I reached the main artery of Sherbrooke. I crossed at the lights to get onto the far side of the street, thinking it would give me a better vantage point.

If McPhee was following me, he would have to emerge at the top of one of the streets leading to Sherbrooke. So I stopped and pretended to be looking through a shop window, keeping an eye on the reflection. So far, there was no sign of him.

Either this was all a figment of my imagination, or McPhee had decided to wait for more optimal conditions. It's easier to tail someone in a crowd than on a deserted street lined with snowbanks.

As my anxiety eased, I grasped that the shop I was standing in front of was an art gallery that featured the work of Indigenous artists. I'd passed it many times but never taken much notice. Now I looked through the reflection at the large painting hanging directly in front of me. It was massive, measuring about eight feet by ten feet. At first it was difficult to tell what the subject was, the colours were muted yet vibrant, but after a minute, I realized it was an extreme close up of a patch of frozen lake ice, seen from directly above. The artist had somehow managed to make viewers look below the snow-dusted surface through layer upon layer of fissured and cracked ice to the black water below.

It made me see—and feel—the intense pressure required to change water to ice. It struck me that perhaps that was what had happened to McPhee. Time and pressure had created a changed mental state—from sanity to something different.

I quickly checked the reflection to make sure McPhee hadn't appeared and then started home, arriving at my building less than a quarter of an hour later to find an unmarked police car waiting outside.

Chapter Nine

Detective Eugene Anderson looked at me across the black table. We were sitting in an interview room at Station 20, on rue Sainte-Catherine, just around the corner from the Gargoyle. I'd walked by the station many times on the way home in various stages of inebriation but had never been inside. Until now.

Anderson was a large man with a gut so pendulous, his leather jacket parted like a river around the protuberance. He was the same man I'd seen earlier at the Hotel Lorelei speaking with the plainclothes policemen. Now he was looking at me with a not unfriendly gaze, giving off a kind-uncle vibe. His partner, Detective Brandt, sat next to him but farther back from the table.

"Before we go any further," Anderson said, "I want you to know that you're not detained. You're not under arrest. You're free to leave at any time. We just want to talk to you about a rather important file that you may have some knowledge about.

"I've seen some of your stories on the NHL lockout. It's good work. Damn shame about the season. Winter without hockey? I hardly know what to do with myself now. I take it you're a Habs fan."

"I am."

Earlier, when I'd arrived back at my apartment building, both men stepped out of the vehicle and Anderson said in a friendly way, "Mr. Denny Durant?"

I said, "Yes, who are you?"

He showed me his badge and introduced himself. "I'm wondering if you could come with us, sir, down to the police station."

I asked what for.

"We'd like to talk to you about a file."

I asked what kind of file.

"Easier to talk about it down at the station."

"Easier for you, maybe."

He just smiled agreeably.

I asked how long it would take. He said it wouldn't take long at all, then asked if I had anything else to do that evening, because, "we know your children aren't with you. And we know you've already written your story for the *Gazette*."

That threw me. The choice they were offering me—to go down to the station for a friendly chat or not—was an illusion. I decided I might as well get it over with. "Sure, okay, let's go talk about the file."

Now he sat across from me, inquiring gently, as if I had a problem and he was doing his best to help me solve it. "Mr. Durant, could you please help us understand why a beer mat with your phone number written on it was found at the scene of a murder?"

It took me a moment to reply. "I don't know what you're talking about."

He took out his phone and showed me a picture of the beer mat. It was the one I'd written my number on for McPhee.

I did my best to maintain a poker face, but my heart was beating fast and I could feel the heat rising to my face. Had McPhee left my phone number at the hotel intentionally or had it been a mistake, one made under duress? The old McPhee would never have made that kind of mistake. The more I learned about the new McPhee, the more I preferred the old one.

When Anderson and Brandt turned up at my apartment, I knew immediately it was about McPhee, and I was curious about how they had discovered the connection between him and me. During the ride to Station 20, I told myself to play dumb and not give the police McPhee's name until I'd learned more about what he was up to. But the beer mat changed things.

"Yes. I wrote that. What do you mean it was left at the scene of a murder?"

"Well, just what I said, Mr. Durant. It was left at a murder scene, the same one you reported on earlier today. The murder at the Hotel Lorelei this morning. When police arrived on the scene and began to investigate, they found this beer mat in the room."

I decided to tell them as little as I could. "I wrote my number on that beer mat for a friend of mine."

"And where was that sir?"

"It was at the Gargoyle."

"The Gargoyle on Crescent?"

"Yes."

He pulled a black spiral-bound notebook out of the inside pocket of his jacket and scribbled down the information.

"Which friend in particular did you write it for?"

I remained silent. Anderson turned up the avuncular charm. "We're very interested in finding out who this friend is, Mr. Durant."

I stalled by asking a question. "Do you think my friend had something to do with the murder?"

Anderson scrutinized my face, like we were at a poker table and he was considering going all in.

"You know, Mr. Durant, I said you're not under arrest, but I do have enough to arrest you right now."

I let the shock play on my face. "On what charge?"

He held out a hand and began counting on stubby fingers. "Obstruction of a police investigation, accessory after the fact, withholding evidence. Take your pick."

"I don't understand—"

But he cut me off, and the kind-uncle mask fell away for an instant before returning.

"Please try to see things from my point of view, Mr. Durant. I need to understand how you're involved in this murder. I don't think you did it, but I think you're involved in some way. So I could look at you as an accessory after the fact, or I could look at you for obstruction. I'm sure I could think of some others."

He waited for about twenty seconds for me to say something, but I didn't have a ready reply, so he continued to sum up his position.

"Your phone number was found at the scene of a homicide. When that kind of thing happens, when we find evidence like that, we like to take a step back and see what we have. In this case, we gave the number to our analysts, and they were able relatively quickly to put a name to that number. The name was yours, Mr. Durant."

"And I told you—"

He cut me off again. "We need to know why you went to the Hotel Lorelei on Christmas Day and pretended to report on a murder while at the same time, somehow, your phone number was found written on a beer mat inside the room where the murder was committed."

"You think I killed someone, left my phone number there and then wrote a news story about it?"

"Maybe you didn't murder anyone, but maybe you and the murderer were plotting together."

Anderson and Brandt stared at me expectantly. Did they already know McPhee's identity or were they fishing?

"You already know who did this, right?"

"Maybe we do. Maybe we don't. The man who was killed would have many people who would like to see him dead. What we need to know right now is how you're involved."

I sighed. "I wasn't pretending to be a reporter. I am a reporter. I filed a story with the *Gazette*. It's online right now. You can check it."

"Yes, Mr. Durant. We've seen your story."

I knew that I had to tell them about McPhee. But I also knew that I might be able to get something in return.

Through all of this, Brandt had sat as still as a stone and stared at me. But Anderson now turned to him. "Serge, how would you describe the body of the victim?"

"Very badly beaten," said Serge, whose eyes never left my face. "Like he'd been hit with a thousand hammer blows."

"Serge, how long have you been a cop?"

"Twenty seven years, Gene."

"Have you ever seen anything like what you saw in Room 110 at the Hotel Lorelei?"

"No, and I hope to never see anything like that ever again."

Anderson turned back to me and continued his gentle attack. It was like being trampled by puppies. "Whoever committed this murder knew what he was doing. Whoever committed this murder is still on the loose. It's my job to find him before he commits another murder."

I said, "I understand, but I had nothing to do with this murder."

"That may be so. I don't think you're the murderer. For one thing, whoever killed the man in the hotel room used his bare hands. Your hands are not those hands."

I wasn't sure whether to thank him or to take offense. "Look, the man I wrote the number down for, he's an old friend. And I feel like I'm betraying him by giving him up."

"I understand," said Anderson. "And I respect your loyalty to your friend, but your friend may be a cold-blooded killer."

"I'm aware of that," I said. "He is also a highly decorated army officer and one of the best men I ever knew. I can't just throw him under the bus."

It was a gamble. I was betting that Anderson might calculate that it would be easier to give me something than to go through the hassle of arresting me. He leaned back and held his hands out, palm up. "We seem to be at an impasse."

I was getting tired. It was almost midnight. But Anderson held all the cards.

"I feel like he's in trouble. I can't explain why."

Anderson said, "He's in a lot of trouble."

So you think he did it?

We don't know yet, but whether he did it or not, we still need to talk to him."

"I believe he's in some kind of emotional crisis."

"Once he's under arrest, we can assess that."

"If I tell you who I gave my number to, will you help me?"

Anderson slammed his fist on the table so hard his notebook jumped. The puppies had morphed into a German shepherd. "You are withholding material evidence in a murder investigation. You need to come forward with the information or I will have no choice but to place you under arrest."

I held his gaze. He wasn't the first cop to try to intimidate me with a fit of anger.

"How do I know my friend was involved? What makes you think he's involved?"

With an unmistakable air of triumph, Anderson swiped to a picture on his phone and held it out. It was a surprisingly sharp black and white image of McPhee walking down what looked to be a hotel corridor.

"Is this your friend? This man was observed on the hotel's video security system leaving Room 110 at about 1:30 a.m. Christmas morning. A few hours later, a maid walked into that room and found the body. She is still in the hospital being treated for shock."

I nodded, feeling the foundations of my position, never very solid, beginning to crumble.

"Look, I'll tell you everything I know. But I've written one story about this and I intend to write more. So maybe we could come to some arrangement where I help you and you help me."

"Help you how?"

"If I give you his name, will you give me the police file so that I can use parts of it in my story."

"You said two minutes ago that you don't want to throw your friend under the bus. But you will if we give you the police file?" Anderson and Brandt looked at each other and laughed.

I felt my anger start to rise. "You're looking at this guy as a potential killer. I see the soldier who served his country with courage and distinction in Afghanistan. You don't know what happened in that hotel room. He could have merely been in the wrong place at the wrong time. At the very least, he deserves to have someone tell the whole story. If you have information that can help me do that, I want that information."

"I can't give you the police file."

"Have you identified the victim?"

He smiled. "I'll tell you what, Mr. Durant. You tell me the name of your friend, and I will give you the tombstone details of the victim. You can include that in your reporting."

It was clear I was not going to get anything more in exchange, and I was feeling exhausted by this point, so I stopped resisting.

"My friend's name is Michael McPhee. He's a former officer, a major, with the Royal Canadian Regiment. He was released from the military several months ago. As far as I know, he's still based in Petawawa."

He wrote it all down. "And how do you know Mr. McPhee?"

I told him how I knew him from my time in Afghanistan and hadn't seen him for six years before the previous evening.

"You were with the military?"

"I was in Afghanistan as a reporter, covering the war."

"Continue please."

"Two nights ago, McPhee came to the bar where I was, the Gargoyle, and we had a couple of beers together. He asked me for my phone number. His phone was dead, so I wrote my number on that beer mat. Later, in the middle of the night, he made several calls to my cell phone to say he was having some kind of trouble at the Lorelei."

Can you show me the phone log?

I did.

Anderson wrote in his notepad and then took a photo of the log, presumably so that he could trace the number.

"Did you keep the voicemail?"

"No, I didn't."

He looked at me for a long minute. "That's unfortunate."

He made another note "Why didn't you come to us right away with this information?"

"Like I said before, I didn't know whether or not he was involved."

Brandt took out his notebook and began to write while Anderson continued with the questions.

"When was the last time you saw Mr. McPhee prior to Christmas Eve at the Gargoyle?"

"In 2006 at Kandahar Airfield."

"And you haven't been in contact with him since then?"

"No."

"It's a bit of a strange coincidence, isn't it, that he walked in and saw you there on Christmas Eve, while you're having a beer?"

"Very strange," I said.

"Do you think it was a coincidence?"

"I don't know."

I didn't want to tell them about the envelope full of documents McPhee had given me in case they tried to confiscate them.

"What else can you tell us about Mr. McPhee?"

"I don't know much," I said.

"You said you had a couple of beers. What did you talk about."

I recalled the broken man sitting next to me at the Gargoyle, the man who had lost faith in the mission. "He wasn't doing very well. He talked about trouble in his marriage. He talked about his mental health being bad. He said he was in town to meet a friend."

At this, Anderson and Brandt exchanged glances.

Anderson said, "How did he seem to you?"

I considered this a moment. "Like a boat about to sink."

"So not in great shape?"

"That's right."

"What time did he leave the Gargoyle?"

"I think it was just before midnight"

"Where were you between 1 a.m. and 6 a.m. on Christmas Day?"

I was taken aback. "I was at the Gargoyle until about one in the morning. Then a I went back to my place with a friend."

"Your friend is...?"

"You need her name?"

"I'm afraid I do."

"Her first name is Johanna. Her last name is...actually I don't know what her last name is. She's from Finland. She's a graduate student at McGill."

He gave me a wry look. "So, for all intents and purposes, you don't have an alibi."

I thought fast. "Virginia, the bartender at the Gargoyle, can vouch that I went home with a woman named Johanna."

There was a pause as the detectives looked at each other.

"Did McPhee say where he was staying or give any indication of what his plans were while he was in town?"

"He said he was staying at a place on Sherbrooke. He didn't say anything about his plans."

"What did he tell you about the woman he was supposed to see that night?"

"Just that she was an old friend. He said he was killing time before he met her and that's why he popped into the Gargoyle. That's when he saw me."

"Do you plan to meet McPhee again?"

"No."

Then both men stood up. "Okay, Mr. Durant, thank you for your help, we'll be in touch. You're free to go."

"I can't go."

"Why not?"

"You haven't given me any details about the victim."

He sighed and reopened his notebook. "Do you have a pen and paper?"

I took my pen and notebook out of my jacket pocket.

"This doesn't get attributed to me, okay?"

"Okay."

"Victim's name is Frank Raymond Leclerc, age thirty-five, of Montréal."

I wrote that down. I spelled it out to make sure I had it correct. "Date of birth?"

Anderson sighed again. "March 20, 1977."

"Was he known to police?"

Anderson glanced at Brandt. "Intimately."

Chapter Ten

When I woke up at six the next morning I was disoriented. It was still dark. A police siren sounded in the distance. Snatches of a dream came to me but none of the pieces fit together. The only thing I could remember was surfacing in some large stretch of water.

I'd slept only for a few hours. By the time I got back from Station 20, it was well past midnight and it had taken me a while to unwind.

Now, lying there in the dark, questions about McPhee wouldn't leave me alone. What had he been doing in Room 110 at the Lorelei? I could understand if he was having a hard time, but why drag me into it with him? Had he deliberately left my phone number behind in the room? Was he the killer?

I lay in bed for a while hoping to get back to sleep, but it didn't work. Instead of stewing, I decided to give being productive a try. I had a long, hot shower, and by the time I got dressed, light was beginning to show in the eastern sky. After feeding Elliott, I grabbed my things and left the apartment.

I stopped at the dépanneur and bought the four main Montréal newspapers—the *Gazette*, the *Devoir*, the *Journal de Montréal* and *La Presse*—and continued on to my local coffee shop on rue Guy in the building that was part of Concordia University. The coffee wasn't anything special, but the price was right for students and freelance journalists.

That morning, the place was almost empty because the students were still on Christmas break. I sat at a table near the windows that overlooked rue Sainte-Catherine and watched the sparse traffic for a while. There was a 24-hour McDonald's restaurant on the corner. The sign above the front doors displayed the temperature—a balmy 13 degrees below zero. After a few minutes, I pulled out my laptop.

As a freelancer, I needed to have a number of revenue-earning balls in the air at all times. I once calculated that to make ends meet, I needed ten or eleven stories on the go simultaneously. If I wasn't writing stories, I was pitching them, and if I wasn't writing or pitching them, I was chasing being paid. Many otherwise good and decent people felt it was acceptable to delay payment to one-man shops like me longer than they would to, say, the power company or the paper manufacturer. They might argue that without electricity or newsprint, they wouldn't be able to produce a newspaper. But the same could be said about content: without our stories, they wouldn't have a newspaper, or at least a newspaper anyone would want to read.

Freelancing wasn't an easy way to make a living, but it beat having to punch a clock in some soul destroying salary job. That was how I thought about it anyway. I had invested most of my share of the funds from the sale of our home in blue chip stocks. The rest I'd stashed in a high-interest savings account in case I needed it to get me through the lean times, which were always just around the corner.

I opened the spreadsheet I used to track stories and set about updating it. I currently had fourteen projects in various stages of production—three were just started, seven were at about the midpoint and four were almost complete. I added the story about McPhee I had filed yesterday to the completed stories tab, and gave it the status "send invoice." It was a quickie that together with the video would earn me about $250.

Three of the four stories that were almost complete were about testimony at the Charbonneau Commission, the provincial inquiry into corruption in the construction industry. It had been a treasure trove of stories, including one about the city engineer whose gifts from a major contractor included cash, wine, travel, golf games, hockey tickets and even hang outs with mob bosses. In exchange, the engineer approved millions of dollars in false cost overruns. I wanted to finish these four stories in the week ahead and send them to various editors.

On a separate tab, I had a list of pitches I'd made and to whom, and whether or not they'd been accepted. A few of the pitches recently had, and these I moved to the current stories tab, giving them the status of "not started" and adding the deadline.

And then there was McPhee. What was I going to do about McPhee?

I wasn't sure yet what the follow up story about McPhee would be. As soon as the *Gazette* offices opened, I'd pitch a story about the murder victim, Frank Leclerc, about who he was and why he'd died.

But how was I going to report on McPhee? I would need to go through the documents he'd given me to see if there was a story there. Very often, a person will have what they think is a good news story, but either it's so biased that it fails the objectivity test or its been reported before. It has no news value or it's simply not interesting.

I picked up the Gazette and found, as I expected, that my story on McPhee, which included the update about the case becoming a murder investigation, was on the front page below the fold. Hackett had given it a very light edit, which was fine by me. I reached for *La Presse* but the story on the front page of *Le Journal* caught my attention. Under the byline Robert Provost—the reporter I'd seen in the scrum at the Lorelei the day before—was the headline, "Victim in Christmas Day Murder was Convicted Pimp."

I dropped the paper on the table. I'd been scooped by Provost.

There's nothing worse as a reporter than having somebody else get the story before you. There were two reasons for that. Number one, it called into question your effectiveness. Somebody with better sources was able to move more quickly, more adroitly, to work those sources to get the information and to report it. Number two, it added to your workload because now you had to verify everything your competitor had reported just to match the story. You also had to somehow seize back the initiative. Your value as a reporter lay in your ability to set the news agenda, to produce the stories that everyone talked about. When you got beaten to it, you somehow had to steal the story back.

Who was Provost's source? How had he found out who the victim was? Was that from Anderson? Provost must have known the victim's identity well before I'd spoken to Anderson to make his deadline.

I checked the paper's website. *Le Journal* had done a video about the Christmas Day Murder, mentioning everything that was contained in the print version of the story. It was brief and contained few images, but considering they would have had very little time to produce it, they'd done an impressive job.

In the story, Provost said Frank Raymond Leclerc, born on March 20, 1977, had a lengthy criminal record that included convictions for sexual assault and living on the avails of prostitution. He also said police were looking for a "person of interest" and that they considered him "dangerous."

Anderson must have known that the information he'd given me, the name of the victim, would have very little news value, since Provost already had it and would be reporting on it before me. Unless Anderson wasn't Provost's source.

I grabbed Anderson's card from my jacket and was about to call him when I realized that it would be a mistake to call now with a head full of steam.

I sat quietly for a moment, sipping my mediocre coffee, gathering my thoughts. There was only one thing to do, and that was to match Provost's story and somehow seize the momentum. The fact that I knew McPhee was a complication I wasn't sure yet how to handle. But the fact that *Le Journal* had put out a story meant that we, the *Gazette*, had to match it.

I picked up my phone and dialed. I got the same daytime copy editor as yesterday. "Hackett, *Gazette*."

"Hey Charlie, it's Denny."

"Your ears must have been buzzing."

"Why's that?"

"We were just talking about you."

"Let me guess. You want me to match the *Le Journal's* story about the Christmas Day murder."

"Bingo."

"How about this. I know the name of the guy they're looking for. He's an ex-military officer."

"They said you were good and they were right."

"But there's a catch."

"What's the catch?"

"I don't know if I can report it."

I told him, as concisely as possible, what the situation was. "A guy I know, a kind of friend, is the person they're looking for. He's the guy who originally tipped me to the murder."

"Wait, the guy who killed the pimp called you to tell you about the murder?"

"Not exactly, and I don't know that he killed the pimp. But he's the guy the police want to talk to, the guy in the security footage."

"Why did he call you?"

"I don't know. He said he was in trouble."

"Who is he?"

"He's a former infantry officer I met in Afghanistan when I was reporting on the war."

"How well do you know him?"

"Not well. Before a couple of nights ago, I hadn't seen him or heard from him in more than six years. Then on Christmas Eve, he came into the Gargoyle where I was drinking. He told me he had a story for me about something called mefloquine, and gave me some documents. He said he was going to meet a friend and that we would talk about it later. The next time he called was in the middle of the night. He was in come kind of distress down at the hotel. I didn't know how he was involved, so I just reported it straight. Then the cops showed up at my place last night because the guy had left my phone number at the scene."

"Denny, my head is spinning right off my neck."

"I know the feeling."

"This is above my pay grade."

"I figured."

"Let me call you back."

He must have gone straight to the editor-in-chief, Lydia Gallant, because within five minutes he called me back. This time it sounded like he was on speaker phone in a conference room.

"Denny, I'm here with Lydia in her office. Why don't you tell her what you told me."

So I did.

Lydia said, "Let me get this straight. A guy you haven't seen for six years shows up, says he might have a story for you, gives you some documents on mefloquine, leaves to take care of some business, the next time you hear from him he's calling from a hotel room because he's in some kind of trouble. You go down there, you find out there's been a murder, and the guy's wanted by police?

"Essentially, yes."

"You write the story, then you find out later from the police that the guy left your phone number at the scene?"

"Correct."

"Why would he do that?"

"I don't know."

"Has he been in touch since?"

"No."

"But you tried him?"

"Yes, no answer."

"You gave his number to the police?"

"Yes."

"And the police showed you security camera images of the guy at the scene?"

"Yes."

"They think he's the guy?"

"They say they don't know how he's involved but they want to talk to him."

"Do you think he's the guy?"

"I don't know."

"Who the hell is this guy?"

I told her as best I could. "Mike McPhee was a top soldier in the Afghanistan War. He was a platoon reconnaissance leader and a Patrol Pathfinder, highly decorated. When I saw him two nights ago, he seemed to be really struggling.

So the police know who he is, does anyone else?

I don't know, but I'm pretty sure *Le Journal* has a source that's close to the investigation. That's how they got the name of the vic, so it's probably only a matter of time before they know the name of the officer.

"We know his identity?"

"Right."

"Then let's go with that!"

"Wait."

"Why wait?"

I paused a moment to marshal the facts of my argument. "If we publish his name now, then everyone will know. We'll lose the advantage."

"Okay, but if we don't publish it, *Le Journal* or *La Presse* will get the name and publish it."

"I don't think so."

"Why not?"

"The police are going to want to keep a lid on his name. They don't want the media attention. They'll guard McPhee's identity more closely than they protected the identity of the victim. I say we don't publish his name yet. Give me a few days to figure out what he's up to, to find out what the hell happened to him. This could be a great story. If we publish his name now, we give it away."

Lydia said nothing. Charlie chimed in. "We need a second-day story. We need to at least match the *Le Journal* story, ideally we need to advance it."

"Let me talk to Anderson. Maybe I can work something out with him."

Neither of them said anything. Finally Lydia spoke. "Denny, you have exclusive information. I can justify the budget for exclusive rights to one or more stories. First, give me a story to match *Le Journal* and get us back in the game. Then, you have three days to give me the full story on this McPhee guy and what he's up to. We can't let *Le Journal* own this. I have a feeling about it.

I drained my coffee. "I'll get to work now on the story to match Le Journal. Who should I deal with on the copy on the desk?"

"Talk with April Levy. She'll be the assignment editor on duty this afternoon. She'll put you in touch with the night editor who will handle the final copy. Try to file by 9 p.m., latest." Lydia gave me the phone number for April Levy and we hung up.

I was off to the races.

Chapter Eleven

B ack in my apartment twenty minutes later, I got down to work. I fished Anderson's business card out of my pocket and dialed the number. It went straight to voicemail.

I said, "This is Denny Durant. We spoke last night. Thanks for the tip on the name of the victim. I see from the paper this morning that *La Presse* already had that. I don't know where they got that information, but it must have been someone in your office. My editors want to publish the name of the army officer we spoke about last night. I don't want them to do that. I don't think you want them to do that. But we may have no choice. Please call me back."

The good news was that so far, nobody else besides Provost and me appeared to be covering the story, at least in print. TVA had run Camille's one-minute stand-up piece but then had moved on to other things, giving twice as much time to the fire in the east end. Most of the press corps was still in holiday mode.

My major advantage over Provost was that I knew the prime suspect. But I had no idea what went on in that hotel room. I was going to have to go the long way around. I was going have to track down a witness.

The first person who came to mind was the young woman in the room, the woman in her mid twenties whom the police were still trying to find. Who was she? If the pimp was known to police, was the young woman also known to police? I could start by finding out if the people at the hotel had any insight.

The other thing I would have to determine was what had happened to the Mike McPhee I knew in Afghanistan.

I checked my watch. It was almost 9 a.m., which gave me a few hours to beat the bushes.

Next, I called the police media relations line. I explained who I was and that I was trying to confirm certain facts in the *Journal* story, in particular that the victim was a convicted pimp, and that police were still searching for a person of interest. Having that on the record from police would at least be putting a stake in the ground. I also asked if I could get copies of the images of the people wanted for questioning.

Many of the calls that I made over the next hour were similarly pro forma. It was a box-ticking exercise and nothing more. But I had to show that I was ticking the boxes.

Once in a while you get lucky, and the police tell you something. Quite often, it's something they want out there in order to sow confusion, to get the gang-bangers and the thugs talking. Because, as a cop told me once, everyone in that world talked, everyone had enemies and everyone had a score to settle. It was the bread and butter of law enforcement. But mostly, the police tried to stay clear of the media until it was time for the photo-op.

I put in a call to the coroner's office to ask for an update on the autopsy and any toxicology report and left my details on their voice mail. I didn't expect a response, but at least my name would be on their radar.

Then I remembered Joyce Maxwell. Joyce worked at the coroner's office. We had dated for a while before Angie and I got serious. Did I regret choosing Angie over Joyce? I preferred not to frame things in those terms. I checked my phone contacts and hoped her business number hadn't changed.

She answered. "Joyce Maxwell."

"Denny Durant."

A pause, and then, "You split up with Angie, didn't you."

"As a matter of fact, I did. But that's not why I'm calling."

"Why are you calling?"

"I need a favour."

"You got some nerve."

"So I've been told."

"What favour."

I told her what I wanted, but I was out of luck. When we dated, Joyce was a medical adviser to the chief coroner in Montréal. But she'd moved on two years ago to a position in the provincial ministry of health.

"You were lucky to get me at this number," she said, her tone softening. "It's been two years and my number still isn't switched over."

I couldn't resist asking. "Did you ever meet anyone?"

"After you dumped me, you mean?"

"After we went our separate ways."

"I never kiss and tell, Denny, you know that."

I smiled and I sensed she was smiling too.

"Take care, Joyce."

"You too, Denny."

I walked around the apartment to stretch and started to wonder about Joyce and what might have been. It didn't take long to remember why we'd parted all those years ago, so I boxed the idea up, put it on the shelf and got back to work.

The Quebec Legal Information Society maintains a very useful website with a database of all court records, both for civil and criminal cases. I searched for the name Frank Leclerc, and found two records. The most recent was from 2006. Frank Raymond Leclerc had been tried and convicted of assault and living on the avails of prostitution. According to the prosecution, Frank and his brother Felix, who was two years older, had forced a nineteen-year-old woman who lived with them to work as a prostitute in a hotel in East Montréal and to work as an escort for an agency called Fantasia.

The document set out how the young woman, identified as X, was raised by a single mother who had addiction issues and had to give X up to social services when she was only nine years old. X bounced around between foster homes and juvenile detention centers and by the time she met the Leclerc brothers, was more or less resigned to a life on the street. It also laid out how the brothers used violence and threats of violence to control her, including choking, slapping and burning with cigarettes.

The prosecution had alleged that the Leclerc brothers forced X, under threat of violence, to give them all her earnings and in return, they clothed and housed her and supplied her with drugs, both weed and cocaine, which she had become addicted to. They kept her locked in the apartment except for when she was working for them. They posted provocative photos of her in classified sites online, and would drive her to do "out calls" at hotels and have clients come to the apartment for "in calls." Prosecutors estimated she made as much as $700 a night.

This carried on for about eighteen months until the young woman confided her situation to a client who was alarmed by the burn marks and bruises on her body. He alerted police, who arrested the Leclerc brothers.

Frank and Felix must have had a damn good lawyer because the assault charges were thrown out. They were found guilty of living partly on the avails and sentenced to two and a half years, barely more than the minimum allowed for Section 212 offenses.

I made notes on all of this.

The second set of documents was about a case from 2004 involving the Leclerc brothers and another man, Pierre Blanchette, who were charged with assault and living on the avails. The judge had acquitted the men when the key witness withdrew her testimony.

I tried again to reach McPhee on the number he'd used to call me, but again it went to voice mail.

I checked Twitter to see if Conrad "Buzzy" Buzsaki, McPhee's friend from Afghanistan, had read my message. There was no indication that he had. I sent him another one asking if I could call him or if he could give me a call and left my number.

At around 11 a.m., my phone rang. The caller ID said "Unknown." I answered.

"Hello Denny, it's Detective Anderson."

"Thanks for calling me back."

He wasted no time. "Listen, you can't publish the name of this guy."

"Why not?"

"You'd be interfering with a police investigation."

"That's a stretch."

"Do you really want to try me on this?"

"If we don't run with it, *Le Journal* or *La Presse* will. Rob Provost seems to have a direct line to someone in your shop."

"That's been dealt with."

I paused to take that in. "Our editor-in-chief is talking to the lawyers right now to see if we can publish the military officer's name. I don't want it published right now either, but you need to throw me a bone. I need to give the editors something to get us back in the game."

He said nothing, and I could hear traffic noises. Elliott jumped on the sofa and started licking a paw.

"Where are you right now?" he asked

"I'm at home."

"You know Dunne's on Sainte-Catherine?"

"Yeah."

"Meet me there in an hour."

Chapter Twelve

Anderson was sitting alone in a booth against the far wall, drinking coke through a straw. His carefully folded jacket was on the bench beside him. He wore a green T-shirt that stretched impressively over his belly. He saw me and motioned me into the seat across from him.

Anderson said, "I'm supposed to be off today. I wouldn't normally wear a T-shirt on the job."

The waitress came. "I'll have a coffee," I said. "Black."

Anderson waited until she was out of earshot and said, "Appreciate you keeping his name out of the papers."

"No problem. What can we write about instead?"

He took a sip of coke.

"You can't attribute this to me," he said.

"Deal. I'll say it's from a police source who didn't want to be identified because they're not authorized to speak publicly."

"I don't care how you say it, as long as my name's not on it."

I waited for him to continue. My coffee arrived.

"What do you know about Frank Raymond Leclerc?"

"I saw that he and his brother did time for living on the avails a few years ago."

"Are you familiar with Proverbs 26:11?"

"Is that the one about a fool returning to his folly?"

"I'm impressed a journalist knows that. Frank and his brother Felix both did time for living on the avails. After they got out, they figured they'd have different luck doing the same thing in a different part of town. All that time in the joint, they never thought about a career change. They just couldn't wait to get out to start up all over again."

"So you're telling me that Felix is still out there. I'm not sure I can use that in a story."

"It's not just Felix. They were working with another guy called Pierre Blanchette."

I remembered his name from the court documents. "He was the guy they got arrested with back in 2004."

"Exactly. They got back together and rented an apartment in the Point. Business was booming until yesterday."

"I don't think I can use any of this in a story."

"Felix and Pierre have gone to ground. We can't find them anywhere. We also can't find the girl they are using, the girl seen on the Hotel Lorelei's security camera."

"I think I know where this is going."

"Oh yeah?"

"You want me to help you find them."

Anderson reached under his folded jacket and pulled out a manila envelope. "There's more information and some photos in here. I'm not going to suggest how you use the photos, only that it would be in the public interest that the girl at least is found. We'd very much like to speak with her. We're not releasing the picture of your military friend right at the moment. We want to keep that to ourselves until we have a better handle on where he's at."

I peeked inside the envelope. There were what looked like a half-dozen sheets of paper. "So I can use any of this?"

"It's all yours."

"*Le Journal* doesn't have it?"

"If they do, they didn't get it from me."

"Okay, thanks, this is valuable. Where do you think the girl is?"

"No idea. We've never seen her before. We have some people who are intimately familiar with this group of fuckwits and nobody knows who the girl is or where she went."

I stood up. "I may have someone who can help locate her."

Chapter Thirteen

After I left Anderson, I went to the Gargoyle. It was early in the afternoon and there were few customers. Virginia made me one of her famous Virginia Caesars and asked what I'd been up to.

I took a few sips of the Caesar. "Why this drink has not achieved worldwide recognition is beyond me."

She rolled her eyes.

"Do you remember Christmas Eve when I was in here talking to the guy I knew from Afghanistan?"

"How could I forget. That guy was in sad shape."

"Turns out, his troubles only got worse once he left here."

She looked at me, waiting for more.

"He got himself mixed up in something."

I told her about the Christmas Day murder.

She stepped back and crossed her arms. "You're shitting me."

"I am not shitting you."

"What exactly did he do?"

"I don't know yet, I'm trying to find out."

"You're trying to find out? When did you become a cop?" She started wiping down the bar, a sure sign of anxiety.

"I'm not a cop. I'm a reporter. I'm working on the story. On assignment for the *Gazette*."

She shook her head and exhaled loudly. "You just got yourself out of a mess and now you're going to get yourself back into one."

"The story needs to be told."

"Here we go again."

"I'm serious, Virg. This guy was a crackerjack officer, a man of courage and principle."

"Don't give me that bullshit," she replied." He didn't look like a man of principle sitting here like a three-day drunk. He looked like a reprobate."

"He's fallen on hard times. I need to know why."

"It's your funeral. No wait, it could be my funeral too, since he knows where you drink."

She turned and went into the back, probably to bring supplies up from the basement, leaving me alone with my thoughts, and my notes. And my drink. I still had a few hours to write the story before I had to file it. I had enough to match *Le Journal*, but I hadn't yet found a way to advance the story.

Virginia reappeared. "So what kind of story is this going to be?"

I gave her the details of what I knew to that point, leaving out a few things.

She said, not for the first time, "This is a case for the police, not for a beleaguered freelance journalist."

"I am no longer beleaguered."

"I don't believe you."

"Here's the situation. The man has come back from some very traumatic experiences overseas in the service of our country. He is damaged. He went to see a friend last night and something happened. I don't know what happened. The police are obviously investigating. There is a risk that if the police get to him before I can tell his story, it could go horribly wrong."

"What do you mean by that?"

"Let me explain it to you this way. Mike McPhee is an infantry officer. He is a former reconnaissance platoon leader. He's also a Pathfinder. Do you know what that means?"

She shook her head. "No. I don't know what that is."

"The Patrol Pathfinders course is the hardest to pass in the Canadian military. They have a failure rate of well over fifty percent."

"They should take better candidates."

"They only take the best candidates. You have to be in top physical condition to even attempt the Pathfinder course."

"What the hell is a Pathfinder anyway?"

"They're the medium and long-range reconnaissance patrollers. They specialize in insertion and extraction."

"Ouch."

I ignored her. "They go into enemy territory in front of mechanized brigades, they jump out of aircraft, they land behind enemy lines to prepare drop zones, landing zones, beach zones and airstrips."

"What for?"

"So that the follow-on forces know where to land. They help them get the layout of the ground and move to their objectives. For example, they do fast-casting, where they slip quietly over the side of a boat. The enemy might hear the boat passing but they wouldn't realize a Pathfinder team is now in the water and swimming back to shore in the dark to set up a beachhead. They rappel out of helicopters or down cliffs, they can parachute from any aircraft. They can swim out of any ship at sea or near the shore, in and out of submarines. They parachute at night into hostile territory, then they carry their hundred-pound knapsacks, a C-8 rifle and night-vision goggles, plus the 'chute itself, through rocky terrain for dozens of kilometers to a rendezvous point, all without being detected."

"So basically like supermen."

"Yes, but in addition to the physical feats, they also have to be wicked smart. They have to be skilled in combat team tactics and be able to plan detailed missions. They have to be adept in escape and evasion techniques. They have to know how to survive for weeks and months if necessary in hostile territory until they can get back to safety. They need to be able to identify food and water sources that will keep them going."

She was nodding now, nothing left to say.

I continued. "You see a guy with a Pathfinder badge and it's automatic respect."

"And this fella, this McPhee character, is one of them?"

"Yes."

"Okay, well then he probably doesn't need your help."

"That's just it. I can't square McPhee the Pathfinder with McPhee the murder suspect."

"Denny, remember what happened two months ago. You almost got yourself killed chasing a story. No story is worth that kind of risk."

Sammy walked out of the kitchen and spotted me. "All right, mate? How about a spot of curry?"

"What type?"

"Lamb Rogan Josh."

"My favourite."

He returned to the kitchen. Virginia started restocking the cupboards for the night ahead. I sat back and let the action revolve around me for a few minutes. By the time I'd eaten the curry, it was almost 3 p.m. I had to get down to the actual writing of the story.

Chapter Fourteen

I'd spoken to April Levy, the assignment editor, about the story I was filing, and then the night editor to hash out with him what I had and how we would approach the story. It wasn't complicated, and I was able to file a straight-forward 12 paragraphs by 8:30 p.m.

I stayed on in the Gargoyle after filing, working on one of the other stories. By this time there were a few patrons in some of the booths. The handful at the bar seemed content to drink quietly. Virginia had gone home early and Will had taken over behind the bar. He and I didn't get on particularly well. He resented my relationship with Virginia, I never knew why. Perhaps he didn't like that fact that she gave me discounts on food and drink in exchange for helping out once in a while on the door. And she let me run a tab. Will made me pay in cash.

When he took over, I ordered my usual St-Ambroise, set a bunch of toonies, dimes, and quarters on the bar, told him to keep the change and took a seat in the corner alcove beneath the window, where Bruno and I would be able to chat privately.

He had just been coming off shift when I called him to ask if he wanted to collect on the beers I owed him. He agreed to swing by.

He arrived a half hour later in good humour. Bruno was a large man, a good 220 pounds with a square head and lively blue eyes. He'd grown up on rue Saint-Patrick in the Point, a self-described brawler and baller.

I bought him a pint and ordered him some wings. We made the usual small talk until Sammy delivered the wings and Bruno tucked in. While he ate, I thanked him for helping me out on Christmas Day when I was at the Lorelei.

"You know this guy involved in the Christmas Day murder?"

"Yeah," he said, a wing pinioned between thumbs and index fingers. Food was the best way to keep a conversation with Bruno going.

"Here's the thing. I know the guy."

He stopped eating to glance at me. "What do you mean, the guy who got killed?"

"No, the other guy, the guy on the security footage, the person of interest."

"The army guy?"

"Yeah."

"Fuck me Roman. How do you know him?" Bruno wiped some sauce off his face and fingers.

"I knew him in Afghanistan. He's a military officer. Highly decorated."

"You've shared this with Anderson, I take it."

"Yes, Anderson and his partner, Brandt, paid me a visit last night."

I told Bruno about meeting McPhee on Christmas Eve right here in the Gargoyle. I told him about giving McPhee my number, about getting the phone call the next day.

Bruno stopped eating and wiped his hands carefully on several napkins. "It was a pretty bad crime scene, from what I hear."

"Bad in what way?"

"Bad as in messy. Whoever did it basically ripped the victim's face off. Not that many tears were shed. The guy was a pimp. But you know when sixteen-year vets are making jokes about a crime scene that it got to them."

"This guy, McPhee, was the crème de la crème in Afghanistan. One of the best, most well-respected officers in the whole theater. He was invited to participate in operations with the Americans. Do you know how rare that is?"

Bruno went back to his wings, picking off the stragglers. "So the guy spent too much time there. He comes back not right in the head. Goes on tilt. Decides to blow off a little steam with a Montréal hooker and it goes sideways."

"Yeah maybe," I said, sipping my beer. "But you guys don't have him yet?"

"Not yet. We're kinda stretched at the moment. There's this little thing called the Charboneau Commission."

I laughed. "The gift that keeps on giving."

Bruno had finished the wings and was sitting back with his beer. "Yeah, that one. It's kicking up all kinds of dust."

"How convinced are you guys that the army guy did it?"

"We have his prints all over the room. We have his prints on the thing that had your phone number on it. We have your prints on that thing. There weren't a lot of other prints in the room, surprisingly, considering the number of people coming in and out."

"That doesn't prove that he did it."

"No, just that he was there."

"But you guys aren't putting a big push on finding him? If you think he did it, the ex-military homicidal maniac currently at large in the city isn't priority one?"

"There's urgent and there's urgent urgent. Take your pick, buddy. Besides, the feeling is that he flew the coop. He's out of the country somewhere by now, lying low."

"That could be." I signalled to Will for two more beers. He pretended to ignore me so I got up to get them, reaching into my pocket for another load of shrapnel.

"This'll be my last one," said Bruno when I returned with two pints. "Early day tomorrow."

"What can you tell me about the victim?"

"Frank Leclerc. Low-level hood. He and his brother were running girls. They had about a dozen they shuttled back and forth between hotel rooms around Saint-Jacques, sometimes over in the West Island. But their main place of business was the Lorelei. You wouldn't believe the shit that goes on in there. The owner is a canny operator. We've tried to bust him a number of times and haven't been able to do it yet.

Frank and Felix got busted a few years ago operating out of the East End, down around Notre Dame. So when they got out, they moved the operation to the West End."

"You mind if I take a couple notes?"

"Go ahead."

He kept talking while I fished out my pen and notepad.

"The two of them, Frank and his brother have, or had, a partner called Pierre Blanchette. These guys are bad news, and they're into everything. I don't know what happened on the night of the murder. Frank was usually the calm one. He was the one who does all the technical work—posting the ads, taking the reservations, booking the hotels. Felix is usually the muscle. He waits around in the car while the girl is servicing the client, just to be on hand if there's any trouble.

"Blanchette is the drug link. He has affiliations with the bikers and the mob. So these guys are selling, they're also feeding drugs to the girls to keep them working. Your classic cycle of dependency and manipulation."

"Nice guys."

"There's a multi-agency effort to establish exactly how it all works—or at least there was until somebody beat the piss out of Frank. Now Felix and Blanchette have gone underground. We can't find them."

"What's Felix like?"

"Mad as a box of frogs. Frank ran the business. Felix couldn't run shit."

"Who are the women?"

"It depends. Sometimes they get dancers to do the dirty work for them. Sometimes they use Facebook to connect with out of town women. They lure them to Montréal, 'Baby I love you so much,' shower them with gifts. Next thing they know, these girls have a nasty coke habit and they're legs up in a hotel room for twenty guys a day. Every cent they earn goes to the pimps."

"You gotta wonder how they fall for it."

"Sure, but a lot of these girls are lonely. Unhappy at home. Desperate to escape their butt-fuck town in New Brunswick or wherever. Frank was a good-looking guy and a master manipulator. Fish in a barrel for a guy like him."

Chapter Fifteen

The next morning, I stopped again at the depanneur, got copies of the same four newspapers and went along to the same coffee shop for a cup of the same tasteless coffee. I read my story in the *Gazette,* which was on the front page, above the fold. The night editor had done a nice job of not doing much to the copy that I'd filed. The photos of the victim, Frank Leclerc, and the unknown girl were placed prominently under the headline: "Murder victim was leader of prostitution ring."

Le Journal had nothing on the murder, which made me nervous. I expected a follow-up story from Provost—it was standard practice for a newspaper to follow up a big story with a second-day story to keep it fresh in the public's mind. Maybe he was taking his time to get the larger picture.

The other two papers had very brief items, mostly written from the press release that the police had put out the day before. My story essentially put us back in the game for the time being.

Now, my reporting needed to focus on one of two areas. First, what exactly had turned Mike McPhee from a high-performing officer into a person of interest in a murder case. Second, what had happened in Room 110 of the Lorelei Hotel?

I'd told Anderson that I might know somebody who could help with finding the girl who was in the room with Frank Leclerc and McPhee. That person was my foster sister, Shawna Okwahu. Shawna had made a name for herself as an investigator by solving five cold cases related to missing and murdered Indigenous women. She lived in a community called Black Point River about an hour outside Montréal, but she spent a lot of time in the city, checking on sources, following leads. There was really no end to her work because, although she'd solved five cold cases, more than 1800 women in her database were still missing and presumed murdered.

I'd called her the night before to see if she could meet for coffee early, though I didn't tell her what it was about. I had just finished with the newspapers when she walked in the door, her long black hair moving like a curtain as she made her way toward me.

She was smiling that languid smile that always took me back to the house in NDG where I lived with my mother for that terrible period after my parents split up. Shawna came to live with us and stayed for two years, leaving in difficult circumstances. I was fifteen when she arrived. She was sixteen. After she left, we lost touch. But a story I'd worked on a couple of months earlier had led me to look her up and we had reconnected.

We hugged. "What's up, Denny D?"

"Living the dream," I said.

I got Shawna a coffee and once we had settled into our chairs, she looked at me as if to say, so what the hell is this all about?

"Have I ever told you that I was a reporter in Afghanistan for a while?"

She shook her head.

"It was back in 2006. I was working for a wire service. While I was there, I got on well with one of the infantry officers. His name was Mike McPhee."

She smiled. "I'm sure you'll come to the point soon."

"After I left Afghanistan, I didn't see McPhee for six years. Then he showed up at the Gargoyle a few days ago, on Christmas Eve. He was a changed man. I barely recognized him he looked so rough. We had a couple of beers and he went on his way. It turns out he may have gone to the Hotel Lorelei after meeting me."

"Hotel Lorelei? You mean where the Christmas Day murder happened?"

"So you've seen the story."

"Yeah, I read it this morning."

"He may have been in the hotel room at the time of the murder."

"Get out."

I nodded. "He called me on Christmas Day, five in the morning, to tell me he was in Room 110 of the hotel and something bad had happened."

"I just got tingles up the spine."

"By the time I got there, police were all over the place. And for some reason he left my phone number there, in the room."

"Oh shit."

I let her digest that information for a few seconds and took a sip of coffee before continuing. "So, I wrote a web bit for the *Gazette*. Then when I get home that night—"

"Christmas night?"

"Yeah, Christmas night. There were two cops waiting for me. They wanted to know why my phone number was left at the scene."

"What did you tell them?"

"I had to come clean."

I set the photo of the girl—the photo from Anderson's dossier, the same one that was published in the newspaper—on the table.

"I need to find her. Can you help me?"

"Why not let the police find her?" She was looking at me with those dark eyes—pools of intelligence and understanding, eyes that saw things in ways I never could. She was intimately familiar with the seamy side of the city, all the cracks through which had fallen so many young women. She knew about their lives, their deaths, and very often their whereabouts when nobody else did.

"Why not let the police find all those murdered and missing women," I said.

"I see your point. Why are you so keen to talk to her?"

"She may be able to tell me what happened inside the hotel room."

"You need this for the story?"

"There's a bit more to it."

She drank some coffee but her eyes never left mine. "Share with Sugar Bear."

I looked out onto Sainte-Catherine, to the cars and people. I had to trust Shawna with this.

"When I saw McPhee at the Gargoyle, we talked about how he was doing. He told me he was struggling. His marriage was falling apart. He wasn't allowed to see his kids. He gave me a bunch of documents about a drug called mefloquine. Have you ever heard of it?"

"I don't think so."

"The military gives it to soldiers deployed to combat zones where malaria is present. I haven't had a chance to go through all the documents yet, but I'm guessing McPhee blames mefloquine for his current struggles. The plan was for me to go through the documents and then he and I were going to talk about what was in them. Then this happened."

"So you want to find the girl because you think she might know where this guy is?"

"Essentially yes."

"And you just want me to drop what I'm doing and help you?"

Her eyes were smiling but the rest of her face and body suggested anything but good humour. I was reminded of all the times I'd teased her when we lived together. She would mostly ignore me. Then I'd say something that would trigger her, and she would get this look—the same one she had now. The memory was so vivid, and my emotional response so powerful, that I had to fight the urge to bolt. I even stuttered the first few words, uncertain of my footing with her.

"Well...ummm...I mean...only if you have time."

"Only if I have time. Only if I don't have anything else to do. Why is it you guys think your needs are more important than my needs? Why is it you guys think what I'm doing can play second fiddle. Do you think maybe what I'm doing is not as important as what you're doing?"

"Look, Shawna, I'm not trying to suggest—"

"You're not trying to suggest anything. What's coming out of your mouth right now is a bunch of words, and the words coming out of your mouth right now are saying that you think I can just drop what I'm doing and come running to help you find this girl so that you and your military dickhead can go live happily ever after. You think McPhee is the only guy who's not allowed to see his kids? Who's going to help me when I'm not allowed to see my kid?"

I wasn't sure what to say. "I'd pay you for your time."

That was clearly the wrong thing to say. "You think this is about money!"

"Definitely not." As I said this, my phone buzzed on the table and the name of an editor of one of the magazines I was working for appeared. They probably wanted an update on the Charbonneau Commission story I was writing for them.

"It's about the same goddam thing it's always about when some privileged white man goes to meet a vulnerable young woman in a hotel room for sex."

"I don't know what happened in that hotel room. He might have stumbled upon a crime that was already committed. He might have witnessed a crime in progress and become triggered."

"Triggered my ass."

"It's pretty clear to me he's suffering from something that looks like PTSD."

"You want to know about goddam PTSD?"

I just looked at her.

"I'll tell you about goddam PTSD." But instead of telling me anything, she grabbed her jacket and headed for the door.

"That went well," I said to nobody.

Chapter Sixteen

I walked in a daze back to my apartment. I hadn't expected Shawna to react the way she had. I was sure there was more behind it than my clumsy request. Was she having problems seeing her kid? I knew that Shawna had done some time in federal prison and her ex-husband had gotten custody of their son. But that was all I knew.

I didn't have much time to think about it. The editor from the *Standard* had left me a voicemail saying he urgently needed the story about ties between a provincial minister, construction firms, gifts and municipal contracts. I'd interviewed one of the heads of a construction and engineering firm in Quebec City and he'd had a lot to say on the recent testimony at the commission. It was just a matter of weaving parts of the interview with highlights from the testimony. After an hour of intense work, I filed the story.

I got up from my chair to stretch and get some food. I was still unsettled by Shawna's reaction.

Whatever the reason, it was a setback for my efforts to find the young woman who was likely in the hotel room at or around the time of the murder. She would have been the last person to see McPhee before the murder. Maybe she knew where he went. I needed to speak with McPhee about the documents. Maybe he'd said something to the woman about where he was going or what his plan was. He referred to her as an old friend. How would he have known a Montréal prostitute?

I checked my watch. It was only 10:30 a.m., the perfect time to revisit the Lorelei to ask the staff if they knew anything about the girl, now that I had a photo and a couple of days had passed. I found my keys, and drove over to the hotel.

It was about minus five and snowing. No sun. The hotel's sliding doors opened onto a grim little lobby. A vending machine sat prominently next to a small table and chair, and beside that a meager, fake evergreen was propped lopsidedly in a makeshift stand. Someone had hung a handful of plastic ornaments on it, but the effect was more depressing than festive. A few wispy strands of tinsel completed the sorry effect. On the wall opposite the reception desk, a couch and a ratty love seat vied for space beside an ancient elevator. An emergency exit sign glowed red in the corner. There was a strong smell of Lysol.

There was nobody at the reception desk. I leaned against it, waiting. The door to the office was ajar and I thought I could hear the murmur of conversation, but it could also have been a television or radio on low volume.

There was a bag of garbage in the corner of the lobby. I wondered what was inside it. A coffee urn on a small table by the sliding doors seemed like a thoughtful touch. I couldn't vouch for the quality of the coffee.

A large circular mirror above the desk afforded a view down the hallway of the ground floor. I saw two cleaners at the end of the hallway moving a cart piled with supplies into one of the rooms. I waited another thirty seconds and when nobody appeared, I decided to have a look around.

As I walked down the hallway the hairs on the back of my neck began to rise, because I knew I was getting closer to the room where the murder had taken place. Everything was quiet apart from the occasional muffled bang or thud from the cleaners. The sound of a vacuum. Passing room 104, I thought I heard something behind me, but when I turned, there was nothing there. I stopped in front of Room 110, my heart beating rapidly. I grappled with the feeling that I shouldn't be there, the feeling that I should turn around and walk back. I tried the handle of the door. It was locked.

A voice behind me called out. "Hey!"

I turned, ready to confess my transgression. It was a father yelling at his kid, a toddler who was running down the hall toward me. The toddler stopped and giggling madly, ran back toward his father.

I was starting to feel unwell and headed for a door at the end of the hall. I couldn't wait to get out into the cold air. There was something sick about the Lorelei, something that seeped out of the walls and through the floor—a stagnancy to the air, a poison about the place. I glanced in the room where the two housemaids were making up one of the beds. One of them glanced back at me. She was a black woman, maybe late forties or early fifties, a care-worn face, the face of a woman who had seen her share of troubles and kept her own counsel. I nodded to her, but she didn't acknowledge me.

I walked out the door at the end of the hall, compelled toward an unknown answer by some unformulated question. It was an emergency exit, but as I suspected, there was no alarm, at least no audible alarm. I walked around the corner of the building until I found the fifth window from the end, the window for Room 110. But the drapes were closed and I couldn't get a look inside. What had I hoped to see, the beer mat with my phone number still sitting there on the floor or the bedside table, wherever McPhee had left it? A pool of blood? Body parts? McPhee himself?

I kept moving around the back. There was a service entrance with a metal door which was locked. There were two white buckets, upturned, that I deduced the staff used as seats from the countless cigarette butts littering the ground. Some instinct told me to wait there, and after a few minutes, the door opened, and the black woman I'd seen at the end of the corridor came out. She stood beside me, took a pack of cigarettes from her apron and lit up. It seemed too cold for her to be standing out here dressed like that but she didn't seem to mind. She regarded me with a stoic look. Her skin was smooth, pulled tight over high cheekbones, and the lines around her eyes and mouth were deeply etched.

She said, "You're a reporter, aren't you?"

"I am," I said.

"They warned us there would be reporters."

"Who warned you?"

"The managers."

"I wanted to get a look inside the room."

"I know you did. But that room is locked up tight. Nobody is getting a look inside."

"Why not?"

She laughed. "You're sure in the right occupation, aren't you."

"That depends," I said. I took the photograph of the girl out of my pocket. "Do you recognize her?"

She ignored me. "You don't want Mr. Metzgar to find you out here."

"Who's Mr. Metzgar?"

"He's the day manager. He's not very nice. He's nicer than the night manager, but still..."

"Who's the night manager?"

She didn't answer. "Mr. Metzgar is probably watching you right now."

I looked up and there was a security camera directly overhead. "I'd better go introduce myself."

"Good luck with that," she said.

I offered her my card but she waved a hand as she exhaled. "No thanks."

I left her to finish her cigarette, making a mental note of the name on her tag—Olivia. When I reached the reception desk, a young woman was standing there, eating a sandwich. She hastily chewed and swallowed her food, then said, "I'm sorry, I start my shift at nine, but by eleven I'm always starving." She finished the last mouthful. "Merry Christmas, how can I help you?"

She was thin and attractive in an unassuming way. Large, dark-rimmed glasses dominated her face, and behind the lenses, a pair of blue eyes looked at me expectantly, helpfully. Her youthful, fresh appearance was wildly out of place in these surroundings, like a beautifully cut gem in a bargain basement bin. Her name tag said Katarina.

I smiled broadly and did my best to look unintimidating. I leaned an elbow on the desk and said in a conspiratorial whisper. "I was here two days ago. The police were everywhere."

The gamble could have gone sideways. She could have clammed up or called for the manager. Instead she rolled her eyes. "It's been awful. The room is still locked up."

I could have left it there but she seemed eager to talk.

"They need to bring in special cleaners. Not these ones." She gestured to Olivia and her colleague, now pushing their cart down the hall to the next room. "You know, like the ones who clean up after the crime scenes. They use special chemicals to get rid of everything, so ...."

"Do the police know what happened?"

"Not that I've heard. I just know the guy was, like, killed."

"Were you working that night, Katarina?"

"No. That was my colleague, Rufus. He was on night shift and I'm usually on days now."

I pulled the photo out of my pocket. "Do you know this girl?"

"That's the girl they're still looking for, right?"

"Yes."

"I recognize her. I used to work nights and—"

She stopped and said, "I'm sorry for running on at the mouth like this. You're not looking for a room, are you."

"Well, actually, I'm working on a story."

"Oh," she said. "You're with the newspaper."

"I'm a freelancer, on assignment with the *Gazette*."

"You're not going to quote me, right?"

"No, of course not," I said. "This is all just for background information." I recalled a detail from the information sheets that Anderson had given me. "I understand the victim registered under the name Jean Jeudi."

She smiled. "It was a fake name. People do that all the time here."

"I'm really very interested in speaking with the woman who was in the room."

Just then an older man, late fifties or early sixties, walked in from outside. He was in no way dressed for the cold. He was wearing a light, cotton jacket, no hat, thin leather shoes, the kind with soles that would easily slip on the ice. He carried a takeout coffee and a small paper bag that might have contained a muffin or a croissant. He gave the girl behind the counter a sharp look.

Katarina, obviously troubled, said, "Hello Mr. Metzgar."

Mr. Metzgar walked behind her without returning her greeting and into the office. He left the door open. I heard the sound of a chair on wheels, then Metzgar came out of the office and stood there with a face as sour as month-old milk. "What's the problem here?"

Katarina, clearly rattled, said, "This man is ...." But she wasn't sure what to say.

I held out my hand. "Denny Durant. I'm a freelance journalist."

He shook my hand, but there was no energy in the shake. It didn't rise to the level of a formality. His hands were like ice. "What can I do for you?"

There was no point beating around the bush. "I would like to speak to someone about the murder that took place here two days ago."

He shot Katarina an accusatory look. "What have you told him?"

She grew even more flustered and appeared on the point of tears. "I didn't, I mean, it was—"

I jumped in. "She hasn't told me anything. I just got here."

He pushed past her and started scrolling on the computer. "We have nothing to say," he said, without looking up. "You'll need to check with the police. We've been asked not to speak to any media."

"Of course. I'll just leave my card in case you change your mind." He ignored me, so I placed it on the counter.

"There's nothing we have to say. So unless you're looking for a room for the night, you'll need to leave the hotel."

The conversation was over. Katarina stood to the side awkwardly while Metzgar maintained control of the workstation.

"Of course," I said cheerily. "Thanks for your time. I'll put you down for a no comment, Mr. —?"

"I don't want my name in the paper," he said quickly, not without fear.

"Got it."

Chapter Seventeen

I was getting nowhere with finding the prostitute. I took it as a sign that I should focus my efforts on my other main area of inquiry—what had happened to McPhee before he came to Montréal. I pulled out my phone and checked the Twitter message I'd sent to Buzzy Buzsaki. Still nothing. I checked an online map to see how long it would take me to drive to Cornwall. It was less than two hours.

I figured that Buzzy's Bikes and Buggies would be open and that Buzzy himself would be there. The owner of a small business like his was unlikely to take more time off than the statutory holiday.

It was just after one o'clock in the afternoon by the time I left. There was a bit of snow, light flurries, and the temperature was about five below zero, with enough humidity in the air that an ice fog had formed, meaning I couldn't see farther ahead than a kilometer. Limited visibility. It struck me as a metaphor for everything that had happened since McPhee walked into the Gargoyle.

Until that day, it had been a long time since I'd thought about my time in Afghanistan. Then, as now, seemingly, McPhee had trusted me, and because he trusted me, the men and women under his command trusted me. He wanted the story told of what his soldiers were going through, and so I got many more opportunities to go on operational missions than the other reporters had. It inspired some jealousy but I didn't care. I got good firsthand accounts that the others found hard to get.

After a while, Sarah, the woman I had become involved with, grew pissed off that I was often the only reporter offered the chance to go outside the wire. She kept asking me to bring her along. I kept telling her it wasn't up to me. It was up to McPhee. But she wouldn't let it go. She said it was unfair. She was a good reporter and she was going to use every advantage to get out there. Finally I went to McPhee and asked if he could take both of us along on the next mission.

Buzzy was dead against it. He was in McPhee's office when I walked in. He said there was no way they could handle two reporters because the situation was too fluid. McPhee explained they'd heard that about three hundred Taliban fighters were massed on the other side of the Arghandab River, about 15 kilometres upstream from the base. McPhee was sending a few men on a reconnaissance mission to high ground at Bag Ghar to scope out what they could see. He didn't see a problem with my going.

Buzzy also seemed okay with me joining the mission, however he was legitimately nervous about Sarah going along. He had also taken a fancy to her. She had interviewed him for a story about one of the missions, and afterward he kept going out of his way to talk to her. She was a very attractive woman and a magnet for all these sex-starved soldiers. It wasn't hard to see that Buzzy was smitten.

He knew about my relationship with Sarah. I couldn't help but feel that his objection to her coming with us was more about trying to show he had more power than I did. He probably told himself he was being protective.

To be honest, I was ambivalent about her coming. Ambivalent is the wrong word. I was torn. I knew she was good. She could handle herself if things went pear shaped. She knew the risks. We all knew the risks. Her argument about fairness had been wearing me down. It was true, she had paid her dues.

So I felt a little bit like she deserved the opportunity. I also hoped McPhee would say no.

He said yes. And that's how she ended up in the LAV that day.

Several days after I was released from the hospital and they were getting ready to ship me home, McPhee came to see me to make sure I was okay. He was nothing but supportive. Buzzy, on the other hand, blamed me for Sarah's death.

I was standing there one day on base, taking a long last look at the mountains beyond when Buzzy joined me. We stood side by side, and without looking at me, he said, "You're always going to have her death on your conscience. You're the only reason she was out there." I turned to face him. I thought he might throw a punch but he turned and walked away.

When I returned to Montréal I did my best to forget about Afghanistan. I changed jobs, got married, had kids. I hadn't thought about the war for many years. And truth be told, I'd prefer never to think about it. Now after running into McPhee, after what happened at the Lorelei, there didn't seem to be any way to avoid thinking about it.

I had to come to grips with it. I needed to find out what happened to McPhee, and Buzzy was the only link I had.

Chapter Eighteen

I pulled into a large parking lot populated by old Jeeps, dune buggies and ATVs. A pristine Mercedes Unimog occupied pride of place at the front of the shop. A mechanic in blue coveralls stood inside the garage beneath a Jeep on a hoist. He watched me warily as I approached.

"Looking for Buzzy," I said.

He pointed with a greasy ratchet to the other end of the shop. A man in similar blue overalls was hauling an orange tarp over a Zodiac on a trailer. He had his back to me. I walked over. "Buzzy?"

He said something that sounded like a cross between "yes" and "hello," then receiving no reply, he turned to see who it was. His face clouded over. "You got a lot of nerve coming here."

I was surprised the animosity had survived all these years and my face must have shown it.

"Did you hear me? I said you got a lot of nerve coming here."

He was standing fully upright now. I watched his fists bunch and then he came at me. I braced to take a punch, but he wasn't the physical specimen he used to be. He stepped forward and I saw pain register on his face. He swung but it was a clumsy effort and I easily stepped back. He missed by a good six inches and when he didn't connect, the follow through from the punch took him off balance. He staggered and went down.

I looked at the other mechanic. He was watching, still with the ratchet in his hands, but didn't make any move to intervene. I figured there was no option but to see it through. I took off my coat, set it on a tire that was leaning against the wall, and put up my hands. "I just came to talk to you about McPhee."

He was back on his feet but breathing heavily now. He might have wanted to say something but maybe it would have been too much effort. We danced around each other for a while, but he was hobbling more than dancing. It looked like he couldn't put full weight on his right leg. He gradually recovered his breath and came at me again, wrapping me up in a bear hug. He tried to get a couple of upper cuts to land. One of them glanced off my ear.

I pushed him off me, stepped forward and caught him square on the nose with a good right hand. He went down and stayed there for a minute, but when he came up he was holding a screw driver like a knife. He must have grabbed it from his pocket. I kicked it out of his hand. He stopped then, and stood bent over, wheezing and holding his knees. I was breathing heavily by now too and there was sweat running down my face.

He stood up, staggered to a counter at the back of the shop about a dozen feet away and slid open a cupboard door. I thought he might be going for a gun. I got ready to run for it. He brought out a bottle and two plastic glasses instead. It was rye. He unscrewed the cap, half filled the glasses, and handed one of the glasses to me.

"That was for Sarah," he said. "I swore I'd beat you up, and now I have. Or I tried. I gave it my best."

He motioned to his office. "Come on, we need to talk."

Chapter Nineteen

H e sank into his chair behind a desk so strewn with papers and tools there was barely an inch of space left for his glass.

Without any preamble, he said, "There were times in the middle of Medusa and then in '07 when the Taliban were giving it to us when legit I didn't think I'd make it back. Whenever I thought about my kids I'd start to panic because I thought maybe I'd never see them again. So I started building this place in my mind." He looked around his office, almost in wonder. "I'd imagine it. I'd labour over it when I was riding around in LAVs or Coyotes or Bisons. I'd go to bed dreaming about it. I'd wake up and dream about it."

He took a good swig of the rye and looked at me without malice for the first time. "In 2007, we were out on patrol in the Panjwai. I got a round through the hip. I got lucky because it went right through me, missed all the vital stuff. I was a few weeks in hospital in Germany and then they shipped me back home." He sipped his rye. "Do you remember Pecker?"

"Pecker?"

"Peter Flynn. We called him Pecker. Little guy. Red hair?"

"Vaguely."

"He wasn't so lucky. He was standing right next to me when we got hit. He didn't come back."

We sat silently for a moment.

"I can talk about it with you because you know what it was like."

Everyone loses weight in Afghanistan because of the heat, so my memory of Buzzy was of a guy probably five foot eight and 170 pounds, and my notes said

Buzzy was smaller than McPhee, stocky and tough. But the Buzzy behind the desk had put the weight back on and then some.

He said when he got back he applied for a medical release and he was discharged from the military about a year later. I figured he was just going to keep talking until I said something, so I jumped in. "I ran into McPhee on Christmas Eve."

He made no comment, just looked at me, waiting for me to continue.

"I was having a beer in my local pub in Montréal and he wandered in. He seemed quite different from the last time I'd seen him."

Buzzy let out a long sigh. "Mad Mike now isn't the same Mad Mike we used to know."

"How do you mean?"

Buzzy raised his right hand to his face and made a pinching motion at his sinuses, as if he was rubbing sleep out of his eyes. "How long do you have?"

"As long as it takes," I said.

"I guess the easiest way to explain it is, he's been through some hard times."

"I'm probably going to write an article. Do you mind if I take notes?"

"Go ahead. Do you need to use my name?"

"I can say you're someone who's familiar with the situation."

"Yeah, so, McPhee. He and I..." It was clearly an emotional topic. He smiled, almost laughed, in the way some men have of laughing off a difficult subject. "I wouldn't say we had a falling out. We just stopped having much in common. He really...well, he changed." He took another swig of rye before continuing.

"The truth is, I'm not sure what happened. Mike and I go back a long way. He was a year ahead of me in high school. I idolized him. The guy was always a standout at whatever he did. He was always the best student. Top of his class in everything. And a great athlete. Football. Hockey. Wrestling. It wasn't like he was popular. He never drank or smoked or did drugs. People didn't know how to take him really. He was just so... driven. It was like he was being pulled toward something. Pulled on a hook."

"What did his parents do?"

"His dad was a teacher, like a university professor or something. He commuted to Kingston for a while but then he lost his job and he stayed home. His mom... I'm not sure how to describe his mom. She never had a job or anything, but she was damn opinionated. They had a big property over there around Glenview Heights, and they grew stuff and kept animals, goats and chickens and such."

"Homesteaders," I offered.

"Yeah, I guess so. Anyway, Mike and I would go to the gym together. He was a fanatical weight lifter and that's how I got into it too. He mentioned wanting to go into the military, and I stupidly figured that would be a good thing to do too.

"We both went through the ROTP. He went to the military college and I went to Brock, but he was a way better student than I was. He was just so intense. We both did the BOTC. He majored in Middle East studies and learned Arabic."

"BOTC?"

"Basic Officer Training Course. He wanted to be an infantry officer and that's what he did. He graduated and got posted to Petawawa.

"I just barely squeaked through engineering science at Brock. I frigged around way too much. But the military still took me and I ended up at Petawawa with Mike."

Buzzy poured a little more rye into my glass, then refilled his own. "We both did well, both got married and had kids. He was on a fast track and I also found my footing there. I made rank and was starting to think that military life didn't involve fighting. Then along came 9/11."

We paused, each of us retreating to touchstone memories of the event.

"Life changed completely after that. It was only a matter of time until we were deployed. Mike was on an elite track—you know he did the Pathfinders course right?"

I nodded.

"Twenty four guys started the course and six graduated. Anyway, he got sent to Kabul in 2002, attached with 1 RCR for their Roto 0. In case you don't know, that means the first rotation of a particular regiment or company."

I did know, but I said nothing and let him continue.

"I was deployed in 2006 and by then things had shifted to Kandahar. I was Mike's second in command."

He looked away for a moment, reminiscing. "I still remember the smell of that place. Kandahar. Diesel, AV gas and burning garbage. I remember when we flew into KAF. Nobody told us they'd be doing contour flying on the way in."

"What's that?"

"The plane follows the contour of the earth to make it less of a target for anti-aircraft fire. The pilots basically fly 100 feet above the ground. You look out the window you're eye level with the camels. You go, 'there's a cactus,' and you're like, 'what the fuck?' The pilot is banking hard right, then hard left. You're all packed in together. Some guys are puking, some are praying."

He shook his head at the memory. "We were there to relieve the Patricia's. We saw some of them on the ground when we got there. Some of them were in tears, hugging each other, saying things like, 'We fucking made it, man.' And I was saying to myself, what am I getting into.

"The same night, we did a ramp ceremony for the Patricia's. That was a kick in the nuts, seeing that flag-draped coffin get loaded."

I gave him a moment to recover. "That was your only tour?"

"Yup. I left a good chunk of flesh, blood and bone over there. I figured that was enough. But Mike did more tours after I got out and I didn't see him much when he was home.

"His wife, Emma, and my wife, Georgina, were close. They still are. That's how I get my information about Mike now. The best way to sum it up is, something happened to him. He went way down a dark road."

"When?"

"His first tour after I got out went fine, as per usual, from what he said. He and Emma had another kid. But when he came back in 2008, everything had changed for him."

"How so?"

"Something happened in Panjwai District, I forget if it was Zangabad or Mushan, but when he got back, to say he was disenchanted would understate matters. It's like he'd seen the light."

"When I saw him, he seemed slightly... deranged," I said.

Buzzy smiled again and nodded. His hands gripped the rye tightly, his knuckles were more scarred than any I'd ever seen. I wondered if it was from his injury or from working in the garage.

"Have you ever heard of mefloquine?"

"Mike mentioned it to me," I said. I didn't want to mention the envelope full of documents. I didn't want to give away too much. It's hard to fully trust a man who just tried to stab you with a screwdriver. I decided to play dumb.

"What is it?"

"It's a malaria drug. If you're in the military, you have to take it. Or at least, if you refuse to take it, they can declare you undeployable."

"Seems extreme."

"The military's rationale is that, by not taking it, you risk contracting malaria, and that could put you out of commission or even kill you. It's a liability. And to be honest, it's a pain in the ass to replace people who get sick. It could take three or four weeks to get someone over from Canada, so most commanders make sure their people take it."

He smiled grimly. "I never saw a mosquito over there. But anyway, after Mike came back from the 2008 tour, Georgina gets a call from his wife, Emma. Long and the short of it, she's saying Mike's not himself. He's drinking. The kids are scared of him. He's having crazy nightmares. He can't work."

"I go to see him on the base. We have some beers. I just want to shoot the shit but he's on permanent send."

"Permanent send?"

"He won't shut up about it, about mefloquine. He says it's poisoned him. He says nobody will take him seriously. All the doctors tell him the drug is safe, but he's not buying it. I mean, he was off his head about it."

"Did you have any problems with the drug?" I asked him.

"I remember some strange dreams, but no, not really. Most people didn't have problems. But some people did."

Another pause. Buzzy finished his rye and poured himself another splash.

"You break a leg. That can be fixed. Or like me, you get shot through the hip. You can get that fixed. You can get physio. I mean look at me, I'm almost good as new. But what Mike's got, I don't think there's much help for that."

I didn't say anything.

"Mike talked about the crazy dreams he kept having. He talked about this rage that he couldn't escape and that kept coming out of the worst times. Maybe he was drinking too much. He said it was the only thing that gave him peace.

"Anyway, I wasn't as good as I should have been about checking in on him. I was busy building the business and, to be honest, I didn't like him much when he was like that. He was always ranting about something. Definitely not the same guy I remembered.

"Emma eventually had to leave with the kids because he was basically unhinged. Then he just started taking off. He'd be gone for days at a time. Nobody knew where he was. I don't think he's been back here in weeks, maybe months. Georgina's not mentioned anything about him."

He seemed to have come to the end of his story, so I said, "When he walked into the bar where I was, he told me things hadn't been too good for him. But I need to tell you something that you have to keep on the DL." I told him about McPhee being a suspect in the Christmas Day murder.

"Ah shit. Did you tell the cops you knew him?"

"Yeah, I kinda had to, but I want to keep his name out of the news."

"You know, I may be out of line saying this, but if he gets into a jam in Montréal, you can bet your ass he'll be armed to the teeth."

"Great."

"Just saying. He will not be going quietly."

There was a pause, and my mind turned to the trek home. I didn't fancy being on Highway 401 with fresh snow making the pavement slick and dangerous.

Then Buzzy said, "He knows all about you."

"All about…?"

"He knew you were writing articles. He talked about it the time I went to the base to see him. He showed me a story you'd written. He said, 'Remember him? He was there with us in Afghanistan.' Then he forwarded me some stories a few weeks ago, something about an overdose. I didn't pay much attention, to be honest. I've been way too busy with the shop."

I began to wonder what else McPhee had known beforehand about me, what other strings he'd been pulling.

"Mike didn't do much without a plan behind it, even if the plan was wack-adoo."

"If I do write about this, do you think his wife would talk to me?"

He studied me for a minute. "I doubt it, but I can ask Georgina to ask her."

"I'd appreciate it."

"You know, I think something went bad on his last tour and he blamed himself. I heard through the grapevine that a good friend of his, Eric, was killed and McPhee may have been at fault. Poor decision making. McPhee mentioned Eric to me a couple of times."

"You didn't know him?"

"No, but I know the feeling. Your average citizen can never really understand how close you get to the guys you serve with. That bond. People think the 'Band of Brothers' thing is all hype, but it's really not. I still get choked up thinking about what happened to Pecker, and that was years ago. It never leaves you. The guys you serve with, they're closer than family. You end up not fighting for your country, but for the guys in your unit."

Buzzy finished the last of his rye. I finished mine and stood up to go. He said, "I'm sorry about—" and he gestured out to the shop, where we'd had the fight.

"Don't worry about it."

He walked me to my car. We shook hands and I thanked him for his time. I handed him one of my business cards.

"If you ever want to give this thing a lift kit, let me know," he said. "These Highlanders are great for off-roading."

"To be honest, Buzzy, I'm happy to stay on-road these days."

As I pulled out and pointed the Highlander in the direction of home, I realized I was leaving with more questions than answers.

Chapter Twenty

By the time I got to the 401, snow was falling fast and thick. I imagined a snowball fight between God and Satan. It was impossible to see where the road stopped and the shoulder began. Traffic had slowed to a crawl. I focused on following the barely visible tail lights of the car ahead. Occasionally a moron with a death wish would career along the outside lane, the one everyone was avoiding, and be lost in the whiteness.

Somewhere to my right was the St. Lawrence River, but it might well have not existed. From time to time the flow of traffic carried me past a large yellow truck, spitting salt out onto the road, and then a little farther ahead would be the plough, pushing as much snow off the road as possible.

I thought about my encounter with Buzzy. We had become adversaries in Afghanistan after Sarah told me he had walked up to her on the base and stated directly that she would make a good bedmate for him. I believed her at the time, but now it seemed unlikely. Could she have been mistaken? She didn't seem like the kind of woman who would pit one admirer against another. Not that I knew her particularly well. We'd been together for only a few weeks in extreme circumstances. She barely knew me, and our feelings ran deeper because of the circumstances. The theatre of war. We had a short, passionate relationship. Then she died. And now Buzzy and I had mended fences.

Assuming Buzzy's information was true, the upshot was that McPhee was unhinged. He was convinced mefloquine was at the root of his difficulties—that the government he had served for so long and served faithfully and risked his life for and gone through the worst kind of hardships for, was trying to poison him. And now he was on some kind of mission in Montréal.

I tried to get that through my mind, tried to imagine what that idea, if fully believed, would do to a person. Mike was always extremely dedicated to an idea and capable of doing a lot of damage. In Afghanistan, the idea was that we were fighting an enemy who deserved to die. Who was the enemy now?

Who was Eric? What had happened to him in Afghanistan? Who was Eric's sister? Who could I ask?

My phone rang, and even though now was not the time to be looking at a screen, I glanced at it in case it was Anderson calling to tell me they'd located McPhee or Johanna, eager for another rendezvous. It was a name I didn't recognize, Dorian something. I brought the phone to the steering wheel so that I wouldn't lose sight of the road and clicked speaker-phone.

"Hello."

There was a momentary pause, then a male voice said, "Is this Denny Durant?" It definitely wasn't Anderson. The voice was Montréal francophone.

"That's me. Who's this?"

"I hear you're looking for information about what happened at the Lorelei on Christmas Eve."

"Yes, that's correct. Who told you that?"

"It doesn't matter," he said. "I have the information you're looking for."

Experience had taught me that the only information I could ever trust was the kind of information that I found myself. Information that arrived on my doorstep was never to be trusted.

"Interesting," I said. "I'm driving at the moment. Can I call you back?"

"You know La Cage in LaSalle?"

"Yes, I think so."

"Meet me there tonight at eight."

"What's your name?"

"You don't need to know my name right now. Have you talked to the cops?"

I didn't like the sound or the tone of the voice, the brusqueness of it. It was the type of voice that preceded a punch.

"No, I haven't spoken with the police. Why do you ask?"

"Are you sure about that? You don't sound too sure."

"Yes, I'm sure. Why would I go to the police?"

"Meet me tonight at eight. I'll give you the information."

"What's your name?"

But the line went dead.

Chapter Twenty-One

After I got back from Cornwall, I had the feeling of the ground slipping away, of being on a sheet of ice and unable to find my footing. I had the vague sense that regardless what had happened to McPhee, I had been absent not just from the people I'd known over the years, but from myself as well. Where had everyone gone? Where had the time gone? Where had my life gone?

The man had called again around five o'clock, almost as soon as I stepped out of the Toyota back home. Again, he insisted I meet him that night and gave me precise instructions that only heightened my sense of foreboding. It seemed like a setup.

I thought about calling Anderson to let him know that somebody was promising information, but I didn't want anything more to do with Anderson or the police or anything outside of my immediate realm, which was journalism. And it's not that unusual to get someone calling you promising information.

I ate a desultory dinner at Mr. Yu's Noodle House down the street from my apartment while finishing off yet another story about the Charbonneau Commission, this one about another lawyer who had resigned, and at seven-thirty climbed back into my vehicle.

The clean up crews had made good progress removing some of the record snowfall from the city's main arteries, and I made decent time along the Expressway to the 15, and then the 15 to blvd Leverendrye, but it was slow going into LaSalle. The smaller streets off Airlie were almost impassable.

I finally located La Cage and managed to find a clearing in the snow bank that was large enough to park in. I still had ten minutes before the rendezvous, so

I let the car idle while I decided whether it was really worth it. I had to weigh the possibility that he did have useful information against the probability he had some ulterior motive.

But I really had no choice. There was a chance the gruff caller had something useful to share with me, so I had to take that chance. Besides, we were meeting at a public place. I presumed there would be other people there. What was he going to do, shoot me in a crowded bar?

It was now almost eight. I found the bar wedged between an Italian and a Vietnamese restaurant. I brought the chill with me as I stepped inside and a shiver ran up my spine when the door closed behind me.

The place was virtually empty. It seemed even more empty because it was cavernous with a huge bar at the back. As I approached the bar, I saw there was another whole section with screens playing everything from European hockey to basketball to soccer. Judging from the uniforms, it looked like at least two of the major leagues in Europe were showing.

The stranger had told me to sit at the table across from the bar, next to the cash machine. That's what I did. I sat down and took off my coat. As my eyes adjusted to the dimness of the interior, I saw a few tables were occupied by men, mostly middle-aged, similarly dressed in T-shirts and sweaters or hoodies, the majority with logos of sports teams—the ubiquitous Canadiens but also the New York Giants or the Chicago Cubs. They were scattered here and there randomly about the place.

One of the tables in the other section was occupied by three men, huddled in conversation. One of the men glanced up, detached himself from the group and walked over to the bar. He was a grim, grey looking geezer with no hint of humour or hospitality. He seemed put out that I was there. I would have thought, judging from the lack of customers on a Saturday night, he would have welcomed the trade, but apparently not.

Nonetheless, he went behind the bar and started fiddling with something, possibly a phone. I expected that maybe he would come to the table but it became clear after a few minutes that if I was going to get something to drink, I'd have to go to him.

I asked for a St-A. The man grabbed a bottle from the fridge and set the beer in front of me. I handed him a twenty. I expected him to ring it up in the till and give me some change. Instead, he pulled out a wad of bills from his pocket, added my twenty, gave me a ten and resumed fiddling with his phone.

"Quiet night," I said, to find out if he could actually speak.

In a thin voice he said, without looking up, "No hockey."

I might as well have been talking to a hologram, it wouldn't have made a goddam bit of difference. I went back to my table, where I sipped my beer and scrolled through my phone. It was eight-fifteen. I decided to finish my beer and call it a night if the person with the information hadn't shown by then. About ten minutes later, the door opened and a man appeared. He was wearing a toque low over his eyes and a scarf that covered his neck and chin, but I recognized him from the photograph that Anderson had given me. It was Felix Leclerc.

He looked quickly at me and then at the man behind the bar. Some discreet signal appeared to pass between them. Felix walked out into the main bar, had a good look around, then walked back to the counter. He removed the scarf and hat. He was shorter than I expected. His nose was small and pointed in the attitude of a burrowing animal, a quality the photograph wasn't able to convey. He had dull eyes set close together in a pugnacious face set atop narrow shoulders with barely the interruption of a neck. He moved with a graceless determination. There was nothing fluid about his movements. It was all appetite.

The man behind the bar wordlessly placed a beer on the counter and returned to his table in the far corner. Felix took the beer. There was no exchange of cash. He walked over to where I was sitting and stood there.

Felix and I were alone in this section of the bar. It wouldn't have surprised me if somebody appeared out of nowhere and put a 'Closed' sign on the door. He stood in front of the table, maybe three feet away. He was holding my business card. He said, "You Denny Durant?"

I stood and extended my hand. "I am."

He pocketed my card. "Save it, chum. This isn't a meet and greet."

He had the social graces of cardboard. The voice was a low growl designed to issue communiques directly from the lower brain stem. I sat back down. He looked like just the type to shoot me in front of witnesses inside a sports bar.

It seemed obvious that Metzgar, the Lorelei manager, had given Felix my business card and told him I'd been poking around. But I hadn't told Metzgar much about what I was looking for.

He sat down in the chair opposite me and said without smiling, "You were asking about what happened with the murder down there. I heard you were going to put something in the paper about Frank."

I remained non-committal.

"Here's the thing," he said, after downing some beer. The bottle rested on his teeth as he drank. Coors Light. He looked around furtively. He appeared to be cycling between anger and anxiety. I waited for him to speak. "I told you I had some information about what happened at the Lorelei. I'm telling you now face to face. You don't need to know what happened at the Lorelei."

There was something missing behind Felix's eyes. "Oh no? Why is that?"

He leaned a little forward. A hint of a smile played on his face. He had a smattering of freckles on his pale cheeks. "You don't need to know what happened at the Lorelei, and you don't need to know why you don't need to know."

I almost laughed but decided that laughing could be lethal.

It was as blunt a statement as he could make. And yet I was still trying to get information. I said, perhaps unwisely, "I disagree with you."

He was looking at me with curiosity now, like I was some new species.

"You know who I am right?"

He was a dangerous child. He needed reassurance and violent entertainment all at the same time.

"I have an idea who you are, yes."

"I'm Felix. That's Latin, for lucky. I'm Frank Leclerc's brother."

I took a moment to have a sip of my beer.

"I'm sorry for your loss."

He was expecting me to be more afraid, or to show him more deference, but my thoughts were fixed on getting him to tell me as much as he could about what had happened three nights earlier at the hotel."

I was skating fast on the ice of my daring. "I need to find out what happened so I can figure out who killed your brother."

"I know who killed my brother."

"You do?"

"Yeah, some batshit crazy soldier named McPhee."

I tried not to let the surprise show on my face.

"How do you know McPhee?"

Felix took another swig of beer and looked around. "You don't need to know that either."

"Were you there that night?" I knew it was a dangerous question. Felix looked at me steadily before answering. I was banking on the fact that everyone, sinners and saints alike, felt an intrinsic need to tell their story.

"I was supposed to be there but I had some shit to do that took longer than it should have. If I'da been there, Frank would still be alive and McPhee would be dead." But he didn't look convinced. In fact, he may still have been in shock. Maybe he'd had to identify his brother's body.

He picked up the bottle and drank. I wondered which would last longer, his patience or his beer. He looked hard at me. "Nobody needs to know what happened. Frank got himself killed. It's over. Nobody needs to go digging around in our business. There's nothing to write about."

He mustn't have seen this morning's newspapers. I took out my notebook and pen. "Can I quote you on that?"

"Don't be stupid, chum. I'm gonna deal with McPhee. I almost got him once. I'll make sure next time. And I'll deal with you if you write anything."

I couldn't help but think he was warming to me. "Can I ask you a couple of questions about Frank?"

He was like a cornered cat, ready to swipe at the closest attacker. "You're fucked in the head."

My phone rang. It was Johanna. I let it go to voicemail.

He sat there, temporarily flummoxed. "Who was the girl in the hotel room. Could you at least give me her name?"

A lewd smile played at the corner of his mouth. "You want me to set up a date with Vanessa? She's pretty sweet."

"Yeah, could you put me in touch with her?"

He was getting bored now. He sat forward in his seat, wiped a finger across his nose.

I persevered. "Is Pierre Blanchette part of your crew?"

His expression darkened. He finished his beer in a dramatic flourish and stood up, slamming the bottle down on the table as hard as he could without breaking it. The noise echoed through the bar but nobody paid us any attention. When he looked at me, there was a different actor behind the mask. He glanced over at the bartender in the far corner then turned and walked away, cramming his toque back over his head and winding his scarf around his neck. He left the bar and the door slowly closed behind him. Then a blast of cold air hit me.

Chapter Twenty-Two

I thought Felix would be waiting outside to finish our discussion, but I needn't have worried. There was no sign of him when I left the pub.

I got home just before ten, and I was exhausted. I had planned to do a little more work on the three stories I had remaining for this week, but I was incapable of it. I went to the fridge, cracked a beer and sat heavily on the sofa. Elliott came over and started kneading my stomach with his paws. I thought briefly about calling Anderson or Bruno and telling them about the encounter with Felix, but the idea of dealing with the police was too much.

I thought about what Felix had told me. If McPhee was threatening Felix and Blanchette, that might explain why they were in hiding. That might explain why Felix had been wearing a hat and scarf to cover his face when he walked into the bar.

I recalled Felix saying "Latin for lucky," and I couldn't help but laugh. This whole situation would be ludicrous if people weren't being killed.

Felix had said the girl's name was Vanessa. I thought about that for a minute but couldn't make any connections. I decided to call Shawna tomorrow and let her know that I had the girl's first name. But right now, I needed diversion. I reached for the day's newspaper on the coffee table.

In the past, I would have first checked the NHL scores and read any news about the Montréal Canadiens, but the only hockey stories would be about the lockout, so I flipped through the page, stopping at the horoscope, which read "Just because you're not talking to someone at the moment doesn't mean you've lost the connection. Silence and space between people who share a strong affinity often signifies a strong bond not a deficit."

Who had I lost touch with? McPhee? My kids?

I was starting to doze when there was a knock on the door. I looked through the peephole. It was Johanna. I'd forgotten that she'd called. I hadn't seen her since I dropped her at the Metro Station on Christmas Day, and truthfully I hadn't expected to see her again. I thought we were ships that had merely passed in the frozen night. But she had other ideas. She kissed me warmly after I closed the door.

"Are you busy?"

"No, I was just reading the paper. Nice to see you."

She hoisted up a bottle of good Burgundy. "You could probably use a glass of wine."

I wasn't sure what to say. There was an awkward silence. She laughed. Perhaps she was used to having this effect on her lovers.

"I've been missing you, waiting for you to call." She walked into the kitchen and started looking for an opener. "I've been a little busy with stuff," I said, feeling both affronted and guilty. "I didn't have your number."

"Busy with stuff," she said mockingly. "I left my number right here."

She lifted a square piece of paper from the coffee table and handed it to me. Written in pen was her name—Johanna Nieminen—and her phone number, along with a skillfully rendered elf with massive phallus.

I couldn't help but laugh. "I could use a glass of wine."

She moved sock-footed about my kitchen. She wore tight black jeans and a black blouse, her makeup lightly applied. Black pearl earrings complemented her dark hair and dark eyes. I began to forget about my work.

I put on some music, a Montréal playlist: Nikki Yanofsky, Sam Roberts, Bobby Bazini, Patrick Watson, Erin Lang.

She brought the glasses over to where I was sitting on the sofa.

"What have you been busy with?"

I was impressed, once again, by her directness. Were all Finnish women like this? She seemed like the type who could handle the vicissitudes of life, who could sail through rough waters without capsizing. As we drank, I told her about McPhee, and her expression grew more alarmed the farther into the story I went.

"Did you have any idea any of this would happen?"

"No," I said. "I had no idea."

She put her glass down and snuggled into me. She had brought a warmth and life to the apartment that had been absent for too long. I basked in it, pushing the dark thoughts of Mike McPhee, of Buzzy and Sarah, of war and Afghanistan to the back of my mind. I was feeling grateful to be inside with this woman.

Gratitude. Not something they teach you in school. Not something you ever think about until your life capsizes and you learn it's the only thing that will keep you afloat. I'd learned to cling to it.

Keen to change the subject from McPhee, I said, "What have you been up to?"

"Working on my dissertation."

"What's it about?"

"It's about the use of rhetorical devices to express shame and guilt in Finnish post-war literature."

"Sounds like a riot," I said.

She laughed. "Are you a fan of Kafka?"

"From what I remember, yes I enjoyed his work, but I've only read a couple of his short stories. Something about a cockroach and a hunger artist."

"Kafka said a book must be the axe for the frozen sea within us."

"Meaning?"

"Meaning he thought we should only read books that affect us like a disaster or like a suicide."

"What about reading for pleasure?"

"Forget about it. Kafka used several rhetorical devices to end the reader's detachment, to draw them in and to, as he put it, 'freeze the laughter.' My dissertation traces how various writers of the post-modern period in Finland used these same devices."

The mention of disaster turned my thoughts back to McPhee.

"Do you think he's still in the city?" Johanna said, guessing what was on my mind.

"Talk about freezing the laughter," I said. "Yes, I do think he's still in town."

"Why do you think so?"

"Because he believes he's on a mission, and the mission isn't done yet."

She must have sensed my change in mood because she sat upright, then said, "You know, my father was a journalist?"

"Oh?"

"Yes. So I'm used to seeing someone preoccupied with a story."

My phone rang. The caller ID said 'Frank.' I didn't want to answer it but the journalist in me picked up on the third ring.

"Hello?"

"Hey Denny, you've been doing some good work."

"McPhee?"

"That's right."

"Where the hell are you Mike?"

"I can't tell you that, Denny. But hey, you know what?" The tone of his voice was jocular, fatalistic. I began to get a sick feeling. "I've got another story for you."

Chapter Twenty-Three

I pulled up outside the club where McPhee said I would find the new story. It was a seedy little joint in a strip mall off of Decarie Blvd. I had expected to see a scene alive with emergency vehicles and police just like at the Lorelei, but that wasn't the case. The only flashing lights were the festive ones around the windows of the Lebanese restaurant next door. It looked like an ordinary Thursday night in late December.

The club was at the end of a row of shops and restaurants. It was called Luxotica and advertised nude dances, cheap pitchers of beer and all you can eat chicken wings. I imagined the dancers going home after a shift covered in buffalo sauce from the greasy fingers of the patrons.

I found a parking spot and backed into it so I could watch the club for a while and assess what to do. I was still expecting the police to show up, but the longer I sat there, the more I wondered whether McPhee was pulling my leg. I'd hated to leave Johanna. I wanted to go back.

She had taken it like a good sport, and I insisted she stay, telling her I didn't think I'd be long, but now I wondered if that had been fair. I didn't know how long I would be. Then it struck me how waiting in the car now was ridiculous. I should go in and have a look. If nothing was happening, I would go home.

When I opened the door and stepped inside, it was like walking into a wall of sound. Scantily clad women roved around the place, stopping at various tables to chat and flirt with the customers, nearly all of them men. I hadn't been sure what to expect, but this was definitely not a crime scene. So far the only crime was the music. I decided to have a quick beer, just to make sure I didn't turn around and leave too quickly.

The bartender was a leathery woman in her early fifties. Maybe she knew something.

I took my time digging out my wallet to pay for the beer. "How are you?"

She looked at me with undisguised contempt. Her smile couldn't have been tighter if it had been zipped on. I was just another middle aged man whose only option for titillation was to buy it. In other words, a scumbag.

She finally came out with "Doing great." She had to shout because the music was so loud.

"Were the police in here earlier?"

She looked at me like I was a lunatic. "No." At the mention of police, a man standing a few feet away and still dressed in his construction worker outfit looked around. I needed to be more careful.

Our transaction complete, the bartender walked rapidly away to the other end of the bar. I retreated to a small table by the door to drink my beer and then head home.

It wasn't long before two scantily clad women approached. They must have sensed fresh meat. "Where you from?" they said in unison.

"I'm just having a beer, ladies."

One of them peeled off and rejoined the circuit, but the other one took a seat. She was a young woman, with long limbs and short blond hair. She would look good in glasses. My first impression was that of a college student.

"Have the police been in here this evening?"

"No, why?"

"Just checking. I heard a rumour earlier."

"What, you an ambulance chaser?"

"I'm actually an injury lawyer. I like to show up at crime scenes offering my services."

"Oh yeah? Injury lawyer. That sounds fancy."

"Very fancy. I normally wear a top hat but I left it in the car."

"You sure you don't want a dance?"

"Positive."

She moved on.

In the back corner of the room, three men were sitting at a table, ignoring the dancers, looking as if they were waiting for someone. They didn't fit in. They looked frightened, or apprehensive, but in an aggressive way. They seemed to be looking at something on a cell phone and arguing.

I realized with a start that the man holding the phone was Pierre Blanchette. I couldn't be sure, but there was strong a resemblance to the photo of him Anderson gave me. Two pimps in one night. My stars must be aligning.

Another woman came by my table but I waved her off. Blanchette got up from the table, said something to one of the men, which he seemed not to like because he was about to stand up when the third man put a hand on his shoulder to keep him in his chair. Pierre grabbed his coat from the back of the chair, took a long swig of beer, set the bottle down on the table and walked past my table, out the door. I considered calling Anderson. He did say, after all, that the police wanted to find Blanchette. But there wasn't time. I quickly looked back at the table. The two men were deep in conversation, apparently oblivious to or not caring that Blanchette had left.

I followed him out to the parking lot on the chance I could talk to him, or at least see where he was going. I wanted to ask him if McPhee had contacted him as well. I wanted to ask him about Vanessa. But he seemed to be in a hurry. Maybe he was going to meet Felix. The cold air outside took my breath away. I walked around to the parking lot, zipping up my coat, checking to see if there was movement anywhere.

I'm not sure what caught my attention, whether there was a noise, but something made me turn to my right. At the back of the parking lot there was a car parked at an odd angle. The passenger side door was open. There was just enough light for me to make out that a man was standing against the car, using the roof as a platform for a high-caliber rifle. I looked to where his rifle was pointing, and saw Blanchette, standing at his car door, unlocking it and about to get in. I instinctively started to yell, but the shot cut me off. One moment I was looking at Blanchette, and the next moment the top of his head had vaporized, and it was just a body pinned up against the car, starting to fall. The second shot spun the body around, and it fell to the ground beside the vehicle. When I looked back at the shooter, he was already in his car and flying out of the parking lot. I watched the tail lights as it entered Decarie, swerved around an oncoming pickup truck, blew through a red light and disappeared down the ramp heading north on Highway 15.

There was no doubt in my mind the shooter was Mad Mike McPhee.

Chapter Twenty-Four

I kicked into gear immediately. I was probably in shock but I just did what came naturally, which was to start making calls. I called 911, and was on the phone with the emergency operator as I walked over to the body. I was dimly aware of a siren in the background. Everything else was quiet, except the echo of the gunshot in my head. I was calm, at least I thought I was.

The operator asked me whether victim was breathing. By that time I was looking down at what remained of the body, which lay in a bloody mess next to the vehicle. I'd seen several bodies before destroyed by military rifles, so this wasn't too much of a shock but it was still a horrible sight.

Gore was spattered on the cars he had been standing between and on the snow bank behind them. A pool of black liquid lay where Pierre's head used to be. It was a glistening mess. There was the smell of something pungent.

"He is definitely not breathing." She asked me to check for a pulse, so I explained that his head had been shot off and there would be no pulse.

A few passersby had gathered around me now, and within a minute or so, a loud siren sounded within feet of us, as first a firefighter, then an ambulance arrived. The people moved away as the police took charge of the scene. I sat down on the curb. I was aware that it was cold, and my coat was undone.

An officer squatted beside me to take my statement. First he asked me why I was there.

"I was in the club and I was heading home. I walked out just in time to see the shooting."

"What can you tell me about the car?"

I tried to remember. "I couldn't see it very well. It was about 100 metres away and the parking lot isn't well lit. If I had to guess, I would say it was a dark colour, two door, foreign make, maybe German."

"Anything else?"

"I couldn't be sure but I think it was an Ontario plate, a veteran's plate. It had the little poppy on the right-hand side."

"Do you remember the plate number?"

"No."

"What was he wearing?"

I thought back. "It looked like a black or navy combat jacket and a baseball hat on backwards but that's all I could see. I glanced at him then he fired, and after that he was in the car and driving away."

"Did you see the gun he used?"

"He had the rifle propped on the top of the car. It was one of those rifles with the kickstands. He took two shots, flipped up the kickstand, threw the rifle in the car and drove off."

"Is there anything else I need to know about what happened?"

"I know who did it. And I think I know who the victim was."

He paused his note taking. "You're telling me you know the perpetrator and the victim?"

"Pretty sure. Can you let me speak with Anderson?"

"Detective Anderson?"

"Yeah."

"Are you a CI?"

"A confidential informant? No. I'm a reporter, on assignment for the *Gazette*."

The patrol officer took in this information. "Okay, wait here."

I called the paper and got the same night editor I'd worked with the night before. I told him there had been another murder, possibly linked to the Christmas Day one. The editor asked how I knew that. I told him I knew that the latest victim was connected to Frank Leclerc, the victim at the Lorelei.

"Who is the latest victim?"

"A guy called Pierre Blanchette. He was mentioned in our story a couple of days ago. Or yesterday." I was losing track of the days.

"When can you file?"

"I don't know."

"Why not?"

"I witnessed the murder. The police want to interview me about it. I'm on the other side of the tape right now, waiting for the lead detective."

There was a silence on the other end of the line as the editor considered the proper form of action to take. Good editors were like quarterbacks on a football field or generals in a battle. They take all the information available, decide what action to take and dispatch the appropriate resources to achieve the goal.

"Okay," he said after a moment. "I'll get someone down there. Let's write two paragraphs now to tide us over. Just give me the facts."

We worked on the two paragraphs for the online version while I waited for Anderson. He read it back to me and I told him it was good to go. He said he'd post it under my byline on the website and to keep him updated. Meanwhile, he was going to hand the story off to the late reporter.

I got to my feet to see what was going on. Police had cordoned off the club and the parking lot with orange tape. There was a huge crowd of people now standing silently outside the club. Most of them had coats on, but a few didn't. The ones in nothing but shirts and T-shirts shuffled back and forth, their hands jammed into pockets. Some smoked cigarettes. The air of death hung over the place.

I felt unsteady on my feet, probably from the shock, and sank back down to the curb. A fireman must have spotted me, because he knelt in front of me so that we were at eye level.

"How you doing, sir?"

"Better than that guy." I nodded in the direction of where Blanchette had fallen. To obstruct the view from the merely curious, the police had parked a vehicle in front of the body.

"I just need to shine a light in your eyes. That okay?"

"Go for it," I said, thinking that shining a light on the scene was what we all needed to do. Why had McPhee wanted me to witness this? Was he trying to shine a light on something? What?

The paramedic quickly beamed the light into my eyes, leaving a pattern of spots and stars in my vision when he switched it off.

"Why do you guys do that?"

"We're testing your pupillary reflexes. It's a good indication of the state of your brain."

"How's mine?"

"Technically okay." He stood up. "But you may be in mild shock. We need to get you warm."

No sooner had he said it than I began to tremble, and the trembling quickly turned into a full-blown shiver. The paramedic returned with a blanket. I let him put it on me but I was thinking about the story.

I looked up at the crowd. The press was beginning to arrive on the scene, Robert Provost among them. Our eyes met. He must have wondered what I was doing there on the other side of the tape, sitting on the curb with a blanket over my shoulders. He gave me a quizzical look and then turned away. There were three television cameras. I spotted Camille Sutton and Victor getting ready to do a stand up. Word must have gotten out about the potential link between the Christmas Day murder and this one.

Anderson turned up a short time later. He stood there looking down at me then nodded toward his car. "Come on."

Chapter Twenty-Five

As soon I sat down in the passenger seat of his car, I realized how tired I was, and that I was also tired of having to deal with death.

I told him what happened. He took notes. He asked to have a look at the phone number McPhee had called me from. I showed it to him.

"Frank," he said to himself.

"Frank Leclerc?"

"Yeah. McPhee must have taken Frank's phone from the hotel room."

That meshed with what I had read in the police documents Anderson had given me, that there had been no cell phone recovered from the scene. Was one of McPhee's skills being able to hack into cell phones?

Anderson was edgy, irritated. He now had two murders to close. And the prime suspect wasn't some dumb gun for hire or an opportunist. This was a hard, principled professional. Anderson had met his relentless foe.

I thought of something. "Blanchette was at a table with some other guys, they were all looking at Blanchette's phone and having a serious debate about something on the screen."

Anderson was nodding slowly, following my logic.

"Frank's phone would have their numbers in it. Felix, Blanchette."

"We'll put a trace on the number," he said, but I knew there were ways to prevent a cell phone from being traceable, and if anyone would know about that, it would be McPhee.

"So he's calling them to arrange meetings..." I let the sentence die, but my next thought was *to lure them into the open because he's hunting them.* That would explain why Felix turned up at the sports bar dressed like that. He was covering his face with scarf and hat to avoid being recognized.

Instead I said, "Have you found Vanessa?"

He looked at me blankly.

"The woman from the Lorelei."

"I can't tell you that."

"I'd like to speak with her."

As he looked away, he made a noise that could have been a chuckle or a belch. I couldn't be sure.

I wondered if I should tell him about my meeting at the sports bar. I decided there was nothing to lose. "I spoke with Felix earlier tonight."

Anderson's expression changed. It looked like he was trying to decide whether or not to be angry. "What did he say?"

"He said if he'd been there that night, Frank would still be alive. He told me not to write anything about the murder or about Frank or about his business."

Anderson snickered. "Good thing Felix doesn't read."

"He told me he almost got McPhee, and that he wouldn't miss next time."

Anderson nodded his huge head, like it was all panning out as he'd expected. "Did Felix tell you this on the phone or did you meet him?"

"We met. At the Cage in LaSalle."

"That tracks. We think he's staying somewhere down around there. Would have been good for you to give us a heads up. We could have arranged to join you."

"But that would have seriously curtailed my conversation with him."

He looked at me with something like amusement. "It took some balls to sit down with a guy like Felix. It could have gone very badly. He's got the shortest fuse in the city. I've seen him go off on guys for walking in the door the wrong way."

"Ignorance is bliss."

"I know you gotta do your job. Just watch yourself."

His tone had changed from our last meeting at Dunne's. He was back to being the kindly uncle. Then he asked, "Are you sure it was McPhee who did this?"

I thought back to the moment of the shooting. "Pretty sure. It happened fast and it was dark, so I didn't get a great look, but my first thought is that it was McPhee. Why?"

"We still can't be sure it was McPhee who did the guy in the hotel room. There's a turf war happening right now, it could have been another group, pissed off at the Leclerc brothers for taking away their business."

We sat with that for a moment, watching the police moving around the scene, some of the patrons moving back into the bar, others deciding to head home. "But why would McPhee be calling Felix, threatening him?"

Anderson mulled that one over for a few seconds, then asked, "If it was McPhee, why do you think he's telling you either right after or, as in this case here, right before, he pops these guys?"

"I don't know. But you know he's a Pathfinder, right?"

"Yeah, I heard something about that."

"Pathfinders find a place for the oncoming forces to land, so perhaps that's what he's doing. He's showing me the way to a story."

Anderson looked out the window at the scene before returning his gaze to me. "That sounds kind of woo-woo to me."

I wondered how he felt every time he came to a new crime scene. Was it a new, exciting challenge to be faced or just another ring around the tree?

"Do you guys have any idea where McPhee might be holed up?" I asked

"Well now, that's the million-dollar question. If we knew that, I suppose we'd have the man in custody. But he's a slippery fish, this guy."

"Maybe it's time to go public."

"That could very well be. A lot of my colleagues think that appealing for the public's help is admitting failure, but I'm not one of them. And now with two unsolved homicides, I think our chief is going to be a lot more concerned about finding McPhee, Charbonneau Commission or not."

"You have jurisdiction, right? It's not like the military police could come in here and take over."

He shook his head. "No, in serious criminal matters like these, even though a member of the military has committed the crime, we have jurisdiction. But the military police are in the background, supplying information and such."

Perhaps that's how he'd heard about Mike being a Pathfinder. "Have you talked to his wife?"

"Why are you asking me all these questions?"

"It's what I do."

There was half a minute of silence while we watched the scene. The coroner had arrived and was in the process of removing the body.

I badly wanted to go home. I badly wanted a drink. Anderson was neglecting his hygiene. His ears needed a good clean and dandruff littered his collar. The acrid smell of his leather jacket was getting to me. At least I hoped that was his leather jacket.

Light from the dash played on his beard and mustache. Sound of cars driving by on the slushy streets. Patrons from the club were filtering back inside. Two television crews were doing live hits in front of the patrol cars, whose beacons were still turning, sending the red lights out and around again, ad infinitum.

He turned back to me. "How do I know you're not involved?"

"You could arrest me and see if the killings stop."

He chuckled. "Don't think I haven't considered it."

Chapter Twenty-Six

M y phone vibrating on the night stand woke me from a dream filled with images of a headless corpse and a smooth shooter. I fumbled for the phone and, through sleepshot eyes, checked the call display. It said "unknown." I answered.

"It's Anderson. We're releasing the name in an hour. You'll receive a press release by email."

"Just the name?"

"That's all I can say. I gotta go." He hung up.

"Shit," I said to Elliott, asleep on my legs.

I got up, splashed some water on my face and put on some coffee. I waited until 6 a.m. and called the *Gazette*. I got the early copy editor.

"This is Denny Durant. The police are releasing the name of the suspect in the Christmas Day murder and last night's murder. They're sending it in an hour."

"Shit."

"No, this is good. We'll have a jump on everyone. I'll send you seven or eight grafs of string in the next thirty minutes you can top and tail with the release."

"Really?"

"Yeah."

I got myself a cup of coffee, opened the laptop and started thinking of what to write. The information the police released would likely take up the majority of the first three paragraphs.

Starting with paragraph four, I wrote a few lines about the murder the previous evening. I added a line about why police thought it might connect with the Lorelei murder.

There had been plenty of stories recently in the local and national press about the struggles of veterans returning from Afghanistan. It was one of the reasons the mood in the country regarding the war was turning sour. The *Gazette* had done plenty of these stories.

I sat back and reflected for a moment. Did I have the right to do this story about McPhee? But it wasn't hard to answer that question. The man had given me documents and left the beer mat at the hotel with my phone number. Why had he done that, unless it was to draw me in to the story? He knew I was a writer. Buzzy said he knew about my career.

Part of me felt that by writing the story, I would be helping my old friend. I cautioned myself to remain objective. My old friend was now an assassin.

I looked again through the summary report Anderson had given me. In addition to what had already been reported, there were more details. For instance, officers on the scene recovered a wallet with identification that allowed them to confirm the man's particulars. Subsequent conversations with hotel staff determined that the room had been reserved and paid for in cash by one Jean Jeudi. The manager of the hotel, Mr. Gary Metzgar, said that the man had shown a valid piece of identification. A trace was made on the ID—a driver's licence from Quebec—that showed the identification was fake. No cell phone was found on the man's person or on the premises. About four hundred dollars in cash, a cigarette lighter and a set of keys was found in his pockets. Hotel staff were cooperative in providing security video of the hallway. It showed an unidentified woman approximately mid twenties and the man believed to be the victim entering Room 110 at approximately midnight. The victim, Frank Leclerc, left a few minutes later. At around 12:30 a.m., another man, mid- to late-thirties, stocky build, subsequently identified by a confidential source as McPhee entered Room 110.

The victim was seen on the footage and by hotel staff running back to the room and re-entering it at about 1 a.m. Less than a minute later, the woman left the room in apparent distress. The security video showed nothing until approximately 1:30 a.m. when a man fitting the description of McPhee was seen leaving the room. However, hotel staff reported not seeing him leave the hotel.

The report said it was impossible to tell from the footage the state of McPhee's clothing. There was blood throughout the room, on the walls, ceiling, the bed clothes and the carpet. There was no sign of a weapon. There were apparently no witnesses. The rooms on either side of Room 110 were unoccupied, as were the rooms across the hall. Evidence collected at the scene included a beer mat with a phone number written on it in pen, several hand towels soaked in blood, a tube of lip gloss, a package of three condoms.

It was interesting information but most of it wouldn't be useful for the story I was currently working on. I took what I had already written, added some of the salient details from the police report and added those to what I had already written.

I added a paragraph about McPhee's specialized training with the Pathfinders and sent it off to the early editor. He needed a bit of time to edit the thing. I told him I would send him the top as soon as the press release hit.

I had enough time to make myself a coffee before the release arrived in my inbox. So it was official. Police said they were looking for the public's help in finding McPhee, gave a physical description, said he was armed and "extremely" dangerous, warned against trying to apprehend him and urged anyone with information to call the Montréal police, the provincial police or the RCMP. There followed a bunch of numbers to call if McPhee suddenly showed up on your front porch.

I packaged this up within ten minutes and sent it off to the editor. Then I kept hitting refresh. We had a full story out there twelve minutes after the police release, well before any of our competitors, and the story was substantially more detailed than anyone else's. Even Provost's story wasn't nearly as detailed, and didn't appear for almost another hour. That would piss him off. No one in the Francophone media liked to get beaten by the Anglos.

Two hours later, I was finishing off another story about the Charbonneau Commission when Lydia called. "Good work on the story this morning Denny. We kicked everyone's ass. Always good to stick it to those jerks over at *La Presse*."

"Um, thanks."

"If you were a staffer, you'd know what I was talking about. This story is blowing up. We've got a decorated war hero going around the city popping pimps. It's *Rambo* meets *American Psycho*. I'm getting calls from everywhere, asking for string, asking for interviews."

"McPhee is nothing like that," I said. "He's articulate, decisive, intelligent and, when I knew him, was a superb leader and complete team player. I have a different angle on the story. Remember I told you that McPhee had given me some documents related to mefloquine?"

"Refresh my memory. What's mefloquine?"

"It's an anti-malarial drug that troops who are deployed to mosquito zones have to take once a week. McPhee blames the drug for his mental decline. I'm not sure what this has to do with pimps in Montréal but I'm working hard to find out."

"I want that story, Denny. When can you get it to me?"

"I need three more days."

"Make it two."

Chapter Twenty-Seven

When I first got back from Afghanistan, when they let me out of the hospital, I was in a bad way and, psychologically at least, things only got worse.

It was the middle of autumn, normally my favourite time of year, all I could see was impending winter, the bleakness of things. The colours of the fall, beautiful to others, to me were merely a prelude to death.

I was at the gateway of despair, my family didn't know what to do, my employer was zero help. Friends rallied around me at first but as the days and weeks wore on with no improvement, they drifted away.

Finally, feeling sick and tired of myself, feeling stuck and mired in an unyielding blackness, I got some help.

A psychiatrist, Dr. Robbins, who worked with many veterans afflicted with PTSD, got me unstuck. Over the next eight months, he helped free me from the quicksand of remorse, sadness and recrimination and got me moving forward again.

I thought maybe he'd retired, since when I saw him he was in his late sixties, but when I searched for him on the internet, he was still there. I figured it was worth a shot, so one of the first calls I made that day was to him. He worked out of his home, and I still had his number. I left a message explaining that I was working on an article about PTSD and mefloquine poisoning in the military and could I take twenty minutes of his time to ask him a few questions.

An hour later my phone rang. It was him. He seemed happy to hear from me, asking how I was doing, about my work. Hearing his voice, I felt my anxieties subside a little. Strange how that happens.

I explained the situation to him as plainly as I could.

"I'm writing a story about somebody who is in the news right now."

"Don't tell me," he said. "It's the man involved in the Christmas Day thing, the veteran who is wanted for murder."

"That's him. Mike McPhee."

"I saw the news this morning. Is he still at large?"

"To the best of my knowledge, he is. I should also mention that I know McPhee from Afghanistan."

"So this is more than just an ordinary story," he said. "You're trying to recover a piece of yourself."

It took me a few seconds to answer. "I hadn't considered that."

Dr. Robbins said he was willing to talk to me, on certain conditions. We agreed that the interview would be for background only, and I promised his name would not appear in the article. We further agreed that I would not mention any kind of psychiatric advice related specifically to Mike McPhee.

Once that was settled, Dr. Robbins asked, "What is it you wanted to know?"

"I greatly admired the McPhee I got to know in Afghanistan. He seemed like an exceptional person. I ran into him just before Christmas by chance and he seemed to have completely changed. He was depressed and lethargic. He seemed to be at the end of his rope. I've since learned that his marriage has fallen apart. The police had to be called to his home. And now he's suspected of murder. I wanted to ask you, Dr. Robbins, what would make somebody undergo such a complete transformation?"

He took a moment to respond. "It's quite difficult for me to say anything definitive without talking first to him in a therapeutic setting to find out exactly what was troubling him. What were his symptoms, as you observed them?"

"He seems unhinged. I've spoken to him on my telephone a couple of times. It's like he's living in some kind of a dream, still acting rationally, but outside of normal constraints."

Robbins again paused to think before speaking. "Sometimes the human mind simply buckles when it encounters something, or several things, that it cannot reconcile. Perhaps a better way to think of it is like a mind unspooling. And this is highly individual. Depending on how tightly wound the mind is, and what the structures are like, the threads of perception could unwind themselves from one spool and wrap themselves just as tightly around another. What is irreconcilable to one person may not be to another person.

"Similarly, a person can get along quite well even in extremely difficult circumstances. And then some element is introduced that disturbs the equilibrium, and suddenly the mind warps. It cycles out of control."

"That may be what's happened here," I said.

"Yes, possibly. It depends on how the person is, shall we say, wired. This can manifest in all kinds of ways. It can become a crushing depression. It can become a mania. It can become terrifying paranoia. However, once this change takes place in the mind, then it's very difficult to return to how things were. I won't say it's impossible, because I've seen it happen. However, it's not easy. It requires very specific therapy."

"What kind of therapy?"

"Most often, we treat the person with a combination of medication and counselling. It would depend on the person, but there are some new drugs that we find can help. Serotonin inhibitors have been shown to help in the case of civilian PTSD but are no more effective than a placebo in military cases. The most effective method of treating combat-related PTSD is usually cognitive behavioral therapy, or cognitive processing therapy in combination with a drug like Sertraline. I've had some success using eye movement desensitization therapy."

That was interesting, but not the information I was after.

"McPhee seems to be paranoid. His wife said that he was having terrible dreams and he thinks he's being persecuted. He's convinced his government is poisoning him."

"Poisoning him? With what?"

"The anti-malarial drug mefloquine."

"Ah yes, I've heard about similar cases. That is something quite different from PTSD, although it shares some similarities. There's anecdotal evidence that this drug has a profoundly negative impact on some people. It's very complicated, but what I think will be proved at some point is that for some people—a small minority—mefloquine does something to the brain chemistry that makes it quite harmful. I've come across it in my practice: people report very serious consequences or symptoms, neuropsychiatric effects, sometimes long-lasting. It's very difficult to distinguish the effects of this from PTSD.

"If your friend is one of these people who is experiencing profoundly negative effects, and if the people he went to for help don't think this drug is the problem, then your friend has a point. The government gave him this drug, and he's now very ill and can't get help."

"Of course, the government isn't intentionally poisoning anyone. But if some people become ill from a prescription medication, then who is responsible?

"Good question."

"Well, it's not for us to decide. It's for the courts. In terms of your friend, my first recommendation would be that he be hospitalized for an extended period for assessment."

"What could happen if he doesn't get treatment?"

"If he's already in a psychotic state, then anything can happen. He may not be able to tell a war scenario from a peacetime scenario. He may feel that he's in the same situation as he was in Kandahar or Kabul."

"Are you telling me he may still think he's in a war zone?"

"It's quite possible. It becomes very dangerous, as you can imagine, especially with a person so highly trained, because those skills don't leave. He still has them. He needs to be off the streets."

Chapter Twenty-Eight

Saturday morning, I woke up feeling stressed. I had a ton of work to do, but the strangeness with McPhee seemed to be talking its toll. The memories of Afghanistan that my notebooks had released refused to return to their storage place. I needed a break from it all. So, rather than getting right to it, I took Johanna ice skating to make up for ditching her two nights earlier.

The Atrium is an indoor rink downtown, near the central station. It is popular with teenagers but on this day there were also many younger kids and seniors, probably because of the holidays. The space was well-lit from the domed glass roof above the ice. Suspended below it were thousands of tiny white lights in the shape of a pair of skates. It wasn't as cold as an ordinary ice rink, but it wasn't warm either. Still, that didn't stop many of the teenagers from zipping around in T-shirts. Few of them wore helmets. A couple of birthday parties were in progress, and a huge penguin mascot made the rounds, terrifying toddlers. Innocuous dance music thumped over the speakers. A few dozen people watched from the stands. A handful of others watched from glassed-in offices that overlooked the skating rink.

Johanna and I skated in leisurely circles around the rink. She was a decent skater, about the same as me. A little rusty but we had the proficiency that comes from spending hundreds of youthful hours carving paths over frozen lakes.

"Is that how you folks skate over there in Finland?"

She gave me a hurt look. "We're good skaters. Finland won the World Championships last year."

"Just a dozen more and you'll catch up with us."

"Anyone can play hockey. Try a real sport like swamp football. We would crush you."

All told, there were perhaps a hundred people on the ice, a lot for such a small surface. A handful of skaters dressed in orange and yellow vests monitored the crowds to make sure nobody got out of hand. Still, many of the teen boys maneuvered dangerously through the slower skaters. They were skating far too fast, weaving in and out of the crowd, no doubt trying to impress the girls their age, the ones wearing tube tops and impossibly tight denim shorts.

I turned toward Johanna to make a comment about swamp football versus swamp politics when I heard the sound of body upon body and one of the teens who had been skating too fast came flying out of nowhere, off balance and collided with Johanna. They both went down.

I helped her up. She brushed herself off. "I'm okay."

The teen lay prone on the ice. I reached down a hand and helped him up. Once he was standing, I grabbed him by the back of the neck, propelled him forward, and said in French, "Do you have something to say to my friend?"

"I'm sorry," he said miserably. "I don't know what happened."

"You were skating like an asshole, that's what happened."

"Yeah, but…" He looked around as though seeking the cause of his wipe out. "Somebody tripped me."

A safety guy arrived. He was an older kid, probably early twenties, and big, a couple of inches over six feet, probably two hundred pounds. By the way he skated, it looked like he had some experience at the major junior level. The best skaters have an economy of effort that belies the speed and power they're capable of.

The teenage kamikaze wasn't going to outrun the safety guy. As they skated away together, the safety guy had the speeding teen by the elbow and was giving him an earful. He escorted him off the ice. Then he came back to us and asked if Johanna was okay.

"It was nothing," she said. "I'm fine."

We skated for another twenty minutes, making small talk, enjoying each other's company, laughing at the penguin mascot. Then Johanna said she could use a hot chocolate. I agreed, and we began to make our way to the gate. She had just turned to me to say something when there was a flash followed by a low, rumbling boom and flames began to pour out of the space where the Zamboni was parked. A woman with her clothes ablaze skated screaming away from the explosion. No one tried to help her. Everyone got away from her as fast as they could. Another explosion blew the glass out of one of the upstairs offices, raining it down on the ice and the skaters.

Everyone was now trying to get off the ice, except for Atrium staff, who were trying to get onto the ice to see what had caused the explosion and to help the burning woman.

I yelled to Johanna, and we joined the mad rush to the nearest gate. A panicky crowd was already forming at the gate, which had turned into a bottleneck. Skaters were trying to get off the ice, staff was trying to get on, and only one person could pass through the gate at a time. We were packed tight in a mass of people. I felt the crush pressing against me from behind. The air had become hazy, and over everything hung the smell of burning metal. I grabbed Johanna's hand and pulled her behind me as I pushed out of the crowd. We skated to a less congested spot, where I hauled myself up and over the low glass, stepped down onto a table and helped her over. As we took our skates off, I looked back at the fire to see what was happening. Half a dozen maintenance workers were spraying the Zamboni with fire extinguishers.

We blended with the throng leaving the Atrium. Police and fire fighters were streaming in. Johanna and I hadn't spoken since the explosion. Now I turned to her. "Are you okay?"

"I'm fine. I need a drink."

We walked out of the Atrium and along the underground corridor that led to the Central Station. The closer we got, the more normal everything appeared and the better the air was, until we emerged into the station's main hall, where it was as if the explosion had never happened.

We made our way to the bar at the far end of the hall, ordered two whiskey sours, sat side by side at the bar, and took stock.

"What do you think happened?" she said. She was paler than usual and her brown eyes a little wider. She took a large gulp of the drink when it came.

"I don't know," I said, but I had a hunch it wasn't a random act.

I checked my phone for news updates. I thought about sending a text to the *Gazette* editors to say there had been an explosion at the Atrium but I had a rule of thumb: never alert other journalists to a story you aren't willing to cover yourself. And I was just happy that we had escaped unscathed and could now recover with the help of a cocktail in this cozy bar. Plus, they would have heard about it by now. They had a team of people monitoring social media. Video would be all over Twitter by now.

Christmas music drifted into the bar and added to the general air of relaxation and ease. We ordered another round of whiskey sours..

"You know, I was supposed to go back to Finland the day after we met."

I took this on board. "What changed your mind?"

She pressed herself against me. "It will still be there when I'm ready to go back."

The second round of drinks was almost done, the whiskey had soothed our ragged nerves. Johanna suggested we go back to my place.

She excused herself to go to the washroom, and while she was gone I asked the bartender for the bill. When it came I reached for my wallet but my fingers closed on something else in my pocket. I pulled it out. It was a small package, no larger than a disposable cigarette lighter, wrapped tightly in brown paper and sealed with clear tape. I spotted Johanna on her way back from the ladies room, so I pocketed the package and paid the bill.

I'd parked near the station, and when we got in the car Johanna looked at me, puzzled.

"What's the matter."

"Nothing," I lied. "Do you mind if I drop you at home? I'd love to spend more time with you, but I just found out there's some work I need to do today. We can see each other tonight if you'd like."

If she was disappointed, she didn't let it show, and while I drove, we chatted about what a day it had been

I dropped her at the residence where she was staying and waited for the door to close behind her before retrieving the package. I ripped off the tape and outer layer of brown paper, revealing a small piece of stiff embroidered fabric folded over something else. I recognized the fabric immediately. It was a Pathfinder badge.

Chapter Twenty-Nine

Back in my apartment, I sat down at the kitchen table and looked again at the package. The Pathfinder badge—a winged torch aflame against a camouflage background—had been wrapped around something else, which I loosened. It was a USB memory stick wrapped inside a piece of drab olive silk.

I smoothed the silk flat on the table. It was about a foot square. Printed on it was a red poppy, but rather than the usual black pistil in the centre of the red flower, there was the small, black shape of a Colt C6, the standard-issue heavy automatic weapon of the Canadian Forces dismounted infantry. I remembered seeing these poppy silks in circulation at Kandahar Air Field, sold in the shops on the base.

I wondered why I had never made the connection before. The poppy—Papaver rhoeas—worn on Armistice Day to memorialize the Allied dead of World War I, and the poppy—Papaver somniferum—harvested in Afghanistan to produce opium, a trade that accounted for a quarter of the national GDP and provided the revenue to the Taliban for their operations.

I was alarmed that McPhee had slipped this package inside my pocket without my noticing. To what lengths would he go to accomplish his mission? Images of the woman on fire at the Atrium played on a loop in my mind.

With some trepidation, I inserted the USB stick into my laptop, waited for the icon to appear and double clicked it. The window showed three folders and a text file titled "Read Me First." I opened the text file. It was concise.

Denny, my mission has taken an unexpected turn, as they always do. I apologize for causing the diversion at the skating rink earlier today but it was necessary. I needed a way to get this to you. The police are watching you because they expect you will lead them to me. Obviously they want to arrest me. I could have dropped off the file at your apartment but the police have that staked out as well. I could have dropped it at the *Gazette* offices but that would have been way too risky. I could have paid someone to get it to you, but that was also too risky. And I believe your phone is tapped.

That stopped me. Could any of this be correct? My thoughts were whirling. I could almost feel myself being lured out onto the thin ice of McPhee's psychosis. That was the last place I wanted to go. I doubted the police had tapped my phone or staked out my apartment. If they had, why hadn't they followed me to the rendezvous with Felix? Why hadn't they arrived at the Luxotica in time to prevent Blanchette's head getting shot off. I kept reading.

I never planned to harm any of the men who have died. I only wanted to help a friend. But things went sideways. And now the people controlling Vanessa are the enemy. They are my Taliban. They need to die.

Find Vanessa. Her address is 2928 rue Bannantyne. She lives there with her mother. She might not be staying there any more. She might be staying with a friend. She might be with that dirtbag Felix. She keeps going back to him.

I was not going to share these journal entries with you. They are personal reflections. They are chronicles of my worst days. They are filled with unspeakable pain. But you must tell my story after this is all over. And it will soon all be over. There is one more thing I need to do. That is why I gave you the first set of documents. This will be my last deployment. Thank you, Brother."

I opened the folder labeled "Notes." There were perhaps a hundred files listed by date. The earliest was January 2008 and the most recent was two weeks ago. I clicked on the most recent one first:

> It's done. The date is made. Then I can put it to rest. A promise is a promise. RIP, brother."

I skipped to one from June 15 2012, a little over six months ago, which read:

> Having more and more difficulty. Feelings are taking up way too much head space. The way people look at me now. Like they know all my secrets. Like they know I'm responsible. Someone is talking shit about me on the base, telling lies. Whalen just nods and says I get it and says you need to take your meds. Not for me. Had enough. Need to get well. Can't get well on that stuff. Already been poisoned once. Won't happen again.

I clicked on another at random, one of the earlier ones. The date was April 11, 2010:

> Went to Whalen today. He says there's nothing for this. Useless shit. Says nothing's wrong with me. Tinnitus he says is from loud gunfire and will go away eventually. Meds for the blues and the rage. I told him the meds make me feel way worse. Em at end of her rope. Says she can't take much more of the spiral. I get it. Not like I'm loving this either. She hints she'll take the kids and go somewhere. Maybe for the best but also couldn't bear it if she does this. There's a lot of darkness now. Hard to sit still. Want to be with the kids but there's so much anger and irritation. Need to keep walking, go somewhere, do something, but what? Focus is shot. Gone to a couple of groups. They help for a bit. Then the

dreams start. Don't want to sleep. Just gets worse. Everything feels broken. Can't remember when it didn't feel that way. Screaming in my head. Need help, but from where? Nothing helps. Em and I in separate rooms now. No love between us. Writing it all down helps but not for long. So angry. Yelled at Brian today. He didn't do anything, knocked a toy with his knee. Lost my shit. Em left the house with the kids. This isn't working.

There were many such entries. They all just confirmed what Buzzy had told me. But I was too angry with him to feel much empathy. I was still disturbed by mayhem he'd caused at the rink, apparently just to slip the memory stick into my pocket. Couldn't he just have handed it to me? Could he not trust me? Was he going through some kind of a psychotic episode?

The third folder was labeled "Pics." It contained several dozen photographs of McPhee's wife, Emma, and their children, presumably taken in earlier, happier times. All of the photographs were labeled with dates, mostly in 2008 and 2009. After that must have been when the dark times started, the kinds of times nobody wants to memorialize.

There was one photograph from 2006. I opened it. It was of three soldiers in camouflage. They were all wearing steel helmets covered in a camouflage material and were carrying rifles with scopes and what looked like heavy backpacks. All of them were smiling. The caption on the photograph itself read "M McPhee, C Buzaki, E Gillespie."

I went to the kitchen, got some water and resumed my post at the laptop. Outside, darkness was falling. I went back to the folder with the journal entries, this one dated 10.27.2011:

Whalen said I should go to one of the groups. Back from the War. Went to a few. Can't go back. Can't look at the other men. They remind me too much of myself. We're all broken. Can't sleep. Want to build a bridge to Em but the river between us is too wide. So I drink. It calms me. But calm rage is still rage.

The next one I opened, dated 4.15.2012, had a more optimistic tone:

> There is a program that Dr. Whalen told me about which is some kind of group therapy. Buzzy thinks I should go. I might give it a try. Maybe a few weeks. It's only twice a week. It's back up on the base. So I wouldn't be gone for too long. Em and the kids could use the break.

But a month later, the darkness seemed to have returned:

> Don't feel part of my family anymore. They don't want me here. My kids look scared when I'm there. They think I'm going to do something to them. Em never smiles at me anymore. Always just gives me a hard look. Like I'm an alien. Need to get away. Wish these thoughts would stop. Worse at night. Crazy dreams. So vivid. Horrible. People coming apart. Blood and bones and flesh. The sounds of it. I sleep in the spare room now. I'm sure I've been screaming but nobody's there. Nobody comes.

I closed the computer and started pacing around my apartment. I was still agitated from the explosion at the rink and reading about McPhee's self-destructive rage wasn't helping. And on top of that, I now had a creeping sense that I was getting sucked into McPhee's insanity.

Why did he think it was necessary to go to such lengths to pass me this memory stick? Surely there would have been an easier way. Pay a kid fifty bucks to hand it to me. Up until then, I thought McPhee had been acting somewhat rationally, but now extent of his irrationality was beginning to dawn on me.

And how the hell did McPhee know I was at the skating rink? He must be following me, tracking me. That meant he had seen Johanna, and knew we were involved. He might have followed us home from the Atrium. That meant he knew where she lived.

Chapter Thirty

Reading the files from McPhee pushed me into a new zone of anxiety. Any lingering hope I'd had that he would come to his senses and call off his mission had evaporated. I knew it would only get worse from here. He really did see himself as carrying out a mission in Montréal, one that I'm sure he believed was connected with his mission in Afghanistan. Somewhere along the way, he'd slipped the bonds of reality. Now there was a highly skilled soldier on the streets of Montréal, picking off those he considered the enemy, and blowing things up to achieve the objective. How many more people would die before McPhee was captured or killed or turned himself in.

From what I knew of his training, he would rather die than be captured. Evading capture would have been built into his training.

I needed to find out more about mefloquine, so I left my apartment, hopped into the Highlander and drove downtown to rue Berri. I still had a couple of hours to do some research.

I found a parking space near the metro station. Seeing the glacier-green tiles of the Bibliothèque et Archives nationales du Québec lifted my spirits immediately. It was one of my favourite buildings in the city. I made my way through the crowded lobby to the digital reference section at the end of the main level. A bank of computers against the back wall gave researchers access to anything published in Québec over the past century and a half. I booted up the nearest terminal and entered the search term "mefloquine." There was no shortage of hits.

I saved about two dozen recent articles and research reports to a new memory stick I'd brought with me, then found a chair on the third floor at the back of the building and opened my laptop. The massive windows overlooked an alley with an impressive array of graffiti.

A quick scan of the articles gave me some initial information on mefloquine, which I put into a new document. I read about how the drug is cheaper because it had to be taken only once a week. I read interviews with soldiers who described having "vile and haunting" dreams after taking the drug. There were accounts of troops lashing out and being "frustrated and very angry." One list of symptoms noted night terror, rage, paranoia, psychosis. One person said the warning label should have included the words "abnormal dreams," and another blamed it for extreme rage.

There were accounts of paranoid thoughts, and of suicidal and homicidal thoughts. Another person said the side effects include nightmares, visual hallucinations, auditory hallucinations, anxiety, depression, unusual behavior and suicidal ideation. The drug was described as a "neurotoxicant." An army physician called it "a horror show in a pill."

Another said mefloquine causes permanent injury to the central nervous system in some individuals. And still another said he was "terrified that guys are getting treated for PTSD. But if they took mefloquine, they could be at risk for the suicidal ideation."

I sat back. My head was swimming. Why had I heard so little about this drug? One thing I'd learned from being around soldiers is they don't complain a lot, or at least they don't complain to people outside the military. Maybe sitting around the knitting circle with fellow soldiers, they might air some grievances, but for the most part, they suffered in silence.

I kept reading and taking notes. A professor said in parliamentary testimony that "mefloquine gets out of the brain by a particular transport protein. There are individuals who lack this transport protein, so mefloquine can reach very high concentrations in their brains, and that puts them at particular risk. It's really the mefloquine in the brain—amount or concentration—that's important."

A Canadian report said its review identified a lack of proper documentation that some military personnel even received the drug, and identified individuals who received the drug who had contraindications.

It warned that patients with active depression or a history of psychiatric disturbances like depression, generalized anxiety disorder, psychosis or schizophrenia, or a history of convulsions, shouldn't be prescribed mefloquine prophylactically since "mefloquine may precipitate these conditions."

Some of the news stories carried a comment from the Department of National Defence that said mefloquine is a safe drug that has been given to tens of thousands of Canadian military personnel with no adverse reaction. It is also used by military personnel of many other countries, including our NATO allies.

It was closing time at the library. I cleared my screen and packed up my things. I walked dazed out of the building into the Montréal twilight. The sky was overcast and the temperature was dropping fast. I thought back to how hot it had been in Afghanistan, reaching 45 degrees Celsius the summer I was there, so hot you couldn't touch a metal door handle without burning your skin. I stood outside the library, letting the cold seep in, letting the icy wind flick at my breath, watching as the building emptied and people headed toward the metro station across the street or farther along to the bars and clubs on Saint-Laurent.

I thought about McPhee at large in the city, executing his mission, convinced he'd been poisoned by the government he served. Was he crazy, or was he correct?

Chapter Thirty-One

I had a thousand things on my mind on the drive home. In addition to the ever present question—where the hell was McPhee?—I still didn't know the whereabouts of Felix. Would he find out about the stories I'd written about him and his brother? Was he going to jump out from behind a snowbank and 'mess me up?'

There were also the usual questions of how I would make the rent this month, which stories I should be pitching, who owed me but hadn't paid me yet, when would I see my kids again?

I was circling the block in search of a spot to park—the door to the underground garage at my apartment was out of commission, again—when behind me the lights of an unmarked police car went on, and a siren chirped one, two, three times to leave me in no doubt that someone urgently wished to have a discussion.

I pulled into the parking lot of a Persian restaurant that had been closed for the past several weeks. Detective Anderson pulled up next to me and rolled down his window. Brandt was in the passenger seat, as usual.

"Good afternoon, Mr. Durant," Anderson said. "So nice to see you. Would you mind joining us for a few minutes for a little chin wag?"

I climbed out of my vehicle and into the back of the black Chevy Suburban. I had been in unmarked cop cars before. Those had been different from police cruisers in only the exterior details. However this could have been a civilian vehicle. I could get out of the backseat if I wanted to because the doors had interior handles. There was no obnoxious Plexiglas shield separating front and back seats, no steel grid over the glass, the back of the vehicle didn't smell like vomit. Except for the industrial strength radio jutting from the dash, this could have been the car of your average Jean.

Anderson opened with, "Mr. Durant, thank you for joining us today."

"Detective," I said.

"We were hoping, Mr. Durant, that you could update us on your progress, whether you have made any advances in your inquiry. I believe you said you're making your own inquiries."

"Nothing really to report," I said.

Anderson swiveled to see me better, laying one arm across the seat back. "Were you at the skating rink earlier today?"

McPhee might be right about one thing, I thought. They were following me.

"Yes, I was there. I'm sure you heard what happened."

"We certainly did. Some pyrotechnics. What do you think that was all about?"

"I read somewhere that there was a gas leak in the room where they keep the Zamboni."

Anderson chuckled. "How convenient. Were you able to make it out safely?"

"My date and I made it out safely, yes. We got out as fast as we could. It was terrifying. I saw a woman on fire."

"It was a very chaotic scene, from what we hear. Anything could have happened in there."

"Yes it could have."

"My partner and I were wondering if you've heard anything at all from McPhee. Or received anything?"

"No."

"We thought maybe McPhee caused the explosion to create a diversion so that he could pass you some information."

I laughed. "Just like they do in the spy novels."

"Exactly like that. Life imitating art."

So that would explain the impromptu interrogation. I reckoned Anderson and Brandt were just working a hunch. If they were going to seize the materials McPhee had given me, they would have done it by now.

"No, nothing at all."

Detective Brandt wiped his nose and cleared his throat extravagantly. He was a dark-complexioned man with a black mustache and salt and pepper hair. He had a quiet, tough look that suggested he could handle himself when the chips were down. I was aware he and Anderson had the power to start the car, take me anywhere, beat the hell out of me and leave me for dead. It coloured the interaction.

I said, "Does that mean McPhee is still at large?"

Anderson looked out the driver's side window before answering. "We have as yet been unable to locate Mr. McPhee, or excuse me, Major McPhee."

I said nothing and the silence grew heavy. There was a faint smell of stale coffee and aftershave.

Anderson finally spoke. "We were hoping you might be able to help us with that."

I said, "If you can't find him, what makes you think I'll be able to find him?"

"That hasn't stopped you from looking for him, has it?"

"Are you following me?"

"Why would you think that?"

"Just a hunch."

It was my turn to look out the window. Rows of cars along the street sat marooned in snow. They were like giant candies with a snowy coating and a crunchy metal interior. Even the trees were encrusted in snow. It gave the landscape an innocent, marshmallow appearance, as if no harm could occur in a place where a soft landing was inevitable.

Finally I said, "I've been making inquiries. But I'm not going to lie, I'm worried about his frame of mind."

Anderson said, in his usual avuncular manner, "You've mentioned his frame of mind before. That's something that could be assessed once he's in custody. Once Mr. McPhee ... I mean once Major McPhee is apprehended.

I was getting angry. "Major McPhee is a Pathfinder. That means he is very good at concealing himself behind enemy lines and waiting for the exact moment to carry out his mission. Major McPhee has a very distinct set of skills. We have to respect those skills. I am not inclined to go looking for Major McPhee. I'm hoping that Major McPhee will see fit to turn himself in."

The atmosphere shifted to one of discomfort. It was Brandt's turn to look out the window.

Anderson cleared his throat. "We don't have the luxury, Mr. Durant, of waiting for this asshole to turn himself in. I have one vic who's missing a face. I got another shot through the head. I might have a woman with third-degree burns. I have a very concerned public. I need to find the guy responsible and lock him up so that people can stop worrying. That's my job. I'm hoping you can help me. If not, we'll have to part company. You go your way, I'll go my way, and we'll see each other somewhere down the road."

"So you think Major McPhee is behind the explosion in the Atrium?"

"Yes, I do."

"What makes you think that?"

"I'd rather not say."

What I really wanted was information about the young woman in the hotel room. Maybe I could negotiate something. "I'd love to know if you found the girl, anything you could tell me about her?"

He looked at Brandt, then at me in the rearview. "What girl?"

"The girl who was in the room. Vanessa. Did you track her down and talk to her?"

"We don't think the girl did this. We don't think ten girls could have done this."

"Maybe she knows where McPhee went."

"Like I told you two nights ago, I can't tell you if we've spoken to the girl. People have a right to privacy."

I thought about what I had read at the Banq. "Why do you think he's doing all this?"

He said, with the first hint of impatience, "Look, it's pretty goddam simple. Your major hired a girl for sexual services. Something went wrong. Her business manager tried to intervene. Major McPhee felt he didn't need to pay or didn't want to pay and took matters into his own hands. It seems pretty clear what happened. This guy is on the loose and he needs to be brought in. So what the girl saw or didn't see really doesn't concern me. My main thing is that I gotta find this guy."

He paused to catch his breath. "I think you know where he is."

"I don't. Why do you think that?"

"We've received information."

He was watching me closely in the mirror. "You've received bad information. I have no idea where McPhee is."

Again, I wondered if he was fishing. They must be getting desperate.

"Look," he said. "We've got a lot of stuff going on, we've got our fair share of stuff. Don't we, Serge?"

Serge nodded. Anderson continued.

"You've probably heard of the Charbonneau Commission?"

"Heard about it."

"Now, we're getting more than the usual number of calls. Lots of things to follow up on these days. No shortage of new leads to old cases and crazy shit coming out of the woodwork—or the sidewalk, for that matter. We're also getting calls about McPhee."

"What kind of calls?"

"People calling to say they've seen him. Sleeping rough in the woods on Mount Royal, wandering along Sainte-Catherine at 4 a.m., getting on a flight to New York, eating a smoked meat sandwich at Schwartz's, sleeping in a hallway of the Underground City, sneaking into Silo 5."

I said, "The abandoned grain elevator?"

"Yes. That eyesore in the old port." He sighed. "I know not a lot of this stuff concerns you, Mr. Durant. And that's as it should be. You're not a cop. You're a journalist. And so we serve different masters. However, I was hoping we could, you know, work together on this, that you could let us know whether or not you have found out anything whatsoever that could help us."

I relented a little, but not by much. "Have you spoken to the manager at the hotel, Metzgar? He's responsible for booking in the prostitutes."

"Yes, we've spoken to Mr. Metzgar."

"What about Felix?"

"Felix may be looking for a little payback. He could be quite dangerous. But right now, my main concern isn't Felix. Or should I say at least not our present concern. We're quite focused on finding Major McPhee."

"Were you able to check my alibi?"

"Yes, we were in contact with Ms. Nieminen. She vouched for you. She sounds like a very sensible person."

The conversation seemed to be at an end. I was keen to get back to my apartment. I wanted to get to work on the bigger story about McPhee. My deadline was coming at me fast. I reached for the door handle.

But the conversation wasn't over yet.

"Maybe you don't know where he is, but have you been speaking with McPhee?" Anderson was staring at me again in the rearview mirror.

I leaned back against the seat and exhaled. "No."

That's when I noticed the Boston Bruins key chain dangling from the ignition. It was impossible to tell if it belonged to Anderson himself, or just to the set of keys that went with the vehicle. Still, I couldn't imagine the Bruins logo would be allowed anywhere near a Montréal police vehicle.

"Are you a Bruins fan?"

"Oh, that. That's just a spare set that was kicking around. I'll throw it in the river as soon as we find the other set."

Brandt grinned.

"I need to run," I said.

Anderson said, "We don't want to come in and search your apartment, because we're afraid of what we might find in there."

I said nothing. They likely knew what I had in there, but they would need to get a warrant, and they didn't seem to want to do that.

"We'd hate to have to bring you into the station. You'd have to stop working."

"Please get to the point," I said.

"There's no point, really. We do talk to a lot of reporters though."

It would only become clear to me in the next few days what he meant.

Chapter Thirty-Two

The next morning when I woke up, put on some coffee and scrolled through Twitter to catch up on the news. The days and nights were blurring into each other, like paragraphs in a never-ending feature story. I stopped scrolling when I came across the following headline in French: "Vehicle Belonging to Suspect in Christmas Day Murder Impounded at Montréal Airport."

The link took me to the *La Presse* website. A video showed a tow truck removing a car from a snow-filled parking lot. The video was time stamped less than an hour ago. One plane landed and another took off in the background beyond a barbed-wire fence. Two marked SPVM patrol cars supervised the operation. A large-bellied man wearing a leather jacket blew into his hands as he watched the tow truck operator affix the blocks to the wheels of McPhee's car, a dark green, late model Volkswagen sedan with an Ontario plate sporting the red poppy emblem. The foot-deep accumulation of snow on the vehicle suggested it had been parked in the same spot for a few days. Had McPhee ditched it there after the shooting.

Scrolling text beneath the images said that the car was believed to belong to Major Mike McPhee (Ret'd), wanted in connection with Christmas Day murder. I turned up the volume on my phone. Camille was narrating the report in French.

"Police have identified the victim as Frank Raymond Leclerc, age thirty-four, of Montréal. They have also identified Michael Gary McPhee, age thirty-nine, of CFB Petawawa in Ontario, as a suspect in the case." The image from a security surveillance camera flashed on the screen. The report continued, giving details of Blanchette's murder, saying police believed it was also carried out by McPhee, who was described in a few sentences, with the usual "armed and dangerous" disclaimer and plea for information from the public. Then Camille said, "Police believe McPhee may have fled the country using falsified documentation."

Camille must have been tipped off that the car was going to be removed for her to be there on scene with a camera. She must have pestered Anderson to give her something, or Anderson hadn't dealt quite as effectively as he'd thought with the leak in his office.

Or maybe Anderson had offered the story to her. It would be good for Anderson to have that story out there, to help change the public narrative, to take the heat off the police. If he was concerned, as he'd suggested in the car, about public anxiety in Montréal over a rogue soldier, then this would help to quell that anxiety.

I put down my phone. Good for Camille. I wasn't worried about her getting the scoop about the car and McPhee leaving the country. For me, the story was developing in another direction. Camille and I were no longer competing for scraps.

My bigger concern was whether McPhee had parked the car at the airport because he really was catching a flight out of the city. Maybe he'd already done a runner. He could easily have obtained a passport through his international network of contacts. Slipping out of the country using fake documents wouldn't be a problem for him. He was obviously skilled at disguising himself—he'd managed to evade police detection for this long, even after his photo had been featured on every front page, television screen and cell phone screen in the city. Or had he left the car at the airport to throw the police off his tail, a diversion like the one he created at the ice rink?

I knew in my guts that he was still in the city.

Chapter Thirty-Three

I still felt that finding Vanessa was the key to finding out what had happened with McPhee. At about 10 a.m. I went to the address that McPhee had given me for Vanessa at rue Bannantyne in Verdun.

It was a Sunday and there wasn't much traffic even for a main street. It was a square, brick, two-level building, built in the forties, that had been sub-divided into four small units. The one I wanted was on the far right. I maneuvered between cars and piles of snow to reach the stairs.

I rang the bell and waited. On the porch by my feet, a bag of trash sat waiting to be taken to the curb, bits of Christmas paper were sticking out.

I heard steps approaching and the door opened a crack. The eyes belonged to a woman who'd grown afraid of who might be at the door.

"I'm looking for Vanessa."

"She's not here."

"Do you know where I could find her?"

"Depends who's asking."

"My name is Denny Durant. I'm a reporter, on assignment with *the Gazette*."

I got nothing to say to the paper." She began to shut the door but I managed to wedge the toe of my boot in before she could. "Please. I'm not going to hurt her, or you. I just need to ask her a couple of questions."

"How did you get my address?"

"If you let me in for five minutes, I'll tell you."

After a few seconds, she opened the door and I stepped inside. The space was surprisingly spacious and modern. Smell of bacon. She stood back, an attractive woman, blond hair with strands of grey running through it. Around her neck she wore a sterling silver chain with a striking lapis lazuli pendant. I'd seen many similar in shops and markets during my time in Afghanistan.

"That's a beautiful necklace," I said.

"My…" she started, then caught herself. "How did you get my address?"

"From someone who appears to know your daughter, someone who may have been at the Lorelei Hotel on the night of the Frank Leclerc murder."

At the mention of the words Frank Leclerc, Lorelei Hotel and murder, she covered her mouth with her hand and leaned against the wall.

"Where do you think I could find Vanessa?"

"I don't know." She had stopped looking at me. She kept her eyes on the floor and remained leaning against the wall, as if standing on her own would require too much of an effort. "We had a fight. I haven't seen her since Christmas day."

"Sorry to hear that."

"I know what she does. I don't condone it."

I didn't say anything, hoping she'd continue. She seemed to need to talk.

"The police were here. A man and a woman. They were looking for her too. I don't know if they ever found her."

"What did you fight about?"

She hesitated. "Family stuff."

"And you have no idea where she is?"

She shook her head. "She runs with a pretty wild crowd. She could be any-where."

There was noise from the hallway, and soon a young man, a teenager, appeared from one of the bedrooms at the back of the condo. He was wearing headphones, his face covered in acne scars, hair over his eyes. He glanced without interest at his mother speaking to a stranger in the front hall.

"Could you at least give me her cell phone number?"

She told me and I wrote it down.

****

At about five that evening, I parked in the lot of a Cabaret restaurant across the street from the Lorelei Hotel. I came prepared to wait, with a thermos of coffee and some leftovers. Between news bulletins on the CBC, I flicked over to 97.7 CHOM FM and a couple of AM stations that still did decent talk radio. There was a lot of conversation about the Charbonneau Commission and the prolonged hockey lockout. Nothing on McPhee.

From my vantage point, I could see through the sliding doors into the reception area of the Lorelei, but I couldn't see behind the desk. I didn't know if Metzgar was in there or not, since it was a Sunday, and I didn't want to risk his seeing me and possibly calling the police.

It was an overcast evening, light snow. Saint-Jacques was a busy street with a constant flow of traffic, but there wasn't much into or out of the Lorelei Hotel.

At one point, a bus pulled up and half a dozen people toting large suitcases emerged, eventually making their way into the lobby. The bus pulled away and all was quiet for another forty minutes or so before a man and a woman walked out. They stood in front of the hotel, looked around to get their bearings and then moved off in the direction of Montréal West and the nearest metro station.

I called the number Vanessa's mother had given me. It rang once and went to voicemail. I left a message, identifying myself, saying I was working on a story for the Gazette and that I wanted to ask her some questions about Mike McPhee.

At around quarter past six, I saw Metzgar, dressed in the same light jacket and dress shoes he'd been wearing on Wednesday, stroll out of the lobby with another man, a few inches taller, hair buzzed short, wearing a black leather jacket, grey sweat pants and white Adidas running shoes. It was Felix. Both of them stood hunched against the cold and lit cigarettes. Felix looked straight ahead while Metzgar talked to the side of his face.

After a few minutes, Felix flicked his cigarette into the parking lot, said something to Metzgar, then got into a blue BMW and drove away. Metzgar took one last puff of his cigarette, crushed it out and went back inside.

I was surprised to see Felix standing out in the open. Maybe he'd heard the reports about McPhee having left the country. Maybe he was no longer concerned that what happened to his brother and his other business partner wouldn't happen to him. Was he speaking to Metzgar about starting up operations again, now that the heat appeared to be off? He probably needed the income.

Nothing happened for a while.

The CBC 7 p.m. news bulletin had this:

"Police believe the main suspect in the Christmas Day Murder in Montréal, Retired Major Mike McPhee, is now outside the country. That's according to a report in La Presse newspaper. McPhee's car was recovered at the airport and police have reason to believe that McPhee boarded a plane for London, England, using an alias and forged travel documents. The investigation is ongoing."

I wondered what the police had found when they searched the car. Buzzy had said he would be armed and wouldn't go quietly. Had police found weapons in the car, and that's why they said he was armed and dangerous?

I drank coffee. At a quarter to nine, a young man wearing a parka and winter boots and carrying a backpack got off the bus and walked into the lobby of the Lorelei. I wondered if that was Rufus, the man Katarina had mentioned who now worked night shift. Fifteen minutes later, the maid emerged.

I was unsure whether she had a car but it appeared she didn't because she started walking down the street towards the bus stop. I pulled out of the Cabaret parking lot, drew up beside her and rolled down the window.

"Olivia, right? Remember me?"

She looked in and didn't seem to immediately register my face.

"I'm Denny Durant, the newspaper reporter. We spoke behind the hotel the other day. I was asking about what happened in Room 110."

"My mama told me never get into a car with a strange man."

"I'm not strange. I'm a reporter. I'm writing a story about what happened at the hotel. Can I give you a lift to wherever you're going?"

There must have been something about my open, honest face because she glanced quickly back at the Lorelei and then climbed into the Toyota.

I asked where she was headed.

"I'm going to pick up some groceries. I've got three kids at home to feed."

I put the car in gear. "I'll take you."

Olivia gave me the name of a grocery store near the Atwater Market and we made our way there through steadily increasing traffic. We'd not got far when she said, "What's it worth to you?" She was staring straight ahead. "I know people get paid for their stories."

We drove another block while I considered. "I can give you one hundred."

"Make it two hundred."

I thought about it. I'd have to put in a claim with the Gazette. "Okay. I'll give you a hundred up front and another hundred afterward if the information is any good."

"Throw in a large double double and an apple fritter and you got yourself a deal."

I hung a left at the lights and headed for the Tim Horton's drive through for Olivia's coffee and pastry. Next stop was at an ATM to withdraw the cash. It better be worth it, I thought.

While Olivia drank her coffee, I counted out five twenties and handed them to her. She recounted them and put the cash in her purse.

"Okay, Mr. Journalist, what do you want to know?"

"What happened in Room 110?"

"Man got his face beat in."

"Were you the one who found the body?"

"No, that was Wilma. She's still off work. She'll milk that for all it's worth."

"Do you know who the girl in the room was?"

"The one the police are looking for? No, I don't. But the girl at the front desk, Katarina, she knows her."

"She does? How do you know that?"

"Because they used to talk. That girl would come out to the front desk between men and ask for more towels and bottled water, and they'd get to talking."

"Between men. So she'd been there before?"

Olivia looked at me. "What do you think they're running down there? That ain't a real hotel. It might as well have a red light outside."

"Was it just Frank Leclerc and his brother or were others using it to make money?"

"There were others, lot of others. Those two managers? They get a piece of every dollar of whoring that goes on in there."

"Metzgar and the other one?"

"Yessir."

"Did you tell this to the police?"

"Did the police give me two hundred dollars?"

"I tried to talk to Katarina but Metzgar was there and I couldn't. How can I talk to her?"

Olivia considered this. "I got an idea. You remember that spot we met the other day, out back?"

I said I did.

"You come by there tomorrow morning at eleven. That's usually when that girl goes for a break. If there's one of those do not disturb signs hanging on the door knob, come in through the side door, the one you went out the other day. I'll be there. The door will be open, so you'll be able to get in."

"What happens if there's no sign on the door outside?"

"Come back the next day, same time."

"Why don't I just meet her somewhere outside the hotel?"

"She only gets ten minutes for her break."

"Not much of a break."

"That girl is too nice to be working at that place."

"Worth a shot," I guess.

"It'll cost you another hundred. Fifty for me and fifty for her."

"Cheap at twice the price."

"Excuse me?"

"Never mind."

Chapter Thirty-Four

Despite my reservations, Olivia's plan the next day went off without a hitch, and by five past eleven, I was sitting inside a room on the ground floor just down the hall from Room 110.

Katarina sat on the bed opposite me. Olivia had closed the door and said she would be right outside, watching, and promised to block anyone who tried to come in, although there was nobody there to try. Metzgar hadn't showed up for work yet, and business at the hotel was very slow. It could have had something to do with the adverse publicity after the murder.

"This doesn't seem like a great place to work, Katarina."

Katarina laughed nervously. "That's what my boyfriend says too. Anyway, yeah."

"Look, I wanted to finish our conversation from the other day."

"You mean about, like, Room 110?"

"Yes, about what happened there. Olivia said you knew two of the people in the room—the man who was killed and the woman the police are looking for."

She shot me a frightened glance. It seemed to take several minutes but finally she exhaled. "Yeah, like, I know who she is. She was there a bunch of times before, and I got to know her a little bit when I was working on the night shift. She'd stay in the room and she'd have, you know, visitors."

"Visitors. You mean the type of visitors who pay money to have sex with a young woman?"

"I guess," she said.

"And the man who was killed, he was her business manager?"

"I guess. I never talked to him. But the girl is nice. She would come out to the front sometimes to get extra towels and stuff like that. And we'd, like, chat and stuff."

"Chat about...."

"Nothing important. Just whatever. The weather. Bands that were playing. We are about the same age, so like, yeah."

"About twenty five?"

"I'm twenty-four. She told me she was twenty-five. She said her name was Vanessa. She never told me her last name or where she lived. But one time she mentioned she was a dancer."

"A dancer, like, a stripper?"

"Yeah, I think so. She told me she had a nom de bikini. Hilarious, right? Like, what, your bikini has a name? But she said all the dancers have stage names. Hers was Satin."

"Satin," I repeated.

"Yes, her bikini name was Satin. I love that. Anyway, she's nice. I don't think she has an easy life."

"What makes you say that?"

"I don't know. Just a sense I got. I mean, why else would you do what she does in those rooms with those guys unless she has to? I would never do that."

"Tough way to make money."

"Plus, she had to give most of it to the guy, whatever his name was. I forget his name."

"You mean the guy who was killed?"

"Yeah."

"Frank Raymond Leclerc."

"Okay, but that wasn't the name he used to sign in with."

"The police have all that information."

"Yeah probably. Mr. Metzgar or the other manager, Mr. Shills, used to deal with all that. One of them would always sign them in."

"Oh yeah?"

"Yeah, Mr. Metzgar's been, like, totally stressed lately."

"Why?"

"I'm not sure but—what was the guy's name? The guy who died?"

"Frank Leclerc?"

"Yes, him. His brother has been around a lot."

"The guy who was talking to Metzgar yesterday, buzz cut, drives a blue BMW?"

"That's him," Katarina said. "My grandmother always says you shouldn't speak ill of the dead but the guy who died, he was not a nice guy."

"Oh?"

"If Vanessa was out front talking to me and he came into the hotel, Vanessa would literally just stop talking, stop smiling, turn around and, like, go right back to the room. And the guy, that Frank guy, he'd give me these incredibly disgusting looks."

I nodded. "Being a creep comes with the territory."

"I didn't want to talk to the police. They were asking all of us if we had information about the girl or the older guy. I didn't say anything. I mean, I don't know anything. And I didn't want to get Vanessa in trouble."

"Completely understandable."

"But you seem nice, and you're not the cops. I figure I should tell somebody. She might still be in trouble."

"She very well might."

****

I was about to get back into my car when I remembered the gas station attendant. I had to check my notes for his name. Joachim B. I walked over.

The man behind the counter was the same man in the employee of the month poster. I picked up a package of chewing gum and placed it on the counter. He rang it in.

As I was paying for the gum, I said, "You're Joachim?"

He looked surprised. "Yes."

He was a tall kid, curly black hair, dirt under his fingernails. I said, "I spoke to your colleague last Monday." He was nodding, still looking scared but now doing his best to understand me. His first language was neither French nor English. "He said you were working the night of Christmas Eve."

Comprehension glimmered behind the dark eyes. "Yes, I was working."

I introduced myself and handed him a business card. "I'm a journalist. Did you see anything that night that was unusual?"

He nodded rapidly. "Yes, I saw something. A man...." He didn't know the word, so he made his fingers into the shape of a gun. "Bang, bang."

"You saw a man shooting?"

"Yes. That's what I saw."

"What time was that?"

"About two in the morning."

"And you called police?"

"No. I called my boss. He said don't call police. He said, always trouble at that hotel."

"What else did you see?"

"Nothing else. A man, he ran away. The car drove away. That was it."

"What kind of car?"

"I don't know. It was dark, I couldn't see."

"And the man?"

"Same. He was a big man, but that's all I could see. I heard voices shouting. I looked out. Heard the shot. Then, they go. It was maybe 10 seconds."

Another customer came into the store. Joachim looked eager to end the conversation. I thanked him and left.

Chapter Thirty-Five

By this time it was getting on toward noon, New Year's Eve. There was a voice I needed for the story, and there was only one way I knew how to get it. So I hit the road.

As I drove, I thought about what I had learned that morning. The girl in the hotel room, Vanessa, was a stripper as well as a hooker. Where did she dance? Was she still working as a dancer? What were Felix and the hotel manager talking about at the front of the hotel? Had anyone else seen the shooting at the hotel, or just Joachim? Did Anderson know about it?

I called Shawna from me cell phone, hoping now that I had a little more information about the girl we were looking for, she would reconsider helping me. She answered on the second ring.

"It's me. I know the girl's name. I know her real name, it's Vanessa, and her stage name is Satin."

"Listen, Denny, I'd like to help you. I really would, but I can't. I've just got too much going on right now." There was a fair bit of frost in her voice.

I tried not to let the disappointment creep into mine. "It's okay, Shawna, I get it."

"And I'm sorry that I walked out on you the other day. Sometimes the four-teen-year-old girl in me comes out."

"Don't worry about it. But why were you so angry with me?"

"It's not just you, it's all you white men."

"Yeah, we're terrible."

She laughed a little, realizing she would think her comment was ridiculous had somebody else said it. Maybe the frost was melting.

"It's my ex-husband," she said

"What about him?"

"He's saying I can't see my son."

"Why not?"

"He says it's because of the work that I do. Says it's a bad influence. He said he told our son about it and my son is scared now, and I just think that's total bullshit."

"I'm sorry. That must be really difficult."

"Hell yeah, it's difficult. I haven't seen him in a year."

"But don't you have a right to see him?"

"He has sole custody. I would need to get a lawyer and I can't afford it."

I wasn't sure what to say so I just listened. I could hear the anguish in her voice.

"You know that kid is half me. I deserve to see him and spend time with him. I've paid for the mistakes I made, but I'm still paying, and I have to keep paying, and it doesn't seem fair to me."

She paused for a moment before continuing. "When you showed me the picture of that girl, and you told me about the man who went to see her at the hotel, it triggered me. Anyway, I hope you can find her. She deserves a better life."

"Let me know if there's anything I can do, Shawna. I know what it's like not to be able to see your kids whenever you want."

We left it there. I was sad for her, and I was sad because I needed her help. But I would have to go it alone.

About an hour later, I stopped at a drive-through for a greasy egg on a bun and some scalding coffee. Brunch of champions. The forecast was for a snowstorm, but at that moment, the heavens were clear, and for a little while, the hard beauty of a Montréal winter was on display—the brilliant white of new snow contrasting with the sky's crisp cerulean hue. Icicles melted in the sunlight as I waited in line, the steady drip, drip like a promise of spring.

I took the time to look up the number for the media relations office at the Department of National Defence, called them and left a message to say I was working on a story about McPhee. I had some personal details of his military service that I wanted to confirm, along with his views about mefloquine. Would the department like to comment for the story? I told them my deadline and left my phone number and email address. I knew the flacks would all be at home for the weekend, but somebody would be monitoring messages.

My next call was to a friend who specializes in deep data dives and whom I sometimes hire to work on stories. I asked her to pull numbers on government spending on the military on a per soldier basis, with a focus on services for veterans. I was curious about whether one of the reasons so many returning vets were suffering was because the government wasn't keeping up with its obligations. How different were those obligations now to the soldiers now that the military had switched to a combat role from a peacekeeping one?

Back on the road traffic was sparse, conditions were decent. I kept to the speed limit as I thought about the story I'd write.

People give up a lot of rights when they join the armed forces, and there's a culture of sucking it up and getting on with the job. This mindset often prevails even after they leave the military. It was one of the things I wanted to talk about with Colonel Dalgliesh, now retired, who was an old friend of my mother's. They belonged to the same bridge club, and for a while I thought they might be romantically involved, but she would never say. My mother was unusual in many ways, and she could be difficult, but she had a wide circle of friends and she never hesitated to share her connections with me. She had given me his phone number.

I reached him on the second ring. Yes, of course he remembered me. Yes, it certainly had been a long time. Yes, he'd be delighted to speak with me about the military for a story I was working on. He suggested we find a moment to chat at the party. I asked him which party. He said the New Year's party tonight at the Robertson's. He used to see my mother there every year but he hadn't been able to attend the last few times. I said that of course I would be there.

Next I called my mother. She updated me on her Christmas visit with her sister in Toronto, and asked me about the kids. My sense was that she would always blame me for the fact she didn't see them as often as she used to.

"I'm planning to come with you to the party at the Robertson's."

"It's not exactly your kind of thing, Denny. Are you that hard up for company?"

She was right. It wasn't my kind of thing. But sometimes one had to make exceptions. "I've just been on the phone with the colonel. I need to speak with him, and he suggested we find time to chat at the party."

"He'll be there?" She sounded like a school girl. "Of course you can come. Pick me up at eight."

My calls finished, I settled in for the drive ahead. I'd brought a voice recorder with me so that I could work on some of the other stories whose deadlines were approaching. Eighty percent of writing happens before the pen hits the paper or the cursor moves on the screen. I talked through some of the ideas, getting rid of the knots, making it easier to write when the time came.

The fair weather held until I got to Cornwall.

I was taking a series of gambles, the first of which was that Buzzy would be at work on a Sunday. That one paid off. He was there. He didn't take a run at me this time. He just kept working, tinkering with an engine.

"To what do I owe the pleasure?" he said in a voice laced with sarcasm.

"I need to ask a favour."

Twenty minutes later we were sitting in his messy kitchen with his wife, Georgina, a heavyset woman with ginger hair. There was something cooking in the oven that smelled delicious. It was the kind of smell that always reminded me of other people's houses, that was redolent of a childhood I'd never had. Their two kids, a boy and a girl, aged about seven and nine were running around.

Buzzy told them to go outside. "You two, go build a goddamn snow fort."

Georgina gave him a cross look.

"They gotta get outside, honey."

The kids rushed to put on their winter gear. Once they were out the door, Georgina turned to me, signaling the time had come for me to explain my presence.

"Has Buzzy told you anything about what's been happening with Mike McPhee in Montréal?" I said

She looked at Buzzy as if for a signal. "He might have mentioned something. And I've seen the news."

"Have you heard from Mike's wife?"

She glanced at Buzzy again before she answered.

"I spoke to her recently, yes."

"I'm assuming the police have been in touch with her, because her husband is a suspect in two murder investigations."

"Two?"

"There was another murder two nights ago."

Georgina shook her head. "Those poor families."

I gave her a minute to process the information. Most people don't want anything to do with murder, and I doubted she was an exception.

"I'm writing about Mike for one of the Montréal newspapers. I have an advantage over other reporters because I know him from Afghanistan. There will be lots of stories written about him that will be hatchet jobs. I want to get the whole story. He's a remarkable person but I believe he's very sick and he needs help. The story would benefit from having Emma's voice."

Georgina's reply was immediate. "She would never talk to a reporter about her husband."

"I know she may have said that, but now that Mike is wanted by police and is on the run, she may think differently. If he doesn't turn himself in, this is going to end badly not just for Mike, but who knows for how many others."

She looked down at the kitchen table, and for half a minute nobody spoke. She was the first to break the silence. "And nobody knows where he is?"

"They can't find him. He doesn't want to be found, and he's got the skills to go undetected for a long time."

She considered this a minute, then stood up and took her phone into the next room. Buzzy and I sat without speaking. I felt like a defendant awaiting his verdict. After a few minutes of this uncomfortable silence, he said, "More coffee?"

I pushed my mug forward. "Sure, thanks."

While he was up, I scanned the room. It was a bad habit, being nosy, but it comes with the territory. My eyes came to rest on the fridge. There were the usual items held there with magnets: photos of the kids and family, a calendar from the local real estate agent, a hydro bill, a post-it note with the numbers 3-7-2-7 written in pen.

Buzzy refilled the cups and sat back down. It looked as if there was something he wanted to say, but then he turned to the window, staring out at nothing. I could hear a voice from the other room but couldn't make out the words.

I looked again at the post-it note. 3-7-2-7. If I transposed the letters to the numbers on an ordinary keypad, I would get 3 RCR, or the acronym for Buzzy and McPhee's old unit, 3rd Battalion, Royal Canadian Regiment.

Georgina came back, shaking her head. "She told me the military police have already been to her house. They've been through everything and took away Mike's computer and a bunch of other things. The kids are upset, and she doesn't want to talk to anyone else about this. She said Mike made his bed. Now he's got to lie in it."

I nodded. "Okay. I understand." I got up and shook hands with both of them. "I'm sorry to have troubled you." I left a card on the table in case Emma changed her mind or in case they heard anything they wanted to tell me about that I could use for the story.

Buzzy came outside with me. I asked him if he was going back to work but he said he was done for the day. They were hosting a New Year's Eve party that they had to start getting ready for. We walked by the kids, who were using plastic shovels to hollow out a snowbank for a shelter. It made me think of my girls and I wondered what they'd been up to for the past few days. Again the dull ache.

The bright blue sky of earlier had clouded over and the air grown damp with the coming snow. Buzzy and I shook hands, a weirdly strained farewell. Maybe he'd been uncomfortable having me in his house, given the history with Sarah. I thanked him for his help and climbed back into the Toyota, empty handed.

Chapter Thirty-Six

I started driving home, but something was niggling at me. Why was Buzzy being so quiet? Was he hiding something? What? And where?

I parked at the Tim Hortons across from Buzzy's shop and waited. At 4 p.m., the other mechanic got into his car and left. I didn't have a ton of time if I was going to get back home and pick up my mother at eight, as I'd promised.

I didn't even know what the hell I was doing there. But the hunch had been so powerful, and Buzzy's behaviour so unusual that I felt justified. Besides, I was getting annoyed, even a little upset, that I wasn't getting anywhere with the story and my deadline was looming.

I stepped out of the car and pretended I was checking the address. When nothing happened, I moved to the door and made as though I was looking for something on the ground. When nothing happened, I tried the door. It was now or never. I punched in the number I'd seen on Buzzy's fridge. The door opened.

I stepped inside and closed it behind me. I'd brought a small flashlight with me from the car.

The first thing I wanted to see was what was beneath the tarp at the far end of the shop. I thought I had seen some kind of an inflatable boat, which Buzzy had quickly covered, and indeed, when I lifted up the tarp, that's what it was. I let the tarp fall and retraced my steps to the stairs to the office. I stopped to make sure I couldn't hear anything from upstairs, and then headed up, pausing when I reached the landing. The only sound was the traffic outside. I still wasn't sure the place was empty. I was about to move when a noise behind me made me jump, but it was only the overhead heater kicking in.

The door to the office was open. The other door, which had been ajar on the day of the fight, was now closed and locked. I looked for cameras and didn't see any. I crept into the office, sat at the old wooden desk, and started combing through the drawers looking for a key to the locked door. It crossed my mind that I would be arrested for breaking and entering if caught, but I reasoned that if my hunch was correct, then Buzzy would have more to fear from the police than I did.

In one of the drawers, in among the junk—half-eaten bags of candy, coins, bitten off pencils, erasers, sunflower seeds— I found three keys, two of them with plastic tags and one without. These I took back out to the landing and tried them in the locked door. No luck.

I tried the door again, assessing whether it would break open if I hit it hard enough with my shoulder, but I realized that was a good way to hurt myself, and I abandoned that idea.

I remembered that old wooden desks sometimes have hidden latches and compartments. My father's desk had, and it had fascinated me as a child, so I felt around inside the drawers. I found nothing, but on the left side of the desk, a single door opened to reveal a shelf that rolled outward, presumably for a typewriter. There was a small hole at the side. I stuck a finger through it, felt a metal rod and pushed on it. I heard a latch opening, and a small wooden board flipped down. I crawled under the desk to get it. Set into the board was a sliding compartment and inside was another key. I tried it in the door, and it worked. The door swung inward.

By now I was filthy and covered in sweat. There was even sweat in my eyes, and the back of my neck was slick. I had to stand still for a minute to let my heart rate slow down. It was dark in the room now that the light had bled from the day, making it difficult to see exactly what was inside the room, so I switched on my flashlight.

Against the far wall was a bed, with a sheet and blanket folded neatly and set on top of the bed, and a pillow on top of these. There was a dresser opposite, a small nightstand next to the bed, and along the wall closest to me, a sofa and a small armchair. It was as neat and squared away as Buzzy's office was messy. It looked like the apartment of an absent ascetic.

Against the wall behind me was a small refrigerator. There were half a dozen beers in there, a few cans of soft drinks and a jar of mustard.

I went through the bedside table, found nothing. I was about to call it a day when I reached under the bed and my hand touched something. I pulled it out. It was a folder holding three sheets of paper. Two of the sheets were maps of Montréal's Underground City. The third was a map of the Old Port. There were some numbers scribbled in the top margin, but they didn't seem to relate to anything on the pages.

I took photos of all three documents, shielding the flash of my cell phone, then replaced the folder beneath the bed. I locked the room behind me as I left, put the key back in its hiding place in Buzzy's desk and headed home.

Chapter Thirty-Seven

My mother insisted I have a glass of wine while I waited for her to finish getting ready. I took the glass but as soon as she disappeared into her bedroom, I dumped most of the wine into the kitchen sink. I wanted to keep a clear head for driving.

"Everything okay?" she called out.

"Yes, everything's fine."

My mother was unusually excited when I arrived to pick her up that evening. There must have been a romance between her and the general at some point, or at least the promise of one. I used to see him often shortly after she broke up with her second husband, Jackson, the stepfather I never liked.

My mother emerged from her bedroom, smartly dressed in white slacks and a navy blouse. She wore a silk scarf loosely around her neck.

"Jeez, Mom, you clean up nice," I said.

"I beg your pardon."

"Nothing. You look good."

On our way to the party, she said, "At least the Toyota is an improvement on your old one."

"Thanks, Mom. I'm glad you're happy with at least one choice I've made."

"You know what I mean, dear."

We sat in silence for most of the ride.

Vivian Robertson had been my mother's bridge partner for twenty years. My mother had more than once mentioned confidentially to me that she found Vivian "a bit stiff," mostly because she didn't laugh at my mother's off-colour jokes or appreciate her frequent profane outbursts, like the time she was dealt a giant hand in a tournament and yelled, "Jesus Christ, Vivian. You won't believe this absolute fucking moose!"

Late in life Vivian had married Gerry Robertson, the former CEO of a railroad. He was loaded. They lived in a big brick house on Lazard Street in the Town of Mount Royal, or TMR, one of the most affluent neighbourhoods in Canada. All I knew about it while I was growing up was that people who lived there dressed beautifully, always knew how to behave, and seemed able to look right through you. It was an alien world to me.

But some things in TMR were like everywhere else in Montréal. Even at almost 9 p.m., we had to drive through a gang of kids playing road hockey under the street lights. The goalies dragged their nets to the side of the road to let us pass.

We were welcomed by Gerry Robertson himself, manning the door. "Come in, come in." He was a balding, round-faced man of medium height and high colour. It looked like the party was well underway.

A massive chandelier dominated an equally massive lobby that featured a wide, spiral staircase and a huge stone fireplace where a fire was burning brightly. In one corner was a self-service bar. About forty guests were milling about or engaged in polite conversation. Lively background piano music kept the mood upbeat. Two servers dressed in black pants and white shirts wandered around, one with a tray filled with flutes of sparkling wine, the other with canapés. I helped myself to a morsel of smoked salmon.

Vivian appeared, and she and my mother embraced. They had worked together at a downtown bank when they were much younger and the friendship had endured.

"Vivian, you remember my son, Denny?"

Vivian held out her hand. "It's so nice to see you again. So glad you could make it."

"Viv, could you fix him up with one of the rich girls around here, please? He's newly single."

"I'm sure he can manage on his own."

I told her what a pleasure it was to see her again and thanked her for inviting me. The formality of the gathering was already starting to grate on me.

I spotted the colonel standing on his own at the bar and excused myself.

"Colonel Dalgliesh," I said, extending a hand. "Good to see you again."

"Ah, Denny. You're looking very well. I somehow always picture you as a boy. It's funny how some images remain fixed in the mind."

He was a tall, distinguished looking man with snow white hair, broad shoulders, blue eyes, an aquiline nose. He wore an extremely well tailored navy suit. He was probably what a retired colonel should look like, except for a less than impressive chin. He obviously maintained himself. I wondered what the prospects were of he and my mother hooking up.

He held a tumbler three quarters full of what looked like whiskey. He lifted it up. "Half scotch, half water. Montgomery swore by it as an aperitif. If it was good enough for Monty, it's good enough for me."

As I fixed myself a drink, the general said, "Does your story have anything to do with the Major McPhee I just saw on the news?"

"As I matter of fact, it does." I told him about how I knew McPhee and my reasons for wanting to report the story. "Do you know anything about his history?"

"I confess, I do not."

"Highly decorated, highly loved and respected by his men. He was awarded the Star of Military Valour for service in Afghanistan. Awarded the bronze star by the Americans. He was an outstanding officer. Three tours of duty. The first two went to plan. When he came back after his third tour in 2008, the bottom fell out. His mental health disintegrated. His family fell apart. His wife had to go into hiding with the kids."

The general was listening intently. "Very troubling."

I asked him if he'd ever heard of mefloquine.

"It's funny you should mention that," he said. "When I was deployed to Somalia, we were the first cohort to use the drug. It was a trial. I remember it caused a lot of problems for some of the men. They complained it gave them nightmares, so much so that I asked HQ to discontinue the drug. They denied the request. I quietly told my medical staff that if any of the men were having difficulties, to advise them not to take the pills. We would sort them out with some replacements. That said, it seemed to work well for most of the men, and the fact it could be taken once a week instead of daily made it much easier to administer.

"Have you ever had malaria, Denny?"

I told him I hadn't.

"I have. It's no fun."

We drank.

He continued. "Somalia was my last deployment. I retired after that. But I've seen stories recently suggesting that the troops are still taking mefloquine."

"They are, although the Americans have withdrawn it from routine use, from what I read. Between you and me, colonel, Mike McPhee believes his troubles begin and end with mefloquine. He believes he's been poisoned by the government."

"Good Lord!"

"Exactly. I wanted to ask you if you know whether the military is thinking about banning the drug and what help there is for people in McPhee's situation."

"I don't know what their position is but I can ask around. I still have friends at DND in Ottawa. But I can tell you this, there will be a massive exercise in ass-covering should it be found that this drug isn't safe. The liability would be gigantic."

"After McPhee was sectioned out of the military, he had to deal with Veterans Affairs, and I don't think it went well."

He sighed. "It's a common complaint in the military." As he was saying this, a look of pleasure crossed his face.

"Well, hello!"

I felt a hand on my shoulder and turned to see my mother standing there looking equally pleased. "Colonel, it's so nice to see you after all this time." They kissed on both cheeks in the Montréal fashion.

I said my good-byes and made my way home. I was looking forward to ringing in the new year with Johanna.

Chapter Thirty-Eight

I called Johanna as soon as I arrived back at my apartment. Twenty minutes later, she arrived, in high spirits, her face flushed from an earlier party.

I took a bottle of wine from the cupboard and poured us each a glass. Before long, we were sitting together on the sofa. It was starting to feel like a relationship that could have a future.

I wanted to forget about McPhee and enjoy some alone time with Johanna, but she brought up the subject. It must have been a subject of gossip at the previous party she had attended.

"I heard your friend McPhee has left town. Someone saw him in California."

"Maybe he did leave, but I have a hunch he's still here."

She was playing with the buttons on my shirt. "Why do you think that?"

"He's on a mission. And it's not done yet."

I hadn't told Johanna about McPhee's memory stick but I decided to confide in her. "You know I spoke to him on the phone?"

Her eyes filled with alarm and incredulity. "When? What did he say?"

"He wants me to write a story about him. He wouldn't tell me where he was."

"That sounds a little bit crazy."

"It is."

"Have you told the police?"

"Not about that."

"Why not?"

I thought carefully about how to say what I felt. "The police are under pressure to arrest McPhee to get him off the street. I'm worried that if they become too aggressive, there will be an armed confrontation. McPhee could be killed, some police could be killed or injured and so could innocent bystanders. I still think there's a chance that McPhee will give himself up. He wants his story told. He wants to know that the government is listening to him."

"But he seems beyond help."

"I can convince him to get help."

"How?"

"I don't know yet."

"Why's that?"

"It's a long story." A sudden weariness came over me.

I refilled her glass. The wine was taking effect. We kissed and would surely have ended up in bed had my phone not rung.

It was Shawna.

"Guess who I found?"

"Satin."

"Got it in one."

"I don't pay overtime."

"You don't pay anything."

"I thought you didn't have time to look for her."

"I ran into someone who knows one of the girls that the Leclerc brothers were running. I spoke with her. She said Satin is a dancer at a club in the Point called Mindy's."

"Is she working tonight?"

"If you call sliding naked up and down a pole working, then yeah, she's working."

"What are you doing now? Do you have any New Year's Eve plans?"

"Let me check my social calendar. Oh, it appears I have an opening."

"See you at Mindy's in forty minutes." I ended the call. Johanna was looking at me with a knowing expression. "You have to leave?"

"I'm sorry."

She nodded. "It's okay. I understand. How late do you think you'll be?"

"I don't know."

"When do you have to leave?"

"I've got ten minutes."

There was that smile again. "That's just time enough."

Chapter Thirty-Nine

When I was growing up in NDG, I was often warned about the kids from the Point, a scruffy neighbourhood, originally working-class Irish, between the Lachine Canal and the St. Lawrence River. When our basketball team went there to play games, there was always an undercurrent of threat and wariness. Not much had changed in the years since. The streets retained a mostly worn, industrial feel. The few visible attempts at gentrification seemed like acts of defiance.

Mindy's was a seedy looking club from the outside. The exterior was plain brick. A neon sign advertising *"Danseuses nues"* dominated the front, though many of the bulbs were burnt out. An all-night diner next door was about half full of customers.

The temperature had risen to almost zero, but the air was damp and the wind pushed the branches of the trees around. Shawna was huddled in the doorway of the diner, shivering. "You took your damn time."

We kissed cheeks. "Something I had to take care of."

It was about midnight when we walked through the front doors. The place was dark, but the music was pounding, hard driving metal, relentless chord progressions, thumping bass. If you could bear the wailing, you might detect a melody. It was music to weld by. The only lights were on a couple of pool tables at the back and a spotlight illuminated a small, circular stage with a chrome pole in the middle of the room.

Shawna and I sat down at a table about twenty feet from the stage. After my eyes adjusted, I saw half a dozen women dressed in virtually nothing but party hats slinking around, stopping at tables, occasionally disappearing into the back with a customer. A few of them looked at me with undisguised greed. Fresh meat.

We waited for a waitress but none came so I made my way through the crowd to the bar. The bartender ignored me for as long as he could. He had a tattoo on his neck that looked like part of a spider's web and his arm was heavily inked with what appeared to be a row of crosses. I waited. Eventually he walked over and planted his fists on the wooden bartop.

"How ya' doing," I yelled with mock cheeriness. "Pint of Murphy's and a coke please."

He poured the stout and walked it dripping back to me. He poured a glass full of black liquid sugar from the soda gun. I handed him a twenty. He kept the change. I wanted to ask him if Satin was on but conversation didn't seem like his strong suit. I brought the drinks back to the table.

"Have you seen her yet?"

"Not yet. Maybe she's on break."

"How do you know what she looks like?"

"Her friend showed me a picture on her phone."

The half-dozen men loitering by the pool tables looked much like the bartender. It was a six-way tie for winner of the ugly tattoo contest. It didn't seem to matter to the few dancers who hung off their arms or sat in laps. One of the girls walked by our table, a thuggish looking blond with small brown eyes and more piercings than Caesar.

She gave me the standard opener. "Where you from?"

"I'm waiting for someone."

She took a chair, ignoring Shawna. "Your wait is over honey. My name is Baby Blue."

She held out a greasy hand. I gave the hand a noncommittal touch and wiped it as inconspicuously as possible on my pants before reaching for my beer. I took a long swig and gave her a level look. "I don't think so, but thanks anyway."

Hostility crackled off her like static. She sat there truculently. Maybe she was giving me a chance to change my mind. I threw caution to the wind.

"Is Satin on tonight? I was really hoping to see her." I broke out my Mr. Charming smile, the kind you see on discount billboards.

"You're looking for Satin?"

"You need me to write it down?"

She hauled herself out of the chair and walked over to the group at the pool tables. She tapped one of the dancers on the shoulder and said a few words, gesturing in my direction. About two minutes later, one of them stood and made her way slowly to our table, watched with a dangerous curiosity by half the swamp contingent.

She stopped at our table and shouted "Yeah?" like a petulant teen. Her long blond hair was plaited behind her neck and twisted over her left shoulder to hang down and hug her left breast. Her bikini top was two triangles of thin red fabric that almost covered her nipples and was held in place by a studded collar. There was a small tattoo of a devil with a halo under her right breast.

I shouted back. "I was hoping to have a word."

This wasn't the type of meeting I had hoped for. Despite the bold show, she seemed nervous. A vein pulsed in her neck and her voice was shaky. Her makeup was starting to flake from the moisture on her skin.

"You another cop?"

"No."

"I already talked to the cops. I got nothing more to say."

I glanced at Shawna, who offered reinforcement. "We're not cops. Your friend Melody said we could find you here."

"That fucking bitch." Satin's arms were crossed. "I have a lawyer."

I tried to reassure her. I gestured to the empty chair. "We wanted to buy you a drink."

"I have one already," she nodded back at the pool tables. "And I don't do couples."

The music was beginning to wear me down. I felt conspicuous. The back of my neck felt hot. Behind Satin a couple of the swamp dwellers got to their feet, probably keying on Satin's body language.

"My name's Denny. This is Shawna."

"So?"

"I wanted to talk to you about a friend of mine you met the other night."

"What friend is that?"

"Mike McPhee. You spent some time with him at the Lorelei."

Her eyes grew wider as I spoke. At the name of the Lorelei, she burst out, "It wasn't my fault what happened."

"I know it's not your fault. I'm a friend of Mike's. I was hoping you could tell me what happened that night. I'm trying to find him."

The pounding music abruptly stopped and the crowd began counting down, "Ten, nine, eight." The door opened and in walked Felix Leclerc.

Chapter Forty

Felix's eyes roved the crowd. He didn't look happy. Was he looking for me or Vanessa?

"Seven, six, five..."

He spotted us and started making his way through the crowd toward our table. I could feel my pulse pick up. I reminded myself to breathe slowly. I glanced up at Vanessa. She must have spotted him too, because her face was white and she was staring at the floor. He was within 20 feet us.

"Three, two, one, Happy New Year!"

Everyone was on their feet, hugging, kissing, laughing. There was a solid wall of people between us and Felix. I could see the top of his head as he tried to find a channel through the crowd.

Vanessa looked at Shawna and me and jerked her head toward the back of the bar. "C'mon." Shawna and I grabbed our jackets and followed as she weaved her way through the revelers to the back entrance. She spoke a few words to the doorman who nodded and let us through. We followed her down a corridor to a door that said 'staff only.' She told us to wait and disappeared into the room. Shawna and I waited silently in the hall. I kept my eyes on the door at the end of the hall through which we had just come, expecting Felix to open it at any moment and charge after us. But in less than two minutes, Vanessa was back out, wearing grey sweat pants, Ugg boots and a short bomber jacket that almost covered her belly button.

We kept going down the hall to a door with a metal push handle that led into an alley. As soon as we were outside, Vanessa lit a cigarette. After exhaling a cloud of smoke, she said, "I'm starving. You want to know what happened, buy me some dinner."

Chapter Forty-One

A few minutes later we were sitting at a booth at the very back of all-night diner a few blocks away from Mindy's. We were tucked into the corner of an L-shaped room, hidden from the view of anyone, such as Felix, on the street.

The waitress came and we ordered. Vanessa looked very stressed. Furrowed brow. Hands balled. Blond hair everywhere. She said, "Tell me what you want to know."

I looked at her, waiting to see if I had her attention. At first, she seemed distracted, fidgeting with the utensils. Then, as if suddenly becoming aware she was sitting in a restaurant on New Year's Eve with two complete strangers, she became very still and stared fixedly at the salt shaker.

I took that as my cue. "Vanessa, I'm a reporter. I write stories. I'm writing a story about Mike McPhee, the man you knew from the Lorelei."

Her face changed. Her eyes opened wide, her lower lip quivered. She looked as though she might say something angry or hateful but no words escaped her lips.

I continued, "I should also tell you, because you may hear it somewhere else, that he is a friend of mine, but I've not seen him for more than six years. So I don't know him well."

Vanessa looked up, but not at me. She appeared to be scouting the restaurant for the waitress. Shawna asked, "When was the last time you ate something?"

Vanessa's expression relaxed. She rubbed her face with both hands, as if she were washing it, then placed both elbows on the table and rested her forehead against her hands, shielding her eyes. "It's been a couple of days."

Shawna and I exchanged looks. Shawna rested a reassuring hand on Vanessa's shoulder. "It's been a time, hasn't it."

Vanessa, eyes still shielded, nodded her head. A single tear splashed onto the tabletop.

The server arrived with huge plates of food. Vanessa straightened up to make room, then attacked the fries. She relaxed a bit once the food hit her belly.

I picked at my own food for a while, then took out a notebook and held it up to her, in a gesture of seeking permission, and she nodded.

"Can you tell me what happened that night?"

She began. "A few days before Christmas, Frank got a message over the website from a client," the word client didn't sit right in her mouth.

"Frank Leclerc, the man who died?"

"Yeah. He handled everything."

"Okay, keep going." I was taking notes with one hand and eating with the other. Shawna was picking at her food.

"Can I get some poutine?" Vanessa said.

Shawna said, "Yeah, I'll order it for you. I need to use the washroom anyway."

Vanessa said a muted thanks, and started in on her burger.

"So Frank would pass along the details to you?"

"Yeah, that's basically it. He would try to schedule as many for one night as possible, just to keep the expenses down, you know, the room and all that."

I wondered what she meant by "all that" but I didn't ask.

She was warming up now and the details were coming more freely. "Frank and his brother Felix hired someone to do a website, because they've got a few girls working for them."

"Why did you decide to work for them?"

She looked at me like it should have been obvious. "I need the money."

Shawna returned and told Vanessa the poutine was on the way.

"Anyway, Frank told me we had a guy and we would see him with a couple of the other ones we had booked for that evening."

"Were you surprised that people were requesting your services on Christmas Eve?"

"Hell no," she said. "It's my busiest day of the year. I'd been going since noon."

The poutine arrived and she attacked it as though the burger and fries had been an appetizer.

"So anyway, I decided to go ahead with it. This guy, your friend, we agreed to meet at the hotel at midnight. I figured, you know, older guy, probably wouldn't take that long. But anyway he shows up. He's a nice looking guy and everything. We make the usual small talk for thirty seconds and I start taking off my stuff and he says, 'Wait a minute.'"

Both Shawna and I were riveted. She knew she had us. The smallest of smiles appeared on her lips. She ate more poutine, probably just to make us wait, before resuming.

"So, usually when a guy says 'Wait a minute,' I know there's gonna be a problem. He's either got a disgusting fetish or he can't get it up. Something like that."

"So he says, 'Look, this may sound weird, but I knew your brother Eric.'"

"I tell him, 'I don't have a brother Eric. I have a brother Milo, but he's fourteen, and why would you know him?' But I'm thinking to myself, I don't want to leave with nothing, so I say, 'Are we gonna fuck, or what, because I still need to charge you for the time?' And he says, 'No, you don't have to do that anymore.'

"Then he says, 'I knew Eric in Afghanistan. He was in my unit.'

"And by now I was starting to get freaked out, because he's so....serious, right? He's got this super serious expression on his face and he's trying to hold my hand. I'm getting freaked out."

Another bite of poutine.

"So I told him, 'Look, I've got another client, so we should probably get on with it.' And I could tell he was getting agitated. He said, 'Your name is Vanessa Young?' I told him it was. And he told me my birthday, and it was the right date. And then he says, 'Your mother is Lucy?' And I said it was. Then he goes, 'Your brother was a good man. He died in my arms in Afghanistan. He was in my unit,' yadayadayada. He named some place where there was a big battle. He told me he dreams about it, and sometimes the blood is running through his hands like warm water, other times it's so sticky he can barely move his fingers.

"And now I know this guy is nuts. He tells me it was Eric's dying wish that someone would get me to stop doing what I'm doing.'

"I say, 'What, stop making a living?' So I get up and go to the can. I text Frank the safe word, right, which is 'freak.' Frank is waiting out in the parking lot in the car, so I know in about one minute the shit's gonna hit.

"I go back out and the guy says to me, 'So I'm here to take you with me.' And I tell him, 'I got bills to pay.'

"He says, 'I owe it to Eric.' I say, 'That might be true. But that's between you and him. I don't know any Eric.'

"Then Frank comes in, he's got the key to the room, for situations like this. Frank and your friend start having words. I know it's gonna get real in there so I'm like, time to go, and I left."

"I get outside the room and I call Felix, because Felix is the guy who normally handles this kind of stuff. I wait out in the parking lot, maybe fifteen, twenty minutes. He finally arrives. There's still no sign of Frank or the other guy. I'm wondering what the fuck is going on. I get into the car, I tell him what happened. He's freaking out because Frank's not answering his phone. He's about to go inside when we see your friend coming out a side door. I say to Felix, 'That's the guy!' Felix pulls a gun out of his jacket pocket, jumps out of the car and starts shooting at the guy. I'm like, 'What the fuck?' The guy takes off, Felix goes after him, and I'm like, 'I don't need this shit.' That's when I decided to make a change, before it was too late."

She took a moment to clean up the leftover gravy with a piece of bread. "That was the moment I realized, 'Girl, time for a change. Time to get off the merry-go-round. Time to get cleaned up. Time to get the Leclerc brothers out of your life.'"

"When did you hear about what happened?"

"It was the next day. It was on the news. I nearly shat myself. I'd gone back to my mom's right after the hotel, but I knew I couldn't stay there because Felix knew where my mom lived, and I knew he would come find me there, probably beat my mom up as well as me, so I grabbed some clothes and went to stay with a friend. Stayed there a few days but we ran out of money so I had to go back to work. Tonight was my first shift back since Christmas. It was okay until Felix showed up."

"Have you spoken to the police?"

"About what?"

"About what happened at the Lorelei."

"Fuck no."

Shawna spoke up. "Look, Vanessa, you didn't do anything wrong. What you did in the hotel room isn't illegal. What Felix is doing is definitely illegal."

She was nodding. "I know."

We let the conversation rest while the server cleared away the plates.

"What are you going to do now?" Shawna asked.

"I don't know. I can't go back to the club. Felix is going to find me there. I need to go back and see my mom. We had a big fight when I went back that night. I haven't spoken to her since. I need to ask her about the stuff this guy was saying. About this Eric guy. The biog thing is, I need to stay away from Felix. He's bad news."

I wrote my address on the back of a business card. "If you ever feel you need a safe place to stay, you can crash at my place. I can stay at my mother's."

She pocketed the card. "Thanks. Can you lend me a hundred bucks?"

Shawna and I looked at each other. "Just wait here," I said.

Chapter Forty-Two

It was about two in the morning when I walked out of the restaurant. I started walking down the street, looking for a cash machine but I didn't see one immediately, so I turned right and kept walking. It was clear and cold, and the sky was studded with stars. I pulled my toque low over my ears. There wasn't a ton of traffic but the streets weren't totally empty either.

Shawna and Vanessa would have plenty to talk about, so I didn't feel a particular hurry to get back. Shawna could have another cup of coffee, maybe Vanessa would get a piece of pie. She seemed to need the nourishment.

I passed a thrift store, a dollar store, a pharmacy, a liquor store and a hardware store. Finally, on the corner, I came to a bank, and the door to its ATM was open. I withdrew some cash and started walking back to the diner, turning over in my mind everything Vanessa had said. She was obviously the "friend" that McPhee had been planning to meet up with after leaving the Gargoyle. But he must have expected her to fall in line with his plan, to come along quietly, to greet him like a liberating hero. Instead she alerted Frank. What happened next was the "unexpected turn" in the mission that he'd written to me about in the text file on the memory stick.

Vanessa's brother, Eric, was the soldier in McPhee's unit that Buzzy had mentioned. Judging from what Vanessa said and from what was written in the personal files, McPhee's chronicles of pain, he must have made a pact with Eric that he would try to get his sister off the streets. Then, when Frank attacked him and Felix shot at him, the mission became, like it had been in Afghanistan, to "get the bad guys."

The shooting Vanessa witnessed, when Felix shot at McPhee, was exactly what Joachim, the gas station attendant, had described. Did Vanessa really not know that she had a brother? Was it Eric who had sent Vanessa's mother the lapis lazuli necklace from Afghanistan?

My reflections were cut short by the sight of a blue BMW pulling up to a traffic light. A figure that looked like Felix hunched over the wheel. I couldn't be sure it was him. The driver pulled an illegal right turn, moving so quickly through the intersection that I couldn't get a good look. If it was Felix, he must not have spotted me. He wouldn't be looking for a solo male. He'd be looking for a man and two women.

I tried to talk myself down, reasoning there must be hundreds of blue BMWs in the city and I was getting worked up over nothing.

Back at the restaurant, Vanessa took the cash and shoved it quickly into her purse. She said a furtive good bye to both of us and left. I offered Shawna a ride home but she insisted on taking the metro because she was heading to Berri. She said she'd been getting text messages all through dinner about a woman newly arrived from one of the Northern communities who was heading for an urban reality check, and she needed to find her as quickly as possible before she became another entry in the database.

Out on the street, we said our goodbyes and parted ways. I headed toward the lot further down the street where I'd parked the Toyota.

The snow had stopped, the temperature had dropped a little and the ground had iced up. I stepped carefully along the frozen sidewalk and was almost at the Toyota when a sound behind me made me turn.

It was Felix, collar up, wearing a black toque pulled low over his pugnacious forehead. His teeth glistened as he lifted something heavy and metallic. I moved just in time and instinctively parried the blow, catching his wrist as he stepped toward me. His feet hit a patch of ice and slid out from under him. He landed with a surprised "oof" and I heard his teeth knock against each other.

My thumb was already on the unlock button of the key fob and I pressed it a dozen times in the space of half a second. I opened the door, jumped in, and

hammered the door lock button. Without a pause, I turned the key in the ignition, jammed the transmission into reverse and floored it, cranking the steering
wheel hard clockwise at the same time, so that the front of the vehicle faced where
Felix was getting to his feet. I shoved the car into drive and there was a gratifying
thump but I didn't stop to see what part of him I'd hit or how much damage I'd
done. I straightened the wheel, backed straight out onto rue de Verdun, and got
moving in the direction of the fuck away.

I glimpsed Felix on one knee in the parking lot, head down. I hadn't killed him.
I didn't know whether to feel relieved or terrified. The fucker had tried to brain
me with a metal pipe. How diabolical was that?

*****

I kept driving. the streets were far from empty, even at 2:30 in the morning. My
nerves were just starting to settle when my phone rang. It was Johanna.

"Happy New Year," I said.

"Hi," she said, panic in her voice.

"What's the matter?"

"I think I'm being followed."

"What do you mean?"

"After you left, I decided to go to a party at a friend's place. I'm just walking
home, and I could swear there's someone following me."

"Where are you?"

"I'm on Prince Arthur, near Saint-Urbain."

"Okay, you're really close to an all-night gas station. Walk to Saint-Laurent and
turn right and you'll see it. Wait for me there. If anything weird happens, call 911."

She said she would and we hung up.

In my mind, all I could see was Johanna in McPhee's crosshairs. I pressed on
the accelerator and blew through an intersection onto Sherbrooke. A few minutes
later, I arrived at the gas station just as Johanna appeared. She hurried to the car
and got in, and we drove back to my place.

This had to end. I had to find McPhee.

Chapter Forty-Three

New Year's Day. I woke up late, around nine in the morning. The attack by Felix and Johanna's ordeal the previous evening had left me with a strong sense of dislocation. I got out of bed and went into the living room, closing the door behind me to let Johanna sleep.

I paced around, wondering what course of action to take. The idea of calling Anderson to tell him what Vanessa had seen and experienced crossed my mind. But he hadn't seemed very interested in speaking with her. I thought about telling him about the attack by Felix. But hadn't he already warned me about the danger of that association? Besides, in the end I had probably done more damage to Felix than he had done to me.

How worried should I be that Felix or one of his associates—if McPhee had left any associates alive—would track me down either at home or at my second home, the Gargoyle. But I reasoned it was unlikely Felix had the skills or resources to find my address. He was more of on an impulse guy, the type who'd prefer to wait in an alley and jump out from behind a trash can.

Should I get a gun? What good would that do me? It wasn't like I could walk around with one in my coat. For one thing, it was against the law for citizens to carry a concealed weapon in Canada. For another, I doubted I could shoot someone in cold blood. Maybe in self defence, but even that was questionable. I had shot a man once. It wasn't something I ever wanted to do again. I called Shawna and told her what happened, and asked her to check on Vanessa if she had a way of doing that.

Then I put Felix out of my mind because I had work to do. My deadline to file the story for Lydia was fast approaching and I needed to start writing. I decided to have another look at the text file from the memory stick. It seemed like so long ago that McPhee had slipped it into my pocket, but only three days had passed since the explosion at the Atrium. I opened my laptop and plugged in the drive with McPhee's documents.

I scanned the text file. What had McPhee meant by, "There is one more thing that I need to do, that is why I gave you the first set of documents." Did the "one more thing" refer to finding and killing Felix? But there was nothing about that in the first set of documents. His mission to find and eliminate the thugs who were responsible for trafficking Vanessa only began when he left the Gargoyle and went to the Lorelei, and that was after he'd given me the first set of documents, all of which related to his battle with Veterans Affairs, his attempt to get a disability claim for mefloquine poisoning and his correspondence with doctors and scientists who had been studying the drug and its effects.

I decided to have another look through the first batch of papers. As I read through, I made notes that I could potentially use in the story. The first document was a letter from a doctor in West Virginia. The doctor confirmed to McPhee that the brain chemistry of some individuals makes the mefloquine toxic, and can have severe neuropsychiatric consequences. The letters back and forth seemed professional and encouraging as McPhee outlined, in a clinical way, his own symptoms, and also how nobody in the military chain of command would confirm a diagnosis of mefloquine toxicity for him. He said at one point that his doctors were leaning towards a diagnosis of PTSD, which he said was wrong.

After a couple of hours of reading, I took a break to make some more coffee. Johanna appeared, looking exhausted. "Last night seems so surreal. I think I was feeling a little paranoid."

I handed her a mug of coffee. "We both were, but it's understandable."

We made small talk for a few minutes, but we were both distracted with our own thoughts and it seemed like there was a wall between us. She finished her coffee and said she needed to get going for a lunch with some friends. I offered to drive her but she insisted on taking a taxi. We agreed that she would call at the first sign that she was being followed or if she felt in danger.

I accompanied her down to the lobby, held onto her as we made our way along the icy walkway, and made sure she got safely into the waiting taxi.

Alone in the elevator, I wondered if I would ever see her again, and felt sad to think I might not. But I pushed the feeling away, along with all the other feelings, locked the door to my apartment, refilled my mug with coffee and resumed my reading.

A letter from someone at Director Military Careers Administration said that the DMCA had reviewed his case, and that he would receive a disclosure package giving him several options before a final decision would be made on his release. After his medical release in 2010, all of the letters were to and from Veterans Affairs Canada, including invitations from Veterans Affairs for career transition services.

Before long, my head was swimming with all of the acronyms and initialisms in the letters and all of the hoops he had to jump through. It would be too much for a sane person to deal with. I could only imagine how difficult it would be for someone who was struggling. McPhee had faced extreme danger almost every day in Afghanistan and had flourished. Yet he seemed to be completely undone by the bureaucracy.

The letters were organized by date and toward the end of the list, there was a document laying out a decision by the Veterans Review and Appeal Board affirming an earlier Entitlement Review decision which affirmed an earlier Departmental Review decision to deny McPhee a disability pension for mefloquine poisoning. The presiding member of the board was somebody called Gordon Musgrave.

Included was some correspondence between McPhee and Musgrave, the deputy chairperson of the VRAB. I scanned the letters. They began civilly enough with McPhee requesting a review of the country's policies on mefloquine and for the addition of mefloquine poisoning to the list of disabilities for which one could receive a disability pension.

Musgrave's response was that mefloquine was an effective drug that had been administered according to the Canadian guidelines and in accordance with the military services of allied countries, and when used as a prophylactic against malaria was safe and effective. The officialese was mind numbing. Not only that, but the letter was terse. It concluded by suggesting McPhee seek professional help from his health-care provider, and a list of several in McPhee's area was appended. I could imagine how that had landed with McPhee.

Then there was a string of letters, around one a month, with McPhee using increasingly strident and hostile language and accusing the government of poisoning him. He repeatedly asked, "How many other good soldiers will be poisoned by this government's reckless disregard of the facts?"

I had to sit back and close my eyes for a long time. The destruction of McPhee's life, whatever the cause, seemed complete. It was like he had undergone a metamorphosis. But unlike Kafka's cockroach, McPhee's transformation was gradual, from mild symptoms of emotional discord to a complete unraveling over the course of about eighteen months.

At about 3 p.m., I resumed my search for Gordon Musgrave. I found his profile on the VRAB website. It said he was a former member of the merchant marine who had done a lot to get a memorial built in New Brunswick for veterans. He lived in Montréal.

That was interesting. It wasn't such a common name in this city. I wondered if it would be possible to find him in the old directory, which was now online. When I entered Gordon Musgrave, I got two hits, both of them for G. Musgrave.

The first one I called and a woman answered in French. "Oui, allo?"

I told her I was looking for Gordon Musgrave. She simply hung up the phone. I dialed the next number. It rang twice before a woman answered. "Hello?"

"I'm looking for Gordon Musgrave."

"Can I ask who's calling, please?"

"My name is Denny Durant. I'm a reporter with the *Gazette*."

There was a pause before she said, "One moment."

It was several moments before a man came on the line. "This is Gordon Musgrave. How can I help you?"

I said again who I was and told him that I was working on a story about Major Michael McPhee. Would he be willing to answer some questions?

Another pause. "Obviously I'm familiar with that name because he's been in the news. But why do you want to speak to me about it?"

"You were a member of the VRAB panel for his review. That decision may be what tipped him over the edge, according to his wife."

"Are you trying to blame me for that man's actions? That's complete nonsense."

"No, I'm not trying to blame you. I'm just wondering if McPhee has tried to contact you."

"Not since he stopped sending those ridiculous letters a year or so ago."

"We're writing a feature story on McPhee and it's quite possible information from some of the letters may be included."

"Go ahead."

"Would you care to comment for the story?"

"Absolutely not."

I started to ask another question but he cut me off. "Look, I'm running late for an event." He ended the call.

I had just opened my browser to search for more information about Gordon Musgrave when my phone rang.

"Hello, Mr. Durant, my name is Emma McPhee. I'm Mike McPhee's wife. I understand you wish to speak with me."

"Thank you for calling. That's correct, I did, but Georgina told me you didn't want to speak with me."

"I've changed my mind."

"I'm glad to hear that."

"I want to speak with you in person. Would that suit you?"

"Of course. Shall I come to you?"

"No, I'll come to you. You're in Montréal, I understand."

"Yes, that's right."

"Good. My train arrives at eleven-fifteen. Can you meet me at the station?"

I said I'd wait beneath the arrivals board, holding a newspaper folded under my left arm. She said she'd looked me up online and knew what I looked like.

Chapter Forty-Four

I arrived at the central station at 11 a.m. and stood for a minute at the eastern end, admiring the blue and white bas relief sculpture that attempted to show the story of early Canada. The words of the national anthem in French ran along the bottom of the panels. Bold figures in white marble were shown engaging in various activities—exploring, playing the fiddle, building heavy infrastructure, dancing, dispensing money from a bank, ice skating, pouring concrete, driving logs down a river and so on. A woman with hair billowing behind her reminded me of the icon on the Pathfinder badge, and I was immediately reminded of why I was standing in the station in the first place.

I'd forgotten to bring my copy of the *Gazette* so at about ten minutes before the appointed hour, I walked to the depanneur to buy one, folded it beneath my left arm and took up my position beneath the departure and arrival board. About seven minutes later, a woman walked up. She was very beautiful, with long dark hair that curled down over a red wool jacket, clear brown eyes beneath a high brow, a small upturned nose and full lips. There was something at once angelic and regal about her. She looked like a princess without trying to look like one.

"Mr. Durant?"

"Mrs. McPhee?"

We shook hands. She looked serious in a way that I didn't think came naturally.

"Thanks for traveling all this way to speak with me."

"Thank you for your interest. I understand you and my husband are acquainted."

She had a faint British accent.

"Yes, we met in Afghanistan in 2006."

In the pause that followed, I suggested we move to the station restaurant where there were booths that would give us privacy.

I brought us two coffees and asked her if she would mind if I recorded the interview, for my own notes. She said that would be fine. I asked her how her family was coping.

She looked around and I wondered if she was concerned her husband would appear out of nowhere. "We're managing. It's been really hard, but like in all military families, there's a really strong network of people who want to help. And Conrad and Georgina have been great."

"I know this is a difficult subject for you. And I appreciate you taking the time to speak with me."

She sighed. I thought she might be on the point of crying but when she spoke, her voice was strong.

"It has been difficult, there's no getting around that. My husband needs help, and despite what he's done, I want him to get help. He's such a brilliant and extraordinary man. It's almost unbelievable what's happened."

"Have the police been in touch with you?"

"Yes, they have. They had me look through the video footage to identify Mike. They asked me questions about when he left for Montréal, what his state of mind had been, where he could be staying. It's all quite terrifying."

"We should get this out of the way. I think you know I am a journalist and that I'm writing a feature story about Mike that will delve into his career, his struggles since he's been back as well as what has happened here in Montréal. But the story needs to have your voice in it. Would you allow me to use it?"

She considered this a minute. "I knew you would ask, and on the way up here I decided that I would say no, but now having met you, and considering the importance of the story, I'll say yes."

I thanked her. "Why do you think Mike has done what he's done over the past week in Montréal? He's a suspect in two murders and is still at large."

"The only thing I can think is that he's on a rampage because he wasn't getting the help, or wasn't able to ask for the help, he needs. He saw so many dreadful things overseas. But he needs to turn himself in, before anyone else dies. There's been enough killing. He needs to turn himself in so that an end can be brought to all of it."

"What would you say to your husband if you could get a message to him?"

"For the sake of your family, for me and for your children, please end this now. Turn yourself in Mike. There is help available. It won't be easy but your family will stand behind you."

"I won't ask where you're staying, but do you feel safe?"

"I haven't felt safe for a long time," she said, and again I thought she might cry, but again she surprised me. Her voice was steady when she said, "We're staying with some friends who have been extremely kind."

"Mrs. McPhee, I knew your husband in Afghanistan. I didn't know him well, but he was very kind to me. He helped me get through a difficult time. When I saw him in Montréal a week ago, he was very different. What do you think happened to him?"

"The most difficult aspect of this whole nightmare is trying to explain to the children what happened to their father, why he's so different. The youngest one, Ben, who's only four, has few memories of when his father was well. But, the older one, Kyle, who's six, feels the most let down and frightened."

"How do you explain it to them?"

She considered this for a moment. "I tell them that Daddy had a very difficult job, that sometimes when people have difficult jobs, they become different people so they can do the job, and when the difficult job is over, they go back to being the same person they were before."

"That seems like a good explanation."

"The trouble is, I don't know if he will return to being the man he was. I don't want the kids to lose hope but I also don't want to give them false hope."

"What do you think happened to him?"

"I don't know. I think he finally saw too much, or experienced too much. Usually he talked to me about what he'd seen over there. But the last time, when he came back, he didn't talk about it. Something in him was destroyed."

I told her what Buzzy had said about the mefloquine.

"A lot of people took mefloquine over there. Very few came back deranged. I don't know if I buy it."

"But Mike thought that he'd been poisoned, somehow, correct?"

"Yes, he certainly talked about it a lot. He was having a terrible time. He really suffered. The dreams were especially bad."

"But he was no longer taking this drug, was he?"

"No, he stopped. You don't take it once you're out of theatre. Or not for very long after."

"And the dreams kept happening?"

"Yes. And I believe he was struggling with thoughts of suicide, though he didn't speak about that very much at all. Please don't print that. He was also drinking a lot, which was very out of character."

There was another pause while she collected herself.

"I watched him over the course of months turn into a man I didn't recognize."

"You said, 'Very few people came back deranged.' Do you think he's deranged?"

"Well look what happened over the past few days. Does that sound like a sane man to you?"

"No, it doesn't. And he didn't seem well when I saw him."

She spoke with a quiet dignity but I was beginning to get a sense of her anger. I wasn't sure who or what the target of that anger was.

"Something happened to him and I don't know what it was. It wasn't something he chose. This isn't the person he would have chosen to be. Something pushed him past the breaking point. I sometimes saw the immense struggle that was taking place within him. There were two people at war within the same man. It was the hero we all expected him to be and the broken little boy that he became.

And his sense of honour wouldn't let the hero disappoint anyone. But the broken little boy needed attention, needed to be cared for."

"Wasn't he able to get help?"

"He did try. The problem was the doctors who tried to help him weren't able to help him. They all said there was nothing really wrong with him. Nobody believed the story about the mefloquine. He'd done a ton of research on this. And he talked to other soldiers. And in time he may be vindicated. But none of the people in the military knew how to help him. He was prescribed medication, but he didn't want that. He kept saying, 'I've already been poisoned once, I don't want to be poisoned again.' But I remember him, near the end of his time with us, before things got so bad, he seemed to be happier for a few days. He kept saying, 'There's help underground.'"

"What did he mean by that?"

"I have no idea, and I still don't. But whatever it was, it seemed to lift his spirits briefly."

"When was that?"

"About three months ago."

"There's help underground."

"Yes."

"Did you tell this to the police?"

"I don't think so, because I really don't know what he meant. Honestly, I thought he'd finally gone over the edge." She sipped her coffee. "The military is a closed system. Many things that happen on missions are covered up and taken care of by the 'family,' so the light never gets in. There's a code. This is both a good thing and a bad thing. It has to be that way, because ordinary people wouldn't be able to deal with what these men and women have to deal with on a daily basis when they're deployed to places like Afghanistan and Iraq. Nobody really understands what they go through.

"Sometimes, the only thing that helps is exposing the problems to the light. But the commanders, they don't want that, because it might make them look bad. Almost every senior officer I've ever met was a psychopath. The military sees a bunch of soldiers or vets who are not coping well as nothing unusual. They'll just say, 'We're all soldiers, and this is the mission. Get on with it. Quit whining like a little bitch."

Her brown eyes bore into mine. "The mind is a delicate thing, Mr. Durant. It can only take so much. When does it reach the tipping point? There are many soldiers who went away to fight for their country and who came back and who are quietly losing their minds. They are not on the military's radar. The support just isn't there for them. It started happening to Michael."

"When did you first realize something wasn't right?"

"Almost immediately after the last tour. He'd done two tours in Afghanistan and he was fine, he was his old self, cheerful, upbeat, full of fun, full of plans, always looking forward. But the last time, in 2008, he was not like that. He just wanted to drink. He was in a lot of pain. I think maybe he made a mistake when he was there, and couldn't deal with it. Maybe some of his friends were killed. Or he saw something that didn't mesh with what he understood was supposed to be happening. The difficult thing, the most difficult thing, was that he couldn't talk to me, his wife, about what was troubling him."

"How was he behaving?"

"He would have these terrible nightmares. He would wake up screaming and sweating, disoriented, crying sometimes like a baby. You know my husband. He's not someone who cries like a baby.

"The dreams in particular were hard on him. This is someone who has been through hell on earth, who has seen people killed in all manner of ways, who has done his share of killing. But the thing he couldn't bear was the thing that was inside of him, that darkness.

"I come from a military family, Mr. Durant, and so I'm aware of what happens and I don't shy away from it. Killing is the heart of warfare. It's what we train those men, mostly men, some women, to do. My husband was a good soldier, a good officer who answered the call and did his duty and he came back and nobody was able to help him when he needed help. The dreams got so bad, that he would try not to sleep." She shook her head. "You can imagine how well that worked out."

I didn't say anything. I've been in the business long enough to know when not to interrupt.

"And then he would try to drink himself to sleep so that the dreams would be less severe. My husband wasn't a drinking man, at least not like that, but it was the only thing that got him through some of those nights. But, naturally, the drinking made him moody, so it was like being around a bear. He would either try not to sleep or drink himself to sleep and it wasn't long before we couldn't sleep in the same bed."

Her voice had taken on a monotonous quality, as if she were dictating rather than conversing with me.

"We have an old shed on our property that Michael had converted into a studio for me to do my painting. There's a bed in there and a sink and toilet, and he ended up spending most of his time there. His own private hell hole.

"The kids would want to go back there to see him but I wouldn't let them, because I never knew what condition he would be in, or to be honest whether he'd even be alive." Her voice was beginning to crack now, and she paused to collect herself.

"I was beside myself, as you can imagine. And it soon became impossible to communicate with him, he was in such a black box of despair. There were times when I was afraid for myself and the children. He started to become violent. He would come into the house, obviously drunk, start shouting, start rummaging for food or drink. He was like an angry bear, a deranged, angry bear. Sleeping in the studio only increased his sense of isolation."

"Did he try to get help?"

"Oh yes, he did, he tried everything at first. He knew he would lose his family if he didn't. The doctors told him it was PTSD. He started cognitive behavioral therapy but that didn't seem to help. They put him on a drug called Sertraline but that seemed to make things worse. He started seeing another doctor who told him he didn't fit the protocol for PTSD and that he was probably depressed and gave him Prozac. That did nothing except turn him into a zombie and he stopped taking it."

"What a nightmare."

"It was. And it's just getting worse, from the sounds of things. There were a few times while he was on his medication and still drinking heavily that he became so intoxicated that I had to call the police. I had to protect the children, but I was also concerned for him. He was traumatized by the dreams, and then his mood was worsened by the drink, and he was getting depressed because he couldn't stop the dreams—he felt impotent—and he saw that his depression was alienating him from the kids and me."

"It was like that for several months, and then he left. He drove away one morning, he just took off in his car. I saw him driving away. I had no idea where he was going or when he'd be back."

"Around when was that?"

"It was shortly after the decision."

"The decision?"

"Yes, the decision from the Veteran's Review and Appeal Board."

I didn't want to tell Emma yet about McPhee's memory stick or the documents he'd given me. McPhee hadn't given me permission to share that fact with his wife. He'd given me implicit permission to use the material in a story, but even now, with my deadline breathing down my neck, I still hoped that I'd be able to interview him to clarify just what story he wanted me to tell with them. I also had some questions about the treatment he'd received from his military doctors. So I said to Emma, "He did mention something about veterans affairs to me."

"They decide cases of compensation. Mike had applied because he was sure that mefloquine had disabled him to the point he wasn't able to command any longer. They denied his application. The ruling was very narrow, and Mike wasn't able to get any explanations. I believe that was the last straw for him. Frankly, his leaving was a relief for the children and me.

"You know, he had guns on the property. He likely still has guns with him. You'll understand, Mr. Durant, it's not my husband I'm saying this about, it's the man that my husband became, a man his family and friends don't recognize."

"What happened when you called the police?"

"Oh, they always came. They were quite good about it. They got to know him, and he got to know them. He was always fine with them, never violent. They knew how to approach him. They would talk about how things were in Afghanistan, ask him if he'd heard the latest from Kandahar or Kabul or whatever. They would appeal to that hero part of him, the one who wanted to protect, not the one who needed protecting. It would kind of snap him out of it. It was like the functioning part of his mind was still in Afghanistan and any mention of it would reanimate it. The functional part would take over from the dysfunctional part."

The interview was coming to a natural end. We'd been talking for forty minutes.

"Does any of this help, Mr. Durant?"

"Yes it does. It all helps paint a picture for me, Mrs. McPhee. But do you know exactly why he came to Montréal?"

"I really don't, but the way he prepared for it, it was like he was getting ready to go back to war. That's what it reminded me of. He was like he used to be when he was getting ready to go back to Afghanistan: strongly focused. He stopped drinking until right before he left. He cashed in some of our savings and bought himself the car.

"He spent a long time packing things into it. I don't know what he was packing or what he planned to do while he was in Montréal, but he did say that's where he was going. I told Georgina and asked her to tell Conrad, but Mike left before Conrad could visit him. One of the things Mike said he wanted to do was to visit you."

"He wanted to visit me?"

"Yes, he was aware of the work you were doing. He kept talking about going to see you, telling you his story so that you could 'blow the doors off this thing.'"

"Blow the doors off what thing?"

"I presume he meant the drug, the mefloquine. He'd seen some articles you'd written about that other drug, was it fentanyl?"

"That's right."

"I remember the day he saw it in the paper here. I think it was from one of the syndicated services. He got rather excited. He told me he knew you from Afghanistan, that you were a good guy. He said he was going to go see you. That you would know how to get the eyes of the world on this thing. He said you were already writing about poison and so here was one more poison you could write about."

I asked when he left for Montréal. She said it was about a week before Christmas, but that he had made other trips to Montréal before that.

"Do you know if he had somewhere to stay when he was in Montréal?"

"I don't know. He only said he need to talk to you."

There was a pause. "There was one other thing."

"What's that?"

"On his last tour, a friend of his was killed, and I believe Mike held himself responsible."

"Do you know who that was?"

"His name was Eric."

"Do you have a last name?"

"No, I'm sorry."

Chapter Forty-Five

By the time I got back to the apartment, there were only a few hours left before the deadline to file. But I couldn't get down to work immediately. My mind was teeming after my conversation with Emma. I had to let all of the questions float to the surface, like air bubbles released from muck.

One of the things that had struck me so forcefully from what Emma said was that McPhee was still acting rationally on some level. He had prepared to come to Montréal as if he was preparing to go on a mission, packing the car supplies, probably guns, maps and other requirements.

Maps. I remembered the maps in Buzzy's spare room opposite his office in the garage. Was McPhee using the spare room as a crash pad? Were the maps of Montréal's Underground City and the old port his, or did they belong to someone else? If they were his, why would he need them? I went through the photos I'd taken of the maps. The letters I couldn't quite make out, it was possible some of them were numbers. They might have indicated 1900R, but I didn't know what that meant. There was something else that looked like WED3.

I remembered what Emma had said, that McPhee had told his kids there was help underground. What did he mean? Had he chosen to hide out there? Had he found somewhere dark and safe? Had he somehow chipped away at the ice in his mind, cleared a path to the surface. Or was it just something he said to amuse the children?

I wanted McPhee to stay unharmed and I wanted him to be restored to his earlier version, but I knew that was unlikely. You can restore things like furniture, but a psyche is another matter, especially one that's been traumatized in the way

McPhee's had. I went over to the window and looked out onto the dark street. The evening traffic moving slowly along, still at only half volume. He was still out there somewhere. So was Felix. So was Vanessa. We were all strutting our hour upon the snow covered stage. I checked my watch. It was time to get to work. I would have to work through the night to finish the story. I put on a pot of coffee and got started.

****

My goal was to use McPhee as a kind of poster boy for the problems the military was having—he would be the face of Canada's new, struggling military. This would give me a chance to highlight the controversy around the neuropsychiatric side effects of mefloquine.

The hook would be that McPhee was still at large a week after he was thought to have committed the first murder. I could report what I knew about the murders and the most up to date information about the victims and the police investigation. It was going to be a long night.

But as they say, the journey of 10,000 miles—or in this case, 10,000 words—begins with a single step. My first step was to make an inventory of everything I had. That turned into a bullet point list of the most important items from the inventory, and after an hour or so, the list began to look like an outline.

At some point, a structure suggested itself, and I began weaving together my material: interviews with military analysts at the college in Kingston, the conversations with Emma McPhee and Buzzy—used with their permission—the journal entries from McPhee himself, the correspondence with Veterans Affairs and the mefloquine experts.

I avoided mentioning McPhee's family or getting too specific about his battles with inner demons. I would be specific about his accomplishments before he became ill. I described the role of Pathfinders, how difficult it was to pass the course and the specific skills that Pathfinders brought to the table.

I made sure to add that the Department of National Defence and the company that manufactured the drug, Hoffman-La Roche, so far hadn't responded to my requests for a comment.

After a few hours, I was hungry, but the fridge was empty. I contemplated ordering in pizza but that was a luxury I couldn't afford. I decided I wasn't hungry, I was just tired and looking for distraction. As a compromise, I made some toast and peanut butter, sat back down at the laptop and wrote six paragraphs about my own recollections of McPhee from my time with him in Afghanistan.

After that, I cobbled together four paragraphs of detailed information about mefloquine, adding that the Canadian military in recent public testimony to Parliament had said that mefloquine was completely safe, appropriate for use in combat deployments to areas where malaria was prevalent.

At around 5:30 a.m., with the story topping 4,000 words, I stopped, figuring it was already much longer than Lydia would want. While my printer whirred, I made another round of coffee, toast and peanut butter. I took the printout to the couch and sitting in an exhausted heap, inspecting the paragraphs carefully, through bleary eyes, for typos and grammatical errors, and triple checking all the facts and citations that could get me into trouble. I made a few minor corrections and sent the file to Lydia with about a minute to spare.

Chapter Forty-Six

My phone rang at 10 a.m. It was Edward Kirk, the *Gazette* features editor. He and Lydia had gone through the story and loved it. He had some questions on sourcing, which I answered.

Sourcing was a key issue in any reputable news organization. At least one senior editor had to know the identity of an unnamed source. If the source wasn't credible enough, the reporter would need to double source the information.

I told Edward I'd interviewed McPhee's ex-wife and his best friend and that both of them had agreed to let me use their material on background. I also said I had a third source who confirms the information. The third source was McPhee himself, but Edward didn't need to know that. I would save that for when I spoke with Lydia and the lawyers.

Dealing with an editor was like dealing with my mechanic. It was likely going to be painful, but my car would run better and I'd be safer on the road.

"When's the story going to print?"

"We want to get it out in the Saturday edition. Should be online on the same day."

It was Wednesday, so that gave them a little more than two days to get it ready for publication. I felt enormous relief that the article was done and delivered, even though I knew there would still be work to do after Edward and Lydia went through it. I would need to keep checking with DND, Veteran's Affairs and the drug company to get comment. And I was still hoping against the odds to speak with McPhee before the story ran. In my heart, I was satisfied that McPhee wanted me to publish the story. I had it in black and white. But my gut told me he hadn't left the country and to keep trying to find him. If I couldn't speak with him before it was time to publish, I would have to check with the lawyers to see if they thought I had sufficient permission to publish.

In retrospect, I should have been more concerned about McPhee's intentions. For some reason, I believed this man who had murdered at least two people in cold blood in Montréal, and was hunting for at least one more, would somehow set aside his homicidal rage and speak to me calmly and rationally for a newspaper story.

Why did I believe McPhee was still in Montréal? Because the mission wasn't complete. If nothing else, Pathfinders are patient. They wait for exactly the right conditions and have the discipline not to force matters. They always think things through first. They know how dangerous it can be to make a decision while in a mental fog. McPhee was in no hurry. He would hide for as long as he wanted.

I understood why the police wanted people to think that McPhee had left town, why he wanted that word on the street. Despite what he said about not caring about Felix, he probably wanted to know where he was, to keep tabs on him, if nothing else, but more likely to see if he had picked up where Pierre Blanchette had left off with dealing drugs. Maybe Felix had access to Blanchette's supply. It was all speculation on my part.

At around one in the afternoon, after a long hot shower, I walked down to the depanneur to buy some groceries and the papers. Back in my apartment, I made a sandwich and went through the news. Camille's latest story was a more detailed account of the police's theory that McPhee had left the country. There was an interview with a flight attendant in London who said she served him gin and tonic on the airplane, and the account of a military analyst who outlined how McPhee could have obtained forged documents.

I didn't feel like getting back to work—I felt like I needed a good, long vacation—but I had bills to pay, so I opened up my stories spreadsheet, picked the next one that needed to be delivered and got to work on that.

But I found it impossible to settle. After about twenty minutes, I gave into my restlessness, getting up to feed the cat and make more coffee. While I waited for the coffee to percolate, I paced.

My mind flitted back to Vanessa. I wondered where she had gone after the restaurant. Did she go to her mom's place to have the conversation about Eric? Did she go back to her friend's place? Did she go back to work at Mindy's? Did Felix find her?

I remembered I needed to send pictures to Lydia for the story, so I opened the third folder on McPhee's thumb drive, where he'd saved all his photos, and flicked through the thumbnails, looking for a good one.

I remembered the picture of the three soldiers, the one from 2006, the one labelled "M McPhee, C Buzaki, E Gillespie." I wondered if E Gillespie was Eric. When I enlarged it, I thought I could see a resemblance to Vanessa, but it was difficult to say. I decided to send the picture to Shawna in case she ran into Vanessa again. She could show it to her.

I sent some pics of McPhee to Lydia and Edward Kirk for the story.

It was getting close to three in the afternoon when a wave of fatigue overtook me and I closed my eyes. Images of Afghanistan flooded my mind, and were followed by images of Blanchette lying in a puddle of blood, the woman on fire at the Atrium, Anderson and Brandt laughing.

When I woke up an hour later, I had an idea. My subconscious mind must have connected some dots while I slept. I checked my watch. There might still be time to stop what I thought was about to happen.

I opened the browser and looked up the number for Gordon Musgrave again and dialed. The same woman answered. "Hello, this is Denny Durant. We spoke the other day. I'm a reporter for the *Gazette*, but please don't hang up. I called to talk to Gordon Musgrave, is he there?"

"I'm afraid he's not at the moment. What is this about?"

I took a flying leap. "Is this Mrs. Musgrave?"

"Yes, this is she. My husband told me you had called. What can I do for you?"

"I don't know if your husband has mentioned it to you, but he was part of the tribunal that denied a disability pension to Major Mike McPhee. Are you aware of this?"

"He did mention it to me, yes, but he said it was nothing to worry about. I'm not sure I believe him, to be honest. My husband can be obstinate, at times."

"I'm concerned your husband might be in danger."

When she spoke again, her voice trembled, "What do you mean?"

"I hope I'm wrong, but I think it's possible that McPhee is planning to harm your husband."

"Why would he do that?"

"It's a long story, but I've learned that he believes he was unfairly treated by your husband and by Veteran Affairs. I'm afraid he's not in his right mind."

"Well, surely the police can handle this. Should I call them?"

"It's not a bad idea, but tell me this. Do you live in a building that's connected to the Underground City?"

"Well, yes, as a matter of fact we do. We live at Victoria sur Park."

"I was afraid of that. Where is your husband now?"

"He's meeting some old friends. They get together every Wednesday at the Legion in NDG."

"Do you know how long he'll be out for?"

"Well, it's darts night. They have a league every Wednesday. They usually meet for a drink and dinner. He usually comes back around ten."

"Are you able to reach him now?"

"I could try, but he's terrible with his phone. He sometimes doesn't even take it. Let me check to see if he's got it." There was a sound of the phone being set down on a table, the sound of receding footsteps. A few seconds later, the footsteps grew louder and she picked up the phone. "Well, no, he's left his cell phone here. He's terrible. He never takes it with him."

"It's okay. I'm sure everything will be fine, but it might be a good idea to call the police. And if there's any way you can get word to your husband—"

But she'd already hung up. I was searching for the address of the Legion in NDG when my phone buzzed with an incoming call. The number was hidden. Some small part of me hoped it was McPhee. "Hello?"

A woman's voice I didn't immediately recognize said, "Denny?"

"Yes." I could hear my own impatience.

"It's Vanessa. From the other night."

"Oh, hi, yes, how are you doing?"

"Not so good. You remember you offered me a place to stay if I needed it?"

"Yes, of course I remember."

"I'm calling to take you up in the offer. I'm pretty desperate."

I was sure from her voice she was telling the truth. "Yes, of course you can stay here. When were you thinking of coming? I was just—"

"Right now. I'm out front."

I walked to the window and looked down. There she was on the sidewalk, carrying a backpack and holding a phone to her ear.

"Oh, okay. Come on up, I'll buzz you in. It's apartment 411."

"Really appreciate it." Her line went dead.

Chapter Forty-Seven

I was having trouble thinking straight. I was exhausted and possibly still in shock. My instinct was screaming to get to the NDG Legion to warn Musgrave. I was sure he was in danger.

But I had to wait until Vanessa was at least in the apartment. I needed to give her the spare house key.

The obnoxious buzzer sounded and I pressed the button to unlock the door downstairs. While I waited for Vanessa to come up in the elevator, I searched for the address of the NDG Legion. It was on Boulevard de Maisonneuve. The building looked familiar, I'd passed it many times without realizing it was a Legion. I thought about calling Anderson to see if Mrs. Musgrave had been in touch, but the thought was interrupted by a knock on the door.

I opened the door. Vanessa stood there, looking sheepish. I led her into my apartment. She seemed exhausted, stressed and nervous. Of course she was nervous. She barely knew me. Her situation must be bad, I thought, if I was the only one she could trust.

"Well, here it is. Please make yourself at home."

It was awkward all around but I was glad that she was there. I understood I was taking a risk. I didn't have much of value in the apartment, but a few of my items were worth something. I was handing over my apartment to a woman who traded sex for money and as far as I knew had a pretty serious cocaine addiction. But I had decided to trust her. It was drastic, but somebody had to do it.

She left her backpack in the middle of the floor—she didn't seem to mind—and started looking around the place, checking her phone every now and then. I asked if she wanted anything, and she said she could do with a glass of water. When I gave it to her, she sat at the table. Elliott came out to see who this newcomer was and jumped into her lap. She began to stroke him.

She saw the photograph I'd printed out sitting on the table and asked who the three men were. I pointed each of them out. "That's Mike McPhee. You'll recognize him. The guy next to him is called Buzzy, and the guy next to Buzzy is Eric. That's the guy McPhee says was your brother.

"I was looking at that photograph earlier today, and I can see a resemblance between you and Eric."

I stood back a moment while she gazed at the photograph. Elliott was rubbing himself against her wrist, seeking more attention, but she was staring raptly at the photograph. I would have stayed to chat with her about it, but I had to get moving. I could be wrong about McPhee and Musgrave but the hunch was strong.

I went into the bedroom to get a hoodie and when I came out, Felix was standing in my living room.

Vanessa was standing by the front door. It was obvious she had let Felix in. She wouldn't look at me. Felix was standing there grinning. He had a knife in one hand.

"Did I mention that Felix is Latin for lucky?" he said. "You should remember that." He paced around the apartment with an air of danger. He picked up my cell phone from the table and wiggled it in front of me. "Thinking about calling 911?" He slipped the phone into his jacket pocket.

He walked over to Vanessa and stood behind her, stroking her hair. You know, it's amazing what these bitches will do for a little white powder."

Elliott had instinctively jumped down and taken refuge under my bed. Felix kept up his pacing, coming nearer and nearer. I should have reacted more quickly when he stepped towards me, but I didn't, and he was fast. He slugged me hard on the side of the face and I went down. I almost blacked out. He was standing over me, glowering. He began ranting like a maniac, spittle was flying out of his mouth and his face was contorted with rage. "You killed my brother. You set it up. You killed Pierre. I saw you there at the club that night. There's nobody called McPhee. That's bullshit."

I was lying on the floor, covering my face, watching the knife. It had started out in his left hand but mid-rant, he switched it to his right, as if he was getting ready to use it. He tightened his grip on it but then his facial expression completely changed. His eyes stopped boring into mine, and he looked up, perhaps out the window toward the light, and the knife fell from his grasp. Then he fell straight forward, right on top of me. I scrambled out from beneath him, and looking down, saw the handle of one of my own knives protruding from his back. Vanessa stood there, still holding the photograph of the three soldiers in her left hand. There was a look on her face I couldn't qualify. Blood was trickling out of the wound in Felix's back onto my carpet.

She was out the door and gone. I heard a doorway open and footsteps receding down the stairwell. She'd forgotten to take her backpack.

I checked Felix's pulse. If he had one, I couldn't detect it. I was shaking, but I felt calm. I retrieved my phone from his pocket. I could already feel my eye swelling up from where he slugged me. I got some ice from the freezer, put it into a dish towel and held it over my eye. I coaxed Elliott out from beneath the bed, and with my free hand carried him down the hall to Mrs. Notley's. A look of alarm passed across her face when she opened the door, but I held Elliot out to her. "Would you mind, Mrs. Notley? There's something I need to deal with."

"Of course, of course."

Back in my apartment, I grabbed the key for the Toyota. The puddle of blood below Felix grew a little while I was away. I left the apartment door unlocked, and as I pulled away from the curb, I dialed 911.

Chapter Forty-Eight

Vanessa was standing by the front door. It was obvious she had let Felix in. She wouldn't look at me. Felix was standing there grinning. He had a knife in one hand.

"Did I mention that Felix is Latin for lucky?" he said. "You should remember that." He paced around the apartment with an air of danger. He picked up my cell phone from the table and wiggled it in front of me. "Thinking about calling 911?" He slipped the phone into his jacket pocket.

He walked over to Vanessa and stood behind her, stroking her hair. You know, it's amazing what these bitches will do for a little white powder."

Elliott had instinctively jumped down and taken refuge under my bed. Felix kept up his pacing, coming nearer and nearer. I should have reacted more quickly when he stepped towards me, but I didn't, and he was fast. He slugged me hard on the side of the face and I went down. I almost blacked out. He was standing over me, glowering. He began ranting like a maniac, spittle was flying out of his mouth and his face was contorted with rage. "You killed my brother. You set it up. You killed Pierre. I saw you there at the club that night. There's nobody called McPhee. That's bullshit."

I was lying on the floor, covering my face, watching the knife. It had started out in his left hand but mid-rant, he switched it to his right, as if he was getting ready to use it. He tightened his grip on it but then his facial expression completely changed. His eyes stopped boring into mine, and he looked up, perhaps out the window toward the light, and the knife fell from his grasp. Then he fell straight forward, right on top of me. I scrambled out from beneath him, and looking down, saw the handle of one of my own knives protruding from his back. Vanessa stood there, still holding the photograph of the three soldiers in her left hand. There was a look on her face I couldn't qualify. Blood was trickling out of the wound in Felix's back onto my carpet.

She was out the door and gone. I heard a doorway open and footsteps receding down the stairwell. She'd forgotten to take her backpack.

I checked Felix's pulse. If he had one, I couldn't detect it. I was shaking, but I felt calm. I retrieved my phone from his pocket. I could already feel my eye swelling up from where he slugged me. I got some ice from the freezer, put it into a dish towel and held it over my eye. I coaxed Elliott out from beneath the bed, and with my free hand carried him down the hall to Mrs. Notley's. A look of alarm passed across her face when she opened the door, but I held Elliot out to her. "Would you mind, Mrs. Notley? There's something I need to deal with."

"Of course, of course."

Back in my apartment, I grabbed the key for the Toyota. The puddle of blood below Felix grew a little while I was away. I left the apartment door unlocked, and as I pulled away from the curb, I dialed 911.

Chapter Forty-Nine

I parked at the Legion and went inside. It was crowded and festive, with groups of older men and women gathered around half a dozen dart boards, and several more scattered about tables and at the bar.

It took me a few minutes of asking around but a man wearing a blue baseball cap with HMCS Athabasca stenciled on the front told me that Musgrave had been called away. "Something important. It was his wife. She called the bar. Told him to come home immediately. That's never happened in thirty years."

"Did he take his car?"

"No, the metro. It's faster."

"When did he leave?"

"Maybe fifteen minutes ago."

I reasoned I still had time. I jumped into the Toyota and headed for Place Victoria. There was underground parking there. On the way I tried Mrs. Musgrave again but there was no answer. I called Anderson. It went to voicemail. "Anderson, there's a guy called Gordon Musgrave. He's with the VRAB, which is a tribunal, part of Veterans Affairs, they adjudicate claims. Musgrave denied McPhee's claim for disability for mefloquine poisoning. I think McPhee is planning to kill him or to harm him. He lives with his wife at the condo tower, Victoria sur le Parc. His wife may already have called you. Please call me back."

I was sure I sounded panicked. But he would be used to dealing with panicked people. I parked at Place Victoria and made my way down to the metro station.

It was now 8 p.m.

I walked briskly down the tunnel into the Underground City network of hotels, shopping centers, office towers—the largest subterranean pedestrian network in the world. On the lower level where we were, even at this hour of the evening, midweek in early January, it was crowded with young people, families.

A massive Christmas tree, beautifully decorated, was still up, a huge fountain shot jets of multicolored water dozens of feet into the air, almost reaching the flock of stainless steel geese suspended from the ceiling.

I followed the network of tunnels to the spacious lobby beneath Victoria sur le Park. A few pedestrians came and went, none of them looked like Musgrave, or McPhee. I felt a mixture of relief and disappointment as I considered that my hunch could be wrong.

I was hungry, but I didn't want to leave to get food. I checked my phone to make sure it was charged and saw the battery had less than 15 percent power. But I couldn't go back to the car for the charger, so it would have to do. I found a bench in the corner and settled in to wait.

I thought about Felix, lying in a pool of blood on my carpet. Had emergency services already been to my apartment? I thought about Vanessa, now on the run. I should tell Shawna what happened. I made a mental note to send her a text.

A news alert pinged. I clicked on the story. My mouth immediately went dry.

It was a Le Journal piece. The headline said: Gazette reporter and Suspected Christmas Day Killer were 'close friends' in Afghanistan.

By Robert Provost

Denny Durant, a freelance journalist now working for the *Montréal Gazette* as a special correspondent, and Mike McPhee, a recently retired major in the Canadian military and suspected Christmas Day Killer, were close friends in Kandahar, Afghanistan, *Le Journal* has learned.

Durant, who has published several stories about McPhee in the Gazette, covered the war in Afghanistan for a national newswire. McPhee did four tours in Afghanistan and was a highly decorated officer. While it's unclear if McPhee and Durant maintained their friendship after returning to Canada, sources tell *Le Journal* that the two were in contact just hours before the murder took place at the Lorelei Hotel, and further, that police may have found evidence pointing to involvement by Durant.

I looked up from the phone. My mouth was hanging open. What Anderson had said in the Suburban began to make sense. He spoke to a lot of reporters. He'd obviously been speaking with Provost. He must have leaked him the story. But what purpose would that serve?

I didn't have time to think about it. There was Musgrave, walking down the hallway toward me. I recognized the shape of his nose and forehead from the photo in the Veterans Affairs website. He was walking quickly, like he had somewhere to be.

I stood up and began walking to intercept him. I stopped to let a security guard pass. I wasn't more than 10 feet away from Musgrave when a felt a powerful arm go around my neck and I was wrenched backward. The grip tightened, and something pushed the back of my head forward at the same time as the front arm cut off the circulation to my brain. Within five seconds, I'd blacked out.

Chapter Fifty

When I came to, I saw the security guard wearing a blue and white jacket and a blue baseball cap. A ring of keys dangled from his belt, a badge hung around his neck on a red lanyard, and a radio handset was clipped to the front of his jacket. It was McPhee.

He had somehow incapacitated Musgrave and was lowering him like a baby into a large, rectangular road case, the kind rock bands use to move speakers around in. I tried to get to my feet. McPhee looked up from what he was doing and when he saw that I was conscious, he set the limp Musgrave down, took a few strides toward me and kicked me hard in the solar plexus. The pain was incomprehensible. I crumpled like an empty chip bag to the floor. As I gasped for breathe, he grabbed a handful of my hair, lowered his face to within a few inches of mine, looked straight into my eyes and said, "Stay down. Denny. Stay there, old buddy. Don't get up. Because the next one won't be so friendly."

He released my hair and walked away. I vomited. I heard a cart being wheeled away and all was quiet. I concentrated on breathing. I was sure my spleen was busted. I imagined puddles of blood and fluid splashing around inside me, organs pulverized.

I lay still, just like he said. The conversation in the Suburban with Anderson came back to me. About all the calls they were receiving from the public. They included McPhee sleeping in the underground city. I imagined him disguised, huddled in a corner, keeping tabs on Musgrave. Watching him come and go, figuring out his routines, planning the job. Planning the backup plan, and the backup for the backup. How many weeks had he done that, waiting patiently, watching? It's what Pathfinders do.

My breath came back in tiny gulps at first, a teaspoon, then a tablespoon, then a quarter cup. Soon I could breathe at about half capacity. After about 10 minutes I could stand. The first time I stood up, I vomited again. I knelt for a minute or so, then tried again.

I wondered why nobody had used the elevator or come through the lobby in the twenty or thirty minutes I'd been there. Then I realized. McPhee had disabled the elevator and locked the door that led into the lobby. I pushed against it and it opened out. I staggered on shaky pins into the hall. I had recovered sufficiently to break into a light shuffle, and I crossed the Esplanade du Palais, past the entrance to the Place d'Armes metro station and fast-limped into the Palais de Congress. I thought it would be closed, but it was not.

I didn't know for sure which way he'd gone, but I had another strong hunch. It would explain why he needed the map of the Old Port.

I trotted past the strange pink trees of the Lipstick Forest and through a curved hallway with brickwork that under different circumstances, I might have admired for its artistry. My footfalls made crazy music as I ran, faster now, almost normally, into the soaring glass atrium of the Intercontinental Hotel. I jogged across the lobby and then finally outside into the Montréal night, the Bourse Tower rising in front of me. I sucked in the cold winter air, willing it to douse the burning sensation in my lungs.

I looked down rue Saint-Pierre toward the river. On my left, a grey sedan rode up out of the underground parking, followed by a blue SUV, then a white panel van. The first two vehicles made right hand turns and passed in front of me. The van turned left toward the river. I couldn't see inside, but I knew it was McPhee. I thought of Gordon Musgrave inside the box, struggling for breath. As the van disappeared down Saint-Pierre, I imagined the fate that awaited him at the hands of McPhee.

My first instinct was to run after the van, but I knew I'd never make it. I looked around, hoping to see Anderson, but he was nowhere. Too busy leaking stories to the press.

I started to run again but my lungs just weren't up to it. I had to catch up to him somehow.

At the side of the street, a taxi pulled over to pick up an elderly couple who were standing under a hotel awning. The driver popped the trunk and stepped out of the cab to help the couple with their bags. I cut behind him, slid into the driver's seat and threw the transmission into drive. The driver screamed "Hey!" and grabbed me by the shoulder before I could get the door closed. "Sorry, Fifth Estate!" I stepped on the gas and tore away, closing the door a little ways down the road.

In the side mirror, I saw the driver running after me, then stumbling and finally falling onto the icy pavement. The lid of the trunk flapped up and down, obscuring the rear view, as I bounced over the cobblestones.

I bumped along Saint-Pierre across rue Saint Paul, then Place de Youville. I made a wrong turn on William, left instead of right, and had to circle all the way back, losing valuable time.

Emerging onto rue de la Commune, the long street that parallels the river and the promenade, I caught sight of the panel van parked discreetly on a narrow causeway that ran to Silo 5, the abandoned grain elevator that sat between the Lachine Canal and the St. Lawrence River.

Away from the streetlights, it was almost impossible to see. I rifled through the glove box for a flashlight but there was nothing. Beneath the passenger seat I found an emergency kit that contained a small but powerful penlight. It would have to do.

I left the taxi parked and running at the side of de la Commune and continued on foot. Snow had accumulated in small drifts and kept falling heavily though the wind had died down. I thought I knew what his plan was and I had to reach him before he got into the building.

I made my way to Silo 5 over the low fence to a walkway along the canal. I jumped down onto a connecting quay and then took a bridge that led over another canal to Silo 5. The massive concrete and steel structure had been left to rot in the middle of the Old Port of Montréal, a decaying emblem of a bygone era.

There were signs along a metal fence warning away trespassers, however there was an entire section of the fence cut clean away. I walked along the train tracks to the side of the building where there was a broken window that looked at one time like it would have been boarded up, but the boards had been removed.

I waited a few seconds, then climbed through the window and when my feet touched the floor, stood there a second just gaping. From what I could see, the building was bigger than any cathedral I'd ever been in, and cluttered with steel girders and concrete columns, massive funnels, ducts, and conveyor belts thick with dust. It felt unreal, like a movie set depicting another age, an industrial age.

It was also quiet like a cathedral, one whose worshipers were extinct. Some light from outside made its way in, so that once my eyes adjusted, I could discern the outlines of forms—steel columns, pipes, ladders, enormous bins, all of which once would have conveyed vast amounts of resources from the offloading point to the waiting ships which would then take it down the St. Lawrence to the world beyond.

I took a moment to settle myself, to take my bearings and to wait. I wasn't sure what traps or alarms McPhee had rigged up to detect any intruders. So far, there was no indication he'd seen me.

I still had faith that I could talk to him, that I could bring him around to my view that he still had lots to live for his family, his country, his future. In retrospect, I know now that I was under an illusion.

In the stillness, I could hear faint sounds coming from the far end of the space. I switched on my penlight and moved out across the floor, crossing beneath the massive bins that would at one time have held ton upon ton of grain.

I walked unsteadily, following the sound until it grew gradually distinguishable. It was McPhee's voice. Ranting. I crept forward until I could hear clearly what he was saying.

"It's up to you, Musgrave. You need to fix this. It's not up to me. It's up to you.

"You know what this drug does to people. You know the damage it causes. You've seen proof of it. I am proof of it. I am living, walking, talking, proof of what this drug does to people.

"I was your best soldier. I was exemplary, not just in some things, but in all things. I was as close to the perfect soldier as it's possible to get, and this drug has ruined me. You have ruined me. You need to take responsibility."

He turned and said in a calm voice, like we were meeting in a pub on a Sunday, "Hello, Denny."

Musgrave was taped to a chair. Two floor lamps cast an amber glow over the bizarre scene. I video camera rigged to a tripod eyed Musgrave from a few feet directly in front of him.

Musgrave looked like a stuffed man, like a man whose limbic system was frozen in one expression of existential disbelief.

I said, "Mike, what are you doing?"

McPhee stretched a hand to indicate the man in the seat. "Mr. Musgrave here was just giving his video testimony about the horrors of mefloquine, because up until now, he didn't realize how dangerous a drug it was and what it does to people. But I think now he's getting it."

"Is this really the best way to do things?"

"There is no other way, Denny, there is no other way. I've seen better men die for more feeble reasons than this. I led men into battle against an enemy that was much less deserving of death. But a government that fails to take responsibility for the damage it has done to those who have served it most loyally and faithfully, and at immense personal cost, doesn't deserve that loyalty."

"Mike, you can't force and kill your way to loyalty."

"That's true, but what I can do is bring Mr. Musgrave here to the point where he understands that it starts with individuals. One by one, people must atone for the mistakes of their government.

"Mr. Musgrave is also a servant. He's a public servant who served his government faithfully, just like you did."

"He served behind a desk, then he went home every night. I served in the Valley of Death. I led men through fields of marijuana and grass so tall you couldn't see over it. I led them straight into a kill box. They followed me because they trusted me. Before mefloquine, I would have calculated the risks accurately, known when to follow orthodoxy and when not. I would have seen the signs that the enemy was still there, waiting for us. They hadn't pulled back. They were still there in Zhari, waiting for us.

"But here's the thing. One of my commanders said he saw a kite flying across the river. Over the radio we heard talk about mirrors flashing. This is how the Taliban sends signals. I should have made the call to pull back and reassess. But that day, I got it wrong and it's not a mistake I ever would have made before mefloquine. Because of that, men died. I didn't die. I should have died."

He was interrupted by a voice, weak at first, but strong enough so that we both turned. It was Musgrave croaking out something. McPhee stepped closer to hear. "Excuse me?" he said.

It was Musgrave. "I served. Merchant Marine." He said the year but I couldn't hear. McPhee straightened up and just shook his head. I noticed he was holding a syringe.

"What's that in your hand?"

He held up the syringe. "This is mefloquine. It's not supposed to be taken as an injection. It's supposed to be taken as a tablet orally. But I rendered it into a form that can be injected. I offered Mr. Musgrave the opportunity to test it for himself, if he was so certain that it was not harmful."

Behind McPhee, on an overturned box sat a monitor showing the view through a night vision camera. It was pointed at a window, the one I'd crawled through a half hour ago. He'd seen me coming.

I was racking my brain to think of something to say to get him off this trajectory. "Mike, I think you're close."

"What do you mean?"

"Look how you've conducted this operation. You've got me writing about it. You've got the eyes of the city and the country on your story. I'll continue to write about mefloquine and what happened to you, because from what I've read, there's evidence to support you."

He was watching me with interest.

"Turn yourself in to the police, either military or civilian. If you don't, I'll be writing about how you took matters into your own hands. But if you don't stop this, nobody will see past the crimes you committed. What? Are you going to stick an old man full of a drug that you think is poison? Who are you going to win over with that move. Stop this and get some help."

His eyes never left me, though I could tell he was getting ready to jab Musgrave.

"Vanessa wants you to get help. She wants you to tell her about Eric. You need to tell your kids your story. You want them to remember their father as the man who went on a rampage in Montréal?"

He was still holding the syringe in the air. "No, Denny. I'm too far outside the wire to get back inside now. I'm an eyesore, just like this building. An anachronism. I've served my useful purpose.

"There's no help for this. Permanent neuropsychiatric damage. Tell Vanessa that her brother was a good man who cared about her. Tell my kids their father always completed the mission."

"Then I need you Mike, to help me with the story." I took a step toward him, as if to grab the syringe out of his hand. In a motion so smooth and unhurried it could have been hydraulic, he took a pistol from his belt and levelled at me.

When you're a finger's pull away from death, time slows down. I noticed the light glinting off the barrel, the dirty grey colour of the metal, the absolute intensity of McPhee's blue eyes staring me down.

"You don't need me to help you write the story. You have my full permission to write it as you see fit. If I turn myself in, I won't be heard. I'll be silenced, and more good men will die, like Eric, and I can't have that on my conscience. Trust me Denny, they're going to hear this."

We stared at each other without speaking for a few seconds. I felt strangely detached. I began calculating escape routes. The spell was broken by a low groan from Musgrave, who must have fallen unconscious but who was now coming to.

I felt like I had to stall McPhee, had to buy time. "Felix is dead. Vanessa killed him in my apartment."

A pause, then a short burst of laughter. "It's true," I said. "You can turn on the news. The police will think I did it—"

Something flickered on the monitor, drawing my eye. McPhee turned to look. There was a light as if from a flashlight, then a man in commando uniform, then a handful of men crawling through the window.

McPhee looked at me with a strange, almost happy expression. "Go time, Denny." He produced a knife from a side pocket and in three seconds cut the tape binding Musgrave to the chair.

Musgrave collapsed to the floor. McPhee strode to a box, withdrew one rifle similar to the one that I had seen him shoot Blanchette with, stuffed the pistol into his belt and replaced the knife in his pocket.

"Denny this place is wired. It's going to blow and you've got ten minutes to get yourself and Musgrave out of here. Tell these bozos to get themselves out of here as well. I'm not coming out. That's non-negotiable.

"I know what I'm doing. You've got ten minutes starting now. He took a phone from his pocket, pressed a thumb to the screen and, stepping on a switch duct taped to the floor, doused the two lamps. "Good bye, old buddy."

I lost sight of him sprinting into the far corner of the space. I thought I heard the sound of boots on metal stairs. I looked at my watch reflexively, but what did it matter if it was noon or midnight. The world would end in ten minutes. I fought the urge to sprint to the window and escape. I had to wait with Musgrave. So I yelled instead. "Help! Over here!"

Musgrave looked in extreme distress. His face was pinched and in the dull light I could see sweat pouring off his face.

The beam from the flashlight blinded me. A voice said, "Identify yourself."

"Denny Durant. Reporter. This is Gordon Musgrave. He needs medical help."

"Lay on your stomach and put your hands on your head."

I yelled, "This place is going to blow up in ten minutes." I tried to be calm but I was shaking from the adrenaline. I didn't want to be crushed to death beneath tons of steel and concrete. I could see nothing but the beam of the flashlights. In a few seconds, hands grabbed my wrists and I was on the floor with a knee in my back, my hands were being bound with something thin and unbreakable.

"McPhee is hiding in here somewhere. We need to leave now. He wired the building."

"Where is McPhee?"

I pointed with my nose. "He ran that way."

A man was kneeling beside Musgrave. "He's alive." Two others ran crouching to pillars a dozen feet away and shone lights into the vast dark recesses of Silo 5. I was lifted by two sets of hands and along with Musgrave, hustled back toward the window. From some hidden speaker, the voice of McPhee rang out. "Gentlemen, this is Michael G. W. McPhee, Major, retired, Service Number N75-634-801. This structure is wired with 50 kilograms of ammonium nitrate fuel oil. Approximately four minutes and twenty seven seconds ago, I used a radio signal from my cell phone to trigger the electronic C-4 detonator. You have a little over five minutes to get out of this building and clear the area before it implodes

"You will not find me. I am well hidden. I am not coming out. This is the end of the road for me. Please evacuate. If you come to find me, I will shoot to kill."

We arrived at the window. Nothing was visible but darkness and snow. One of the men helped me through and people on the other side grabbed me from different directions. A heavy blanket fell over my head. I was rushed about a hundred metres to a waiting police car. Inside, the quiet was complete.

I heard the front door open, the car shifted as something heavy settled into the front seat, the door closed, the blanket was pulled off my head and I saw Anderson sitting there behind the wheel and Brandt in the passenger seat.

The police radio crackled. "We're clear," said a voice.

Brandt spoke into a hand-held radio. "Copy that. We're bringing the suspect in."

By "suspect," he meant me. "You're under arrest for the murder of Felix Leclerc." Anderson read me my rights but I wasn't listening.

"McPhee is still in there," I said. "He says he'll blow himself up."

Anderson looked around. "I hope he's a man of his word."

Several emergency vehicles with lights flashing were lining the street near where I had abandoned the taxi, which was still there, door open, just as I had left it.

We drove away down rue de la Commune as uniformed police and firefighters bustled around the road, some of them warding off traffic, others getting tools and equipment from the trucks. I imagined McPhee resigning himself to his fate. Would he pray? To whom?

As Anderson picked up speed, I swiveled to look at Silo 5, hoping to catch a glimpse of McPhee somewhere on the roof, perhaps. But there was only darkness and the falling snow.

There was a flash from inside Silo 5, then a muffled boom, then panicked voices over the radio.

"Jesus Christ," said Anderson.

"The crazy bastard went out with a bang," said Brandt.

I wanted to argue to say my friend wasn't crazy, that he was sick. But as I watched Silo 5 burn, I no longer knew who or what McPhee was. I thought of the painting I'd seen hanging in the shop window on Sherbrooke that night—was it only a week ago? The painting of the lake, frozen over. Had McPhee just tried to blast through the ice of his frozen sanity?

Chapter Fifty-One

The police held me overnight, then released me and dropped the charges the next day when Vanessa turned herself in—at Shawna's urging—for Felix's murder. Crews were still digging through the wreckage of Silo 5 for McPhee's body.

I'd spent the past few days trying to process everything that had happened, the violence Mad Mike McPhee had inflicted on the city and some of its inhabitants, the fact he'd brought the war home. On Saturday, I got tired of all the introspection. I decided in the evening to have dinner with friends, which turned out to be as good as any psychotherapy.

I was just leaving the restaurant in the old port to head home when I got a text from Johanna.

"At the Abyss Bar, why don't you meet me for a drink?"

The moon had risen in the eastern sky, chasing the stars away. My breath was visible as I hoofed it along, making pretty good time. Twenty minutes later I arrived at the bar. I could hear the music from well outside the door. It was metal night and the place was packed, mostly with long-haired young men in leather. I looked around quickly for Johanna. No sign.

I moved to the end of the bar as far from the music as I could get, and waited for her to appear. Maybe she was in the bathroom. The bartender shouted at me for my drink order. I hollered back, asking what the house cocktail was. I thought he said Finnish sex on the beach. I nodded my assent. It seemed appropriate. A couple of minutes later, the cocktail arrived. I gave him cash. It was awful. Vodka, peach Schnapps and orange grenadine.

The stage was lit in a blue and green light. I felt like I was looking at a fish tank. The band played and the dancers danced. Where was Johanna? I saw a waitress carrying a tray of food and I realized I was very hungry. My cocktail was abysmal, but the more I drank, the less I disliked it. The song ended. There was loud applause. The barman asked if I wanted another. I said why not.

A few minutes there was a tug on my shirt. I turned and there was Johanna. The band was taking a break so we could actually hear each other. She asked me how I was doing after all of the recent events.

"I'll be fine," I said. We made awkward small talk. I wanted to touch her but I felt a distance between us.

"Did they ever find McPhee's body?"

"Not yet. It's too dangerous to go in right now. They're trying to stabilize the structure."

"I've seen the photos. It's a mess." She fiddled with her drink. Her bold directness had given way to hesitation and uncertainty.

"They're also worried some of the explosives might not have detonated yet."

She nodded and looked away, taking a sip of her beer. When she looked back, her eyes were moist.

"I'm going back to Finland," she said, placing a hand on my forearm.

I didn't know what to else to say, so I said, "I'll miss you."

She nodded. "Maybe we'll see each other again. I still have to finish my thesis."

I felt a heaviness in my chest. I hadn't wanted to get entangled but I had grown quite fond of her.

She was eager to change the subject. "How is your story coming along?"

"My deadline's tomorrow."

She looked crestfallen. "You know, I was supposed to leave the day after I met you, but I canceled my ticket. I wanted to see how things would go."

"I guess I failed the test."

"No, you passed, but you're a journalist, like my dad. I don't want to be with someone who is always thinking about stories, and never about me."

It was a fair point.

She smiled, reached up and hugged me. We held onto each other for a moment. And then she was gone.

I finished my shot and left the bar, feeling, somehow, a little less broken.

I walked along William Street, then took a right down King and ended up eventually back on rue de la Commune, not far from where I'd left the taxi. I crossed the street and leaned against the ballustrade, taking in the sight of Silo 5 in the distance. McPhee's explosion hadn't altered the silhouette of the structure, only destroyed a good portion of the interior. A night crew was working to untangle the twisted mess. There was a sense of urgency on the part of the military to recover McPhee's body, whatever was left of it, but it was plain that such an outcome might not be on the cards.

Horrible images from that night filled my memory. I still hadn't fully recovered from all that had happened in the 10 days between when I met McPhee at the Gargoyle and when he blew himself up.

I let my gaze wander from Silo 5 to the river beyond, and as the lights of the far shore played off the water and began to soothe my emotional wounds, a realization began to dawn on me. "Son of a bitch," I said to nobody, almost laughing, but the laughter was cut short by anger.

Chapter Fifty-Two

Pathfinders often must rely on partisans, people who are faithful to the cause, for information about conditions on the ground before they jumped from airplanes or make other dangerous expeditions. For example, a partisan on the ground might set off a flare with a particular type of coloured smoke to show the Pathfinder the direction and speed of the wind so that he or she can make the correct calculations to jump safely.

It all seemed so obvious in retrospect.

I parked at the Tim Hortons across from Buzzy's shop and turned off the ignition. I let a few minutes tick by, while I asked myself if this was really he best course of action. The answer was probably not, but sometimes anger is the best guide.

I stepped out of my car, locked it and walked across the street to the garage. The big main door was open because one of the mechanics was backing out a four-wheel drive. I spotted Buzzy over in the far corner, talking to a man in a business suit. Nobody seemed to notice me. I glanced quickly at the spot where the Zodiac was last time I was there, and didn't see it.

I ran upstairs and stepped quickly through the open door of Buzzy's office. I retrieved the key from the hiding spot in the desk and moved to the room across the landing. I expected McPhee to be there, lounging on the bed or pacing the room, or maybe reading a book of military history, but he wasn't there. Was he hiding? I opened the closet in the corner. Empty.

A sound made me turn. It was Buzzy. I glanced quickly at his hands to see what he was carrying—screwdriver, knife—but they were empty.

"What are you doing? How did you get in here?"

"He jumped, didn't he?"

"What are you talking about."

"From the roof. Of Silo 5."

"McPhee?"

"Don't play dumb. That zodiac I saw on my first trip. You took it out into the river. You picked him up."

"That would be impossible." He wore the smug look of a successful prankster.

"No, it wouldn't. I checked. The highest point of Silo 5 is—was—68 metres, or almost 220 feet. From that height, a skilled pilot can hang glide almost a kilometre. You could have put the zodiac in at Parc de la Cité. The St. Lawrence freezes in winter, but not completely. Piece of cake for McPhee. He could have landed right in the boat."

He was searching my face, maybe to see what I intended to do with the information.

"He'd already been planning for months to kidnap Musgrave, to video tape his confession about the evils of mefloquine. The plan changed when he beat Frank Leclerc to death. He never meant to do that. He called you that night." I waited but he said nothing. "You picked him up, brought him back here. He told you what he was going to do. But this time, he knew the police would be looking for him, so he needed an escape plan, a backup."

Buzzy walked with his uneven gait to the fridge and grabbed a beer. He didn't offer me one. "The first time I was here, when I told you that McPhee had killed someone, you acted surprised, but you already knew."

He drank, but his eyes never left mine.

"You didn't come at me swinging because of Sarah. You came at me to distract me from the fact that you were putting a tarp on a zodiac. I wasn't supposed to see that."

The smugness was gone, replaced by thin bravado. "You're nuts."

"How could you go along with a plan like that? Did you help him transport the ammonium nitrate?"

I could almost see the anger beating through his veins now. "What do you know about friendship?"

It was an odd question. "As much as the next guy."

"Where I come from, you don't let your friends down."

I handed him the key. "They're going to keep looking for the body, and they're not going to find it, and they're going to start asking questions."

"How do you know there's not a body in there?"

I thought about it. I'd watched the bodies of Frank Leclerc and Pierre Blanchette being removed from the crime scene. I watched Felix Leclerc bleed out on my living room carpet. What other body was there? Had McPhee included Metzgar, the hotel manager, on the hit list?

Buzzy took a long swig of beer. "Maybe McPhee got out of there. Maybe he didn't. I didn't have anything to do with it."

I headed for the door. "I'll quote you on that."

Epilogue

"So what happens now?" Shawna asked. She momentarily paused eating French fries. We were sitting in a bar called the Victorian Arms, on rue Saint-Mathieu, which had become my new local, temporarily at least. On the outside, the Victorian looked like an old-style pub, which is what one would expect from the name. On the inside, however, it was all chrome and glass.

I'd visited the place frequently for the past 10 days, ever since Silo 5. I needed a change of scene from the Gargoyle. I missed Virginia and my friends there, but I felt like I needed time on my own to process all that had happened. The Victorian was only a few blocks west of the Gargoyle, but it could have been in a different city. I was completely anonymous inside, and unlike the Gargoyle, where you only had to be there a short time before you'd get talking to someone, nobody seemed very eager to get to know me, which suited me fine.

I took a sip of beer while thinking how to answer her question. I'd been telling her about my meeting with Buzzy a week earlier.

"I don't know. I keep writing the story."

The Victorian was never very busy, which is another reason I liked it. Four or five middle aged men sat at the bar, quietly consuming pints, and a crowd of students at the back watched a large screen television that showed a European soccer match and played some kind of drinking game involving peanuts and pitchers of beer.

"What's the story about?"

I paused again. I wasn't sure what was behind my reticence. It would be a long time before I felt completely free and unguarded. "My story now is about McPhee and how he tried and failed to fake his own death to avoid prosecution for the murders and also how he went about his mission in the most spectacular way possible to draw attention to mefloquine."

Shawna took a sip of coke. "But wait. He didn't fail. He got away."

"For now," I said. "But I know he's not dead. The police know he's not dead. That wasn't part of his plan. The only person that was supposed to know was Buzzy."

"I guess," she said.

"How long can he really run?" I continued. I seemed to be on a roll. Pieces of the puzzle were still falling into place, even days later. "They've already arrested Buzzy and seized his business. Accessory to murder after the fact. How long will McPhee be able to live with that?"

"How do you know about Buzzy? I haven't seen anything in the papers."

"I keep in touch with Bruno."

"Bruno Castillo from high school? Plug?"

"The one and only."

Back in high school, Bruno had taken a shine to Shawna but Shawna had no interest in him. He persisted, and at one point, in front of all his friends, she said "get out of my face, you plug ugly bastard." The name had stuck.

"Still writing for the Gazette?"

"No." I drank the rest of my beer. "The Gazette couldn't pay me. They ran out of money. Well, actually, it's a bit more complicated. They can only allot freelancers a certain percentage of the total payroll, and they'd already reached the limit. Union rules."

"That's too bad."

"It worked out okay. Rolling Stone has offered to buy the story." I hadn't told anyone yet. I'd only found out a few hours earlier. "They're offering me an advance."

She looked up from her plate of fries. "THE Rolling Stone?"

"Yeah, they've published a lot of stories about vets and mental illness and all the things that can go wrong." A swift up and down of her dark eyebrows was the only visible reaction, but I knew she was impressed. I guess I was too. I'd never written for such a high profile publication, and maybe a few years ago, I would have seen it as some kind of crowning accomplishment to my career. But at the moment, I could only feel as though I had let McPhee down somehow. I still couldn't get over his transformation. I told Shawna about how the military was standing by its position that mefloquine was a safe and effective drug. I mentioned the recent studies by the U.S. military that came to the same conclusion. Other studies, however, painted a different picture. It would take time to play out.

The Colonel, my mother's friend, told me a couple of days ago that behind closed doors, in the upper echelons of the Canadian military, there was a deep concern about the potential liability with mefloquine, and it would very likely be withdrawn quietly and replaced by next generation antimalarial medication. Not only that, but the military would be updating its protocols to make sure something similar never happened again, and so in that sense, perhaps McPhee had scored a victory. I was working hard to get someone on the record for the story I was writing.

"Have you seen your son?"

Her face brightened. "It's amazing what you can do with a lawyer. I get him every second weekend."

"That's great news."

After a few seconds, she asked where I thought McPhee would go. "Can he get himself out of the country?"

"Maybe he already has, but his family's here. I have a feeling he's going to be back and he's going to face up to what he did. No matter what the mefloquine did to him, or what his mental illness did to him, whether it was psychosis or something else, deep down, he's the same guy." But I didn't really believe what I was saying. I'd seen too much.

I paused to take a sip of my beer. Shawna drank some coke. She finished the fries and pushed the plate to one side. She'd cut her hair a little shorter. It was an update to her style, but she still had that same languid look. She told me she'd been to visit Vanessa in the Tanguay Correctional Facility, where she was being held while awaiting trial. "Her lawyer thinks she has a pretty good shot at a reduced sentence or even a suspended sentence." Shawna said there was plenty of help available for her in the federal system. I reflected on how, in a way, McPhee had kept his promise to Eric; Shawna was off the streets.

Then my mind wandered to the image of Felix bleeding out on my carpet. I thought about his brother beaten to death by an enraged McPhee. I thought about Blanchette, shot to death by a cool-handed McPhee. I thought about all the death that McPhee had seen and all the death in the world. I drank.

Shawna grew quiet again. Perhaps her mind was running along the same lines.

"You know, I'm sorry that I didn't protect you better in high school from the jerks and the assholes."

She looked at me to see if I was joking, saw that I wasn't. "Thank you, Denny. That means a lot. It wasn't your job to protect me, but I appreciate it." I wondered whose job it had been to protect her.

We talked for a while longer. She told me about some cases she was working on. It was around 8 p.m. when I said good night to Shawna and headed home.

As I was walking, my phone rang. It was my eldest daughter, Jessica, calling to ask me a question. "Daddy?"

"Yes, my love."

"What did one hat say to the other?"

"I don't know. Tell me."

"You wait here—I'll go on ahead."

I laughed. Her sister, Margaux, told me about the cookies she was making. I had an overwhelming sense of life returning to normal, and of normal as an endlessly changing thing.

We'd said our goodbyes and I'd just turned the corner off Sainte-Catherine onto St-Mark when I heard the engine of a large vehicle behind me. Instead of passing me, however, it slowed and pulled up alongside. The passenger-side window of the black Chevy Suburban came down. It was Anderson. "Mr. Durant, have you got time for a little chinwag?"

I climbed in. Brandt was behind the wheel. They must have just eaten fast food because the air inside the vehicle was redolent of grease. I looked at Anderson as he turned to face me. "What brings you to my particular neck of the woods?"

"Oh, you know," said Anderson. "Just out and about, protecting the populace, keeping the peace."

"Thank God somebody is."

Brandt said nothing, just let out a muffled burp.

I nodded. It was somehow comforting to see them both. We were like survivors of a cyclone that had torn through town, leaving a path of death and destruction in its wake.

Anderson nodded and smiled. "I thought you might like to know the latest news about your friend."

My stomach lurched as I braced for him to tell me a story of some violent end to McPhee's life. But it wasn't that.

"The major has turned himself in. Kind of."

"Really? Where?"

"Up at the base. Petawawa. Apparently he tried to get into his house last night to see his wife and kids. His wife called the police. They came and got him. There was no fuss. He went quietly."

"I'm surprised she was still there."

"From what I understand, she knew there was a risk he would return, but she chose to stay." I tried to imagine what the reunion was like. I wondered if the thing that would save McPhee in the end was the possibility of being with his family. I wondered if anyone outside the military had any idea what home and family represented for people who served overseas.

"Where is he now?"

"The MPs are holding him there until some of our guys can bring him back. We have jurisdiction on this one."

"What's going to happen?"

"Well, he's going to stand trial, but they're going to have to do a psych assessment first."

"Can I quote you on that?"

Anderson laughed sharply. "You can say a person familiar with the situation."

"Are we exclusive on that?"

He looked at me. "I figure you've earned some exclusivity."

I thanked him for the information. He said, "Keep in touch."

As I was getting out, I said, "Why did you leak that story to Le Journal about me knowing McPhee?"

"I believe it's called 'setting the news agenda.'"

I made my way back to the apartment. Elliot was glad to see me. I rubbed his ears as he pressed himself against my shins. I glanced at the spot on the carpet where Felix had bled out. The cleaners had done their best, but a stain like that would never come out. I checked my watch. I had an appointment in a couple of hours to see a new apartment, one with room for my daughters to sleep over.

I picked up the mail and walked over to the kitchen to get him some food, thumbing through the bills, brochures and leaflets advertising cheap loans. On the bottom of the pile was a square white envelope, expensive stationary. I opened it up.

It said, "Virginia Sempre and Richard Prentice request the pleasure of your company as we celebrate the beginning of our new life together." It gave a date in May for the wedding.

I sat down at my kitchen table, moved the Pathfinder badge and the other items McPhee had slipped into my pocket to one side, and began writing out my RSVP.

—END—

Coming up

Book 3 in the Denny Durant Montréal Crime Series!

It's April in Montréal—Denny's favourite time of year. With Mad Mike McPhee in the rearview and Johanna almost forgotten, life is finally smoothing out. A bigger, more modern apartment. Steady work. Even a little extra cash for some much-needed R&R.

But good times never last.

An anonymous tip about a stolen old master painting leads to a bigger story than Denny ever expected—one that puts him in the crosshairs of a gang of refined, ruthless criminals.

Go to www.cjfournierbooks.comto join the mailing list and receive updates on Denny's latest adventures.

Acknowledgements

I would like to acknowledge my late father, Joel Fournier, who—in addition to being a great dad and always encouraging my writing—read the manuscript and offered, even from his deathbed, extremely sound advice. He is deeply missed.

I would like to thank my mother Sheila Fournier, for her detailed feedback during the early stages of the manuscript and again at the proofreading stage, but mostly for being a source of unfailing support and inspiration.

Thank you to my sister, Renée Fournier, who read drafts of the manuscript and provided essential feedback, along with helping to proofread the final version.

Many people contributed their expertise and insights during the research for The Pathfinder. I'm grateful to: Andrew Mayeda for sharing his experiences of reporting on the war in Afghanistan, of working at a daily newspaper in Canada and for offering valuable feedback on the manuscript; René Bruemmer, for helping me understand the day-to-day workings of the Montréal Gazette and for reading excerpts of the manuscript; Major (retd) Paul Hook, a fellow author, for telling me what it was like to serve in Afghanistan and for reading excerpts of the manuscript; PCM for sharing his insights into law enforcement and the art of the police interview; retired police officer and fellow Capital Crime Writers member Art Pittman, for answering questions about police procedure and criminal psychology with his characteristic patience and thoughtfulness; Blair Hickey, retired police officer, for telling me about police procedure, particularly at a murder scene.

I would particularly like to thank G.S., for generously taking the time to share his experiences of combat in Afghanistan and, more broadly, of being a special forces soldier in the Canadian military.

I would like to thank Tammy Hogan for her guidance in the early days of the research for this story and for generously sharing her knowledge of Canadian Forces veterans.

I'm grateful to Anne Morin for offering detailed and highly perceptive comments on the manuscript. My friends Francine Roussy Layton and John Layton read the manuscript and pointed out several places where it could be made better. Mitch de la Barre, Jason Molluso, Glen Pepin and Frederic Tomesco fielded random and diverse questions about Montréal.

To Lesley Thompson, founder of MTL Detours, for comping me a walking tour of the Underground City, and to our guide Martin, for making the tour extremely worthwhile. Highly recommended.

To my editor Dinah Forbes, thank you for your patience, judgment and skill.

To my partner, Jen, for reading the manuscript and providing a steady stream of moral support over the two years it took to write this book.

Finally to my children — Nicolas, Adam and James — for keeping me young, on my toes and accountable.

Author's Note

The Pathfinder is a work of fiction. However, I tried to portray the experience of Canadian soldiers and reporters in Afghanistan as accurately as I could. In addition to the people I spoke with, here are some of the key resources I consulted:

- Fifteen days: stories of bravery, friendship, life and death from inside the new Canadian Army, by Christie Blatchford.

- Come from the shadows: the long and lonely struggle for peace in Afghanistan, by Terry Glavin

- No ordinary men: Special Operations Forces missions in Afghanistan, by Bernd Horn

- The Withdrawal: Iraq, Libya, Afghanistan, and the Fragility of U.S. Power, by Noam Chomsky and Vijay Prashant

- No Names No Pack Drill: An Oral History of Canadians at War in Afghanistan, by Steve MacBeth

- The Canadian Army in Afghanistan, by Sean M. Maloney, PhD

Similarly, while The Pathfinder is a work of fiction, I drew on real-world reports to portray the experience of some members of the military who took mefloquine while on deployment and to portray the controversy surrounding the drug. Here are some of the news articles and research reports I consulted: